Four Play

PADDLE CREEK COLLEGE
BOOK FOUR

HJ WELCH

Four Play
Paddle Creek College Book Four

Copyright © 2023 by HJ Welch

Cover Design by Cate Ashwood

Also Available

BY HJ WELCH

Paddle Creek College (Daddies and kink)

#1 Heaven Sent

#2 Yes, Sir

#3 Little Pleasures

Pine Cove (Small town)

Complete Box Set

Homecoming Hearts (Former Boy Band)

Complete Box Set

Bears-4-U (Daddies and bears multi-author shared universe)

Keep Me

BY HELEN JULIET

Contemporary Fairy Tale Adaptations

The Fairy Tale Collection (Beauty and the Beast, Cinderella, Rapunzel)

Daddy's Fairy Tales (Daddies and kink – Goldilocks, Little Red Riding Hood, The Three Little Pigs, Puss in Boots)

Trigger Warning

This book features mention of past abuse of a main character, including sexual situations that, in retrospect, were not consensual. In Chapter 23, there is a threat of sexual assault that does not come to pass. There is absolutely no on-page sexual assault in this book.

Prologue

"WHERE IS HE?" I BELLOW AS I RUN FULL SPEED THROUGH THE double doors into the emergency room at the hospital in Kabul. I'm fully aware that I'm covered head to toe in dirt, sweat, other people's blood, and soot from the earlier explosion.

The explosion that could well have already killed Treyvon.

My heart is hammering and my vision laser focused as I march toward the front desk. Gabby Ortiz has already thrown her hands up and is marching right back toward me, also covered in other people's blood.

It's been a rough day. I know that. Trey's not the only one who got caught up in that god-forsaken ambush. But like it or not, he's the only one I care about in that moment.

I know I'm an asshole. So sue me.

"Sergeant, calm down," Gabby snaps in her 'I'm not taking any of your shit today' voice. "Don't come charging into my ER like a bull in a china shop. In here, I'm in charge."

"Where is he?" I grit out again, trying to keep the emotion from my voice.

1

I've convinced myself that nobody knows how long Treyvon Caldwell and I have been fooling around for. Or that we're fooling around at all.

Or that at some point when I wasn't looking, that bastard wormed his way into my heart, and I fucking fell in love with him.

If I never get the chance to tell him that…

I ball up my fists and clench my jaw as the doc places a gentle hand on my chest. "Sergeant, he's going to be fine."

Relief washes through me, and gravity almost gets the better of me. But there are a dozen people around us, and I'm not going to lose my shit in front of anyone.

"His foot?" I croak out. The doc might be a miracle worker, but I saw that mangled stump as they loaded Trey onto the chopper all those hours ago.

Ortiz pats my chest. "The *rest* of him is going to be fine," she assures me with a twitch of a smile. It's not actually funny, but when you're surrounded by carnage for as long as we are, you learn to develop a pretty dark sense of humor. Otherwise, the trauma might eat you whole.

Now I believe her and let out a slightly hysterical laugh. "Who needs two feet anyway?" I quip so I really don't lose it. Trey loves running. He's always moving. He's…

He's going to be fine. I've seen hundreds of prosthetics. That shit is fucking science fiction these days.

He's fine. He's going to be fine. He's going to live.

Time to stop dicking around, then, Sergeant Bryant.

I exhale, puffing out my cheeks and flexing my fingers to stop my hands from shaking so much. I haven't eaten or slept in over twenty-four hours, and at this point, I'm convinced this meat sack of mine is being powered purely by adrenaline and fury.

"Can I see him?" I manage to ask in a relatively calm voice.

Ortiz nods, patting my chest one last time before withdrawing her arm. "Sure, cowboy. He's been in recovery for a couple of hours now and woke up a little while ago. Of course, he's only been asking for one no-good asshole since then."

I smirk, secretly absolutely delighted.

"Santa Claus?" I kid, choosing to joke rather than show any real emotion, because that would only lead to sobbing, and I'm not ready for that yet.

Oh, Trey. You stubborn son of a bitch. I knew you'd live. You're not allowed to die unless I god damn say so.

"The Easter Bunny," Ortiz fires back over her shoulder, already leading me through another door back into the ward.

She pulls off her plastic apron, balls it up, and throws it in a trash can we pass, then automatically reaches up for the hand sanitizer dispenser on the wall like she's done that set of actions a million times. I have no doubt she has. I'm really glad that Trey had her and her team there when he needed them the absolute most.

I can't help but falter as she leads me into his curtained-off private bay. Trey is lying in a bed, covered in bandages, hooked up to several machines, tubes, drips, and wires, and what little I can see of his usually dark skin is ashen gray.

But he's alive.

And I know it's superficial, but I'm fucking exhausted, so whatever. His face is pretty much unscathed, and I almost lose the battle with my knees. They really want to crumble out from under me, but I remind them that we still have a job to do. We have to be strong for Trey.

He'd be gorgeous to me no matter what. I know this now. But he still has his beautiful eyes and his perfect smile, and I say a silent prayer up to whoever was watching out for him this morning.

"I know 'fine' is a relative term, Doc," I say as Ortiz and I approach the bed. Trey is sleeping, and I take a moment to appreciate how peaceful he looks despite everything else going on. "Hit me."

Ortiz nods. "First degree burns over approximately thirty percent of the body. Second degree, fifteen percent, and third degree, ten percent. He's going to take a while to heal, and there will be some scarring, but compared to the things I've seen, your boy didn't get it too bad."

That smirk reappears on my mouth. I tried to get Trey to call me 'Daddy,' but he wasn't having any of it, insisting he was just as much of an alpha as I am. He's not my 'boy,' but he's definitely my something.

"He's a fighter," I say, carefully resting my hand on his shoulder that doesn't look too banged up. "Anything else?"

She nods again unsurprisingly. When your RV gets blasted off the ground and slammed back down twenty feet away, there are going to be complications. I'll never forget that sight as long as I live, watching helplessly from two cars down.

"A few broken bones," she continues. "I'm sure once he gets moving, there will be a hell of a lot more sore and torn muscles he'll tell us about. We're keeping an eye on him for a concussion, but we think it's mild. That left leg is a mess, but you knew that already."

"Below the knee, though, right?" I ask with an arched eyebrow. I'm not saying Trey got it easy, but if it missed his knee, that'll make life a ton easier for him.

"Below," she says firmly.

"Good, good," I say, chewing my lower lip. "And, um, is everything okay with…"

I'm not shy. I just know when something's indelicate, and this isn't a light situation. The doc still has her morbid humor, however, and shakes her head, looking all naïve and shit.

"Whatever could you mean, Sergeant?"

I scoff and flip her the bird. "Is his junk intact? I have a vested interest."

A groan makes me snap my head toward the bed, and I see Trey scrunching up his face. My heart leaps into my throat, and I fumble to grab his non-injured hand. "At least buy me dinner first before getting medical reports on my junk," he slurs.

I huff out a laugh that's half a sob. Then I drag up the chair beside the bed and drop into it, my eyes never leaving his face as he groggily blinks his way back into consciousness.

"Hello, gorgeous," I rasp. My eyes are prickling. but I refuse to let any tears fall. He needs me to hold it together for him.

He blinks again and looks down. "You're holding my hand?" he says slowly, then shifts his gaze over to Ortiz. "In front of people?"

I laugh and sniff, meaning I have to rub the back of my free hand against my nose to make sure I don't embarrass myself. "Yeah, baby."

"Baby?"

I don't blame him. We've fiercely guarded this secret for over a year, figuring it was nobody else's business if we were fucking all the hours god would allow.

But now I care. Now it matters.

"Yeah, baby," I say, stroking the back of his hand with my thumb. "I don't give a shit. Everyone needs to know you're mine if you're going to marry me."

The words just tumble out, but I have absolutely no doubts as I watch his stunning dark eyes widen. I know he's on painkillers and this might take him a minute, but he'll get with the program soon enough, I'm certain.

I'm not talking 'be my one and only' and he knows it.

That might work perfectly fine for other folks, but whenever we talked about keeping this thing between us up when we got back stateside, we were both clear that we'd still be interested in playing with others. And I meant it.

So long as he comes home to me. So long as his heart belongs to me.

Because he's certainly stolen mine.

We're a team. I want to share my life with him. We've walked through literal hell together in this place and there's no one I know better or trust more. I never thought I'd be the kind of sonuvabitch who'd want to settle down. I thought I'd sow my wild oats for as long as possible, and I still intend to do that.

But I'll be sharing it all with him.

"Did you just propose?" he says, only running the words together a little.

"Keep up, old man," I tease. I'm actually seven years older than him, but he's been tetchy about his age ever since he turned thirty, and I just love riling him about it.

He closes his eyes and scoffs, reminding me of how much pain he's probably in. "Didn't get down on your damn knee, did you?"

I know Ortiz is quietly observing us, but that just means I have a witness.

Without letting go of his hand, I slip from my chair and onto one knee, amused as his eyes go even wider. "If you think I'm almost going to watch you die and not do anything about it, you really did get banged on the head," I growl. I press the back of his hand to my lips, still not breaking my gaze with his. "You're *mine*, Specialist Treyvon Caldwell. You hear me? I'm never letting you go. So yes, I'm going to put a ring on it and then spend the rest of my life with you. Is that okay?"

He stares at me for a moment, then manages a weak

laugh. "Yes, sir," he croaks. His eyes flutter closed, and his head sags against the pillow, but his grip is still strong in mine.

"Good boy," I tell him while he's too exhausted to protest. "You're *mine,*" I reiterate in a whisper.

And what's mine, I protect.

Now and forever.

CHAPTER 1

Brady

"You're hovering, baby boy."

I blush at getting caught. I am indeed lurking by the door, watching my partners in bed. Daddy is reading, and Papa has his head resting on Daddy's chest. His eyes are closed, and I thought he was sleeping, but at the sound of Daddy's voice, he blinks, then smiles at me.

"Hey there, little pup," Papa says warmly. He beckons me to come closer. "Are you coming to bed?"

It's been two years, and I still get butterflies in my tummy at moments like this. I had boyfriends before I met Rick and Trey, but I never fell so hard or fast as I did with them. They're like a force of nature. I moved in just a month after we all met, and I can't imagine my life without them.

Which is why I'm worried about what I'm hoping to ask them. I'd never want them to think that I feel their love isn't enough.

But they've also taught me that I should always, *always* ask them for what I need.

Shyly, I approach the bed then crawl in between them.

They automatically wrap their arms around me, and Daddy places his book down on the nightstand.

"What's going on, little pup?" he asks. Of course he knows something's off. He's practically a mind reader. It's one of the things that makes him the best Daddy ever.

Papa loops his fingers through mine and kisses the top of my head. With my other hand, I trace my thumb along the scarred flesh on his left forearm. I know he can't feel it—the nerve endings are all shot to shit there. But early on, I wanted to show him that his burns don't scare me, so I often touch them. It reassures us both, especially when I'm nervous.

"Are you in trouble?" Daddy asks in concern, obviously impatient with my lack of an answer. I can't help but laugh. That's so typical of him, wanting to jump in and rescue me before he even knows what's happening. I guess you can take the man out of the military but not the military out of the man.

"No, nothing like that!" I cry, some of the tension leaving my body. He makes a good point. What I want to ask isn't a *bad* thing. At least I hope not.

I chew my lip.

Papa gently pulls down my chin to free the flesh from my teeth. "You're not allowed to blemish your pretty skin, are you, baby boy?" I shake my head. "Who does your gorgeous body belong to?"

I relax even further. "Daddy and Papa," I reply confidently.

"That's right," Daddy says encouragingly. "We're the only ones allowed to mark you, aren't we?"

I nod. I love it when they give me treasures to carry around long after they've caught and conquered me.

"Sorry, Daddy," I whisper. "I'm just nervous."

He arches an eyebrow at me. "Of us?"

I nod again. I know Daddy is normally pretty scary—that's one of the hottest things about him—but I do also love it when he gets that adoring look on his face like I'm the most important person in the world. I know Papa is as well. He loves us both so much. But somehow, he manages to make us both feel incredibly special at the same time.

"Why would you ever be nervous of us?" Daddy asks firmly, making me understand that he might be sympathetic but I also have to answer him.

I try not to squirm in pleasure and in a tiny bit of fearful excitement.

"I'm being selfish," I mumble, trying to wriggle farther under the covers.

Papa laughs and wraps his arm around my middle to stop me. "What did we say about that word?" he asks me with a cautionary tone.

I bite my lip but quickly let it go again before Daddy can tell me off. "You said that 'selfish' isn't a bad word," I recite obediently.

"Exactly," Daddy growls before nuzzling his nose against my throat and placing a kiss there. "So what do you want to ask us?"

My eyelids start to flutter shut, and I can feel my cock getting hard. But—*no!* I have to stick to my guns and be brave!

"I...I want to try *hunting*," I blurt out, immediately flinching away and screwing my eyes shut.

There's a pause of a few seconds, then I feel two different hands sliding up my body over the sweatpants and T-shirt I'm wearing. One on my arm and chest, the other down my flank and my hip.

"You want to chase down a sweet boy?" Daddy asks, his voice hot and husky. Oh-kay. That doesn't sound like a bad thing, does it? I crack one eyelid slightly open.

11

Both my Daddies are looking at me like I'm dinner.

I blush, and, this time, can't stop myself from nibbling my lip for a couple of seconds. "Um," I utter. "Yeah. Maybe? But I don't want you to stop chasing me!" I squeak out in a panic. *Oh, I'm doing this all wrong!*

Daddy chuckles, sounding so sexy, and rubs my tummy. I shiver and work really hard to keep listening to what he says. "Baby boy," he says with a sigh. "You're *mine*, remember? Of course we'll never stop being your wolves or your Daddies. But if you'd like to try flipping the tables a little, we'd love nothing more than to support you one hundred percent. Right, Papa?"

Papa scoffs. "Sounds hot as fuck, little pup," he growls. "You'd be so adorable chasing down another sweet boy."

I pout. "I'd be fierce," I protest.

Both my Daddies laugh gently and definitely not unkindly, but I still pout more. Daddy catches my lip between his teeth just like how I wasn't allowed to.

"So fierce," he agrees once he lets it go. I feel like he's humoring me, but I don't care. I preen anyway. "However, I think your Daddies should give you a little reminder of how it's done before we let you loose on the world."

My pulse spikes again, and my breath catches as I look into his eyes. "You really wouldn't mind?" I whisper.

Daddy shakes his head.

Fuck, he's so handsome. His eyes crinkle, and the silver from his salt-and-pepper hair and beard catches in the lamplight. I really am selfish. I have both him and Papa, yet I still want more. But the way Daddy licks his lips and looks at me through his eyelashes doesn't make me feel like I'm being greedy.

He's turned on by the idea. They both are. I can feel the tension simmering between us in the bed and know that any second now it's going to explode. So I do what I usually do.

I stoke the fire.

"If I found a pretty little cutie who liked being chased," I say coyly, tracing my fingers up Daddy's arm, "I could bring him back here for us to all play with, couldn't I?"

Daddy hums, he and Papa nuzzling against my neck. Their hands are traveling along my legs and tummy, skimming over my thickening cock. "The thought had crossed my mind," Daddy rumbles in a low voice.

It's not like sharing is a new concept to us. My Daddies met me at a play party, after all. We've been to several events in different cities since. They often like to watch me get used by other Doms.

But we always come home to each other. That's the rule. So I'd only invite someone back here if they were really special. If I'm honest, that doesn't seem likely. But I want to *try*. I just want a taste of what it's like to be the predator for once. As much as I love being the prey, I feel like it could be so fun to chase *with* my Daddies for once instead of *from* them.

"I think," Papa says as he lifts my hand up to kiss my fingers, "that you've had pretty good teachers. It's only natural if you want to have a go yourself at being a hunter." He lets go of me and makes eye contact with Daddy. "But your Daddies wouldn't be doing their job if they unleashed you without warning people who you belong to."

He and Daddy share a smirk before Papa swings his body, angling himself over the side of the bed, reaching for one of his prosthetic feet.

I gasp and scramble, already trying to get away, but Daddy's hands are on me like a vise. "Oh, yes, Papa," he growls in my ear. My entire body quivers. "You're quite right. We can give our little pup a two-for-one. A lesson in good hunting, and…"

"And," Papa chimes in, "mark his pretty body all over so he and no one else forgets who his Daddies are."

I'm panting now, the blood thrumming through my veins. My vision is trained on the door where I'm already planning my escape. From the corner of my eye, I can see Papa working on the lower limb that he'd removed to go to bed. We usually plan hunts in advance because of this reason, but I love that Daddy's pinning me in place for just a little longer so we can still be as spontaneous as possible.

My focus is narrowing, and I let the adrenaline consume me. My ears are filled with my pulse hammering and the sound of the shallow breaths I'm gasping. I'm trembling.

"Daddy," I whimper. "Let me go. I'm scared."

He chuckles darkly against my throat. "You should be, little pup. Now...*run.*"

He releases me, and I lurch forward, not wasting a second as I scramble over the mattress and throw myself to the floor. I still hear him laughing as I sprint down the hallway toward the stairs, knowing that there's no escape, but I'm going to try anyway.

This is what I live for.

CHAPTER 2

Brady

I FLY ALONG THE HALLWAY AND DOWN THE STAIRS, MY BARE feet slapping on the wooden floors as I run. My heart is pounding and my skin tingling with the adrenaline. Anticipation thrums within me like a living thing.

There are several different routes I could take, but once I hit the tiles in the entrance hall, I make a split-second decision and turn to sprint toward the kitchen. Our two cats— Merlot and Chardonnay—are sleeping on the cool tiles. But as I fly past them, they bolt, their nails scraping comically on the ceramic floor in their haste to get away from me.

I don't blame them. I probably seem like a huge, panicky mess to them right now. I laugh out loud but don't slow down.

I head out through one of the vineyard's back doors. I tumble out into the evening, taking a moment to catch my breath. It's just before ten o'clock, and the last of the twilight is slipping away before the darkness consumes everything. There aren't any other properties for miles, as we're on the outskirts of Paddle Creek, and the sense of isolation only heightens my fight-or-flight instincts.

I launch myself off the porch and across the patio until my feet hit the cool grass. In the gloom, I skid to a halt, looking left and then right. I'm drawn to the little wooden bridge that crosses over the creek that runs past the property, but that leads into the forest, and I'm not wearing any shoes. So instead, I rush over to the converted barn, hastily jabbing in the security code to open the door. My Daddies will probably guess right away this is where I've gone, but the point isn't actually to hide for real.

I *want* to get caught in the end.

Once, this was home to horses, equipment for tending to the grounds, and stock from the business Daddy inherited along with the house. His folks took the horses with them to California when they retired, and everything else got moved to a smaller storage unit Papa and Daddy built close to the house.

Leaving this big space for us to play in.

There are a few different lighting settings on the panel by the door, and I quickly select the lowest one so I have just enough illumination not to stub my toes on everything. I want shadows to help conceal me. Quietly I slink around the straw bales stacked to make a little maze. I know the current configuration pretty well, or at least I think I do. Part of the fun is that Daddy likes to move things around without warning.

Sure enough, after a minute where I expected to turn right is now a left, but that's okay. I can worry about finding my way out later. Right now, I dart past several huge old tires, still looking for a good hiding spot. Some are cut in half. Others are whole and propped up on their sides. There are makeshift cotton curtains hanging from poles across the tops of the bales that I push my way through, also planks of wood placed strategically across the temporary corridors.

Straw lines the floor, prickling the soles of my feet with every step I take.

Several nooks have mattresses tucked into them. They're fitted with clean sheets and a few throw pillows. Beside these, there are baskets filled with lube, rope and padded cuffs, paddles, gags, blindfolds, and other goodies. My heart skips a beat as I trip over the corner of one, knowing that soon enough, I'm going to be dragged, kicking and howling to that place or another just like it and ravaged to within an inch of my life.

It's difficult to hear anything over my heavy breathing and the slamming of my pulse in my ears, but when I turned this light setting on, it also activated the sound system. There's a gentle thrum of atmospheric noises like leaves rustling, water gurgling, and insects chirping to make me feel like I'm lost in the woods at night. Every now and again, a wolf howls in the distance. I can't tell if anyone else has come through the door yet, so I need to hurry up and find a good place to scurry away.

I turn a corner, thinking there might be a loose bale somewhere close that I can crouch behind. But my heart explodes, and I jump out of my skin as hands come out of nowhere and try to grab me around the waist.

I shriek and dance clumsily backward, watching Daddy grin ferally at me as he advances. He's only wearing sweatpants, meaning that his lean torso and many tattoos are on display. Sometimes we play naked. It depends on how my Daddies decide they want me. Sometimes they strip me before unleashing me, and then it's up to them if they're clothed or not. One time, after a charity gala we all went to, they took great pleasure in pinning me down and divesting me of everything but my open shirt. Then they stalked me in their full tuxes. I'm still not quite sure why that was so insanely hot, but it was.

17

"No," I gasp as I spin around and fumble back the way I came, groping at the straw bales and bouncing off them as I try my best to run. I can feel Daddy behind me, chasing but not rushing. There's an inevitability that fills me with dread and turns my cock rock hard.

I don't know where I'm aiming for other than away from him. I could try and get back outside and run for the house, but the truth is I love it out in the barn. It's wild and raw, and I'm more likely to end up with bruises and scrapes from the hard floor. It smells of dry straw, and once we get going, the scent of masculine musk will permeate everything. I like the background noises that drift over my panicked breaths and the snarls coming from my Daddy. I'm feeling more and more like a hunted animal with every unsteady step I take.

When I shove aside a curtain, I'm not really surprised when I slam straight into Papa's solid chest. I cry out as he seizes my shoulders and digs his nails into my flesh, baring his teeth at me with a glint in his eyes that looks almost like madness.

"There you are," he growls, and my stomach drops to my toes.

"No!" I squeak, wriggling and trying to break free. Of course he's far too strong for me, but that doesn't stop me from trying.

I drop and twist, managing to slip away just enough to lurch backward, but then Daddy's hands are on me again. His iron-like arms capture me around my torso, spinning me around before thrusting me against a bale. Straw flutters down around us like confetti as he roughly hauls off my T-shirt. Then he seizes my wrists, gripping them hard, and sinks his teeth into my shoulder. I bellow in delicious pain, but he just sucks and bites harder.

Papa's nails scrape at my hips as he yanks at my sweatpants. I realize he's dropped to his good knee, and his mouth is at just the right height to swallow my dripping cock the moment he frees it from my clothes. I wail again, overcome with sensation already. Papa's lips and tongue feel amazing, but the straw is scratching my bare ass and back, and Daddy is still marking my shoulder with his teeth. He's also got both my nipples between his fingers and thumbs and is pinching them viciously. That's left my hands free, so I try my best to push him off, whimpering and squirming in my attempt to get away.

"No, please!" I squeal as if that'll make any difference. I'm not exactly small, but my Daddies have over a decade of military fitness training under their belts, which makes overpowering me pretty easy.

They like to feel me struggle, though.

"Naughty pup," Daddy rasps, his grin just like a wolf's as he uses both hands to grab my wrists again and throw them above my head. He crosses them and holds them in place with just one hand. The other he brings to my mouth, forcing the middle finger inside. I groan wantonly as I suck on it, but he doesn't keep it there for long. He slips it out before lowering his arm and smacking the side of my thigh hard, making me jump away from the straw. He uses his arm to hold me against him as his wet digit slides between my cheeks and starts probing at my tight, fluttering hole.

I'm still fighting, but with a hot mouth on my cock and a finger in my ass, my knees are going weak. Daddy captures my lips for a filthy kiss, making it even more difficult for me to breathe. I moan loudly, though, and push my arms against their restraint. Daddy just laughs into my mouth, squeezing me tighter, and Papa digs his fingers into my hips.

Daddy removes his hand, only to spit into it and return to my behind, shoving two digits inside this time. It burns, but

I'm distracted as he starts biting the side of my neck. Papa drags his nails along my back, making me scream.

For several moments, I'm lost in the bliss. But then I don't know if Daddy gives a signal or Papa does it of his own accord, but suddenly he pops off my cock and then yanks my pants all the way down to my ankles, where I instinctively step out of them.

Daddy bites my lower lip savagely before nuzzling his nose against mine. "Do you think you can outrun us, little pup?"

I don't hesitate. I shove him backward and lurch away from both of them, my arms flailing and my feet unsteady as I sprint around the corner. I'm not sure where I'm going. I just propel myself forward, their laughs echoing behind me.

I pant as I fumble my way around the mini maze, sweat dripping from my skin and my knees trembling. I scramble around corners, thinking that maybe I do want to try and find the door. Fresh air sounds really good right about now, and the fight or flight in me is feeling a little too real.

But of course I don't get the chance. I round a corner, only to find myself yanked off the floor by Daddy's muscular arms again. I scream and thrash my legs, clawing with my hands, but he just laughs some more in my ear as he spins us around, then dumps me unceremoniously on one of the mattresses.

It's happening. There's no going back now.

Well, naturally, I can *always* tap out whenever I want. But so far, I never once have.

I want them to completely destroy me.

Papa was already lying on the mattress when I landed on it. He rolls over to pin my shoulders down and claim my mouth with his own, and I taste the salty musk of my cock on his lips. It's primal and feral, and my length jerks in response against my belly. The mattress dips, and within seconds, Daddy's firm hands are sliding up my naked torso, his lips latching onto one of my already sore and budded nipples. I groan into Papa's mouth as I reach out with my fingers, fumbling blindly as I search for them. I quickly realize that they've both removed all their clothes as well, and I clumsily pat my way up their legs and over their hips until I can slide my hands along their hot, hard, leaking cocks.

I love the noises they make. Papa hums, and Daddy chuckles. "Is that what you want, pup? Do you want to feel your alphas inside you?"

I whimper in response as Papa is still overpowering my mouth, rendering me speechless. I don't really need to say anything, though.

They've caught me, so now they can do whatever they want with me.

I expect to feel more lubed-up fingers pushing against my hole. So when Daddy suddenly bites my thigh, I shriek in surprise at the sudden sharp but exquisite pain. It's Papa's turn to laugh as he releases my mouth, only to capture my poor, abused lower lip and let it drag through his teeth. *Fuck.* It's a good thing the summer vacation has already started and I don't have work tomorrow. I know I wanted my Daddies to mark me, but sometimes I need a day or two so my face doesn't give anyone the wrong impression that I've been in an actual fight or something.

"I think our little baby wolf needs some paws to take away with him, Daddy," Papa says, grinning down at me as I pant. I can feel my eyes are wide as I look back at him, nervous but excited for what's to come.

Daddy hums as he gives the tender mark on my thigh one last suck. Then he kisses his way up to my tummy, purposefully ignoring my straining cock. "What a lovely idea, Papa," he says somewhat gleefully. "Shall I do the honors?"

Papa manhandles me until I'm on all fours, hovering above him. He lifts his head and kisses me sweetly but contradicts the gentle action by dragging his fingernails down both my flanks, leaving several stinging lines in his wake. I hiss, but he just laughs and kisses me again.

"Yes, please, Daddy," he says, wrapping his hand around the back of my neck. He pulls my face in front of his so we can kiss some more while his head is resting on a pillow, but it also sticks my ass farther into the air.

I know why, and I make a show of trying to scramble away. Papa just grins some more as he tightens the grip he has on my neck and also wraps his fingers around my sore, blemished shoulder.

"Shh, little pup," he whispers as I feel Daddy moving behind me. "There's no escape. Be a good boy now, and let your Daddies fuck you."

My breathing is ragged. "I *am* good," I rasp, nodding so our noses brush together. "I'm a good boy."

"So good," Papa agrees, caressing his hands along my sides where he just scratched them up. I whimper, wanting to be so good—the *best*—for them both.

The only warning I get is a slight whistling through the air that I barely catch thanks to our heavy breathing and the ambient sounds around us. Even with that little moment to prepare, I still yelp as the wooden paddle hits the fleshy part where my ass cheek meets my thigh. Tears spring into my eyes as I moan, and Papa gives me a kiss.

"So good," he murmurs against my lips. "So good for your alphas."

"Papa," I whimper as another blow falls on the other side. I still cry out, but less this time, falling quickly into the subspace that comes from a good spanking.

"Good boy," Daddy also says. "That's two. I'm going to give you ten in total. So how many more?"

I hate when he makes me do math in the middle of sexy times, but that's part of him being in control. He owns my brain as well as my body. I screw up my eyes and force myself to do the basic calculation. "Eight," I huff out.

Papa beams at me like I just won a spelling bee, and Daddy gently strokes my already warm behind. The paddles all have paw prints cut out of them, complete with little claws. My ass will soon be bright red, but I'll be able to see the paler wolf symbols when I look at my reflection in the mirror.

I love those marks so much.

Every time Daddy brings the paddle whaling down on my butt or the tops of my thighs, Papa rewards me with a tender kiss and tells me how good and perfect I am. His hands constantly skim reassuringly over all my skin, not just the blemished parts. Our hard cocks brush together, mingling my desire in with the pain.

I'm ridiculously turned on, but I know I won't be allowed to come until after my Daddies. That's the rule. The orgasm denial always feels like torture when they tease me for a long time, but it's so worth it in the end.

"Ten," Daddy announces triumphantly, running his hand over my sore rump. "Well done, baby boy. That was so good. You did so well."

I'm gasping for air, dripping perspiration onto Papa, and my arms are shaking from the effort of holding myself up. But I still smile goofily and nod. "Thank you, Daddy," I croak.

Papa uses the hand around the back of my head to ease my face down until it's buried against the side of his neck. He cards his fingers through my hair, murmuring about how perfect and gorgeous I am. My heart gallops in my chest.

I feel like a rock star.

Daddy doesn't warn me as his cold, slippery fingers begin rubbing against my puckered hole. I jerk, but only a little, and Papa holds me still with soothing, reassuring noises in my ear. Daddy pushes two digits in like he had before, not wasting much time before adding a third and stretching me further. I think I know what's coming, but that's the beauty of subspace. I don't have to worry about anything. I just have to relax and let myself be used divinely, however they want me.

Daddy's lube-free hand trails down my spine, our skin damp against each other. "Up you get now, baby boy. Papa's cock is all ready for you to fuck him good and sweet."

Papa kisses me before I rise up and angle my body so I can ride him hard. I might already be trembling with exhaustion, but I know I can do this. I'll do anything to pleasure my alpha wolves once they've caught me. Daddy's hand comes between my thighs, and he coats Papa's dark cock with shiny lubricant. Papa groans at the touch, biting his lip and meeting eyes with Daddy. Their love and arousal for each other is always so palpable. I'm so lucky that they had room enough in their hearts for me, too.

I brace my body by gripping onto Papa's shoulders, then impale myself on his rock-solid length, sliding all the way down until the fat tip hits against my prostate. We both moan, and he pulls me back down again for a sloppy kiss. We grind for a minute as I get used to the feeling of him inside me, but Daddy doesn't waste any time in pushing two of his fingers past my tight ring of muscle.

I cry out, tightening my grip on Papa and grimacing. I always think I can't manage this, that it's too much. However, Daddy always proves me wrong. I just have to be patient, but that's not exactly easy when I'm already so tired and so close to the edge.

"Good boy," Daddy growls as he pulses his hand, and Papa

thrusts up and down. I whimper, but then Daddy wraps his other hand around my throat and bites my earlobe. "Who do you belong to?" he snarls, adding a third finger into what feels like an already impossibly tight space.

"Daddy and Papa," I sob, looking up at the ceiling that has soft, twinkling fairy lights hung all over it. They look like stars. I'm just a little wolf pup being claimed by my pack alphas in the wild. It's the most natural and beautiful thing in the whole world.

"Good boy," he says, still licking and nipping at my ear. "Who loves you?"

"Daddy and Papa."

"That's right, baby boy. So you can go off into the world and find some tasty treat to play with, but who will you always come home to?"

"Daddy and Papa!" I wail. They're both still undulating inside me, filling me up but not quite giving me enough. Tears spill down my face. I feel desperate. "Please, Daddy, *please.*"

"Shh, it's okay, baby boy," he tells me as he withdraws his hand. I feel empty despite Papa still being inside me, but I know that feeling won't last long. Sure enough, after the application of a little more lube, the blunt end of Daddy's cock starts pushing at my hole. "You can take us both, can't you, little pup? We're going to fill you with our cum and mark you as ours."

"Now and forever," Papa agrees, running his hands up my chest and finding my nipples to rub and squeeze.

I drop my head back against Daddy's shoulder, gasping for air and feeling like I'm going to shake apart. "Now and forever," I repeat. We say that a lot. I know we can't all three of us get married, but they make me feel like we already are in so many ways.

Daddy's right. It doesn't matter where I go or who I fuck. I will always belong to them.

With both throbbing cocks embedded in my ass, we start to move as if all three of us were one living being. My sore butt cheeks burn as I bounce up and down, slapping against their thighs, but I love the pain. I am all consumed by them. They are my whole world.

I vaguely appreciate that Papa gives Daddy a nod. Daddy removes his hand from my throat at the signal and instead wraps it around my desperately sensitive cock. "We're going to come in you now, little pup," Daddy grunts, our thrusts making us all a bit unsteady. "You're going to come for us as well, aren't you? Such a good little pup for your alphas."

"Yes, Daddy!" I cry. "I'll be good, I promise. I love you. I love you both!"

"Good boy," Papa repeats over and over as he slams up into me. "Such a good, gorgeous boy."

I feel Daddy falter as his cock starts to pulse and spit inside me. Papa gives a few more thrusts before screwing up his face and doing the same. I make a strangled noise, holding on until I get permission, until Daddy tells me it's okay. His hand is flying over my cock, though. I'm so hard. I need...I *need...*

"Come, sweetheart," Daddy mutters against my ear.

I sob as my release explodes all over his hand and Papa's stomach. I know they've just spent all that time marking me in much more lasting ways, but I love seeing my seed covering them as well.

They're mine just as much as I am theirs.

"Good boy," Daddy rasps as we all start slowly collapsing into a post-orgasm puppy pile. "Such a good boy for your Daddies. We love you."

"We love you so much," Papa agrees as he wraps his arms around me.

My ass is so fucking sore. My skin is bruised and scratched and bitten. I'm beyond exhausted.

And yet I couldn't be happier.

I have my Daddies' blessings to go out and try hunting for myself. And thanks to their efforts tonight, I couldn't forget who I belonged to if I tried.

I am one lucky little pup.

CHAPTER 3

Harper

"You really didn't have to come all this way to pick me up, Grandma," I protest.

But my elderly grandmother just grins as she hurtles us up route 31, heading north toward the tiny, crappy town she lives in. She's hunched up against the steering wheel, peering through glasses as thick as the bottom of jam jars.

"Oh, hush your butt," she says gleefully. "I wasn't going to leave you to the wolves, was I?"

I should have insisted on driving. At this rate, we're going to end up smeared on the asphalt before we even pass Kokomo. But I know what Grandma is like. She's been denied the chance to look after me these past five years, so there'll be no stopping her now. Even as my life flashes before my eyes and I grip onto the cracked leather seat, I can't help the small smile that plays on my lips or the lump that rises in my throat.

As if reading my thoughts—something I'm not unconvinced my grandma can do—she reaches over and pats my knee. "Of course I was going to come get you, sweetheart. I'm just so glad you finally came to your senses. I wasn't going to leave you at the mercy of that wicked man for another second. Why, he was meaner than a bag of rattlesnakes, lord help me."

"Oh, it was just time," I say, trying to keep my tone flippant. But I squeeze her hand all the same, and try and fight the uneasy sense of fear writhing in my belly like the snakes Grandma just mentioned.

I'll be honest—as much as I'm dreading swapping city life for deathly boring suburbia, I'm also extremely glad to see Indianapolis vanishing in the mirrors of Grandma's rickety old VW bug. I bet she'll have a cinnamon apple Bundt cake waiting for us as soon as we step through the front door of her tiny house. My bed will be made with fresh sheets that smell like lavender. She'll chatter at me nonstop and ask me silly questions about anything and everything.

I'll matter. I'll be loved.

I try and swallow that lump in my throat, but it's not budging. I wonder how long it'll take Lowell to realize I've gone for good. I left a letter, but he was never very good at listening to what I had to say.

Well, I basically wasn't allowed to leave his apartment, so me not being there will be a glaring sign, I suppose. But I left most of my stuff behind, not wanting any of the expensive things he bought me over the years. I pretty much only packed what I arrived in Indianapolis with after I graduated high school and went to the big city to chase my dreams.

Humph. Some dreams.

"What's that, sweetie?" Grandma asks. She's got both hands back on the wheel, but as she looks at me, she swerves the whole car. I lurch forward to grab the dash, but she just chuckles and rights herself before she can drive us off the freeway. "Oh, honey. It's okay. You just relax now."

That seems a statistical impossibility while still in this car, but the sentiment warms my heart. She managed not to ever kill me when I was growing up, so hopefully she won't do it now. I take a deep breath and let it out slowly.

"Sorry, Grandma," I say genuinely. "These last few days have been…intense."

That's not really the word I mean, but it seems the most appropriate for now. And if I think on it hard, it hasn't just been the past couple of days or weeks, or even months.

This whole relationship has been rotten for years, but I was too in love to see it. Or at least I thought I was in love. I guess getting showered with gifts and living a pampered life-style will make you turn a blind eye to all kinds of awful shit.

Well, maybe not just anyone. But it certainly suckered me in.

Grandma reaches out to squeeze my knee without causing a multicar pileup. I smile ruefully and slip my hand against hers once more, holding it as tight as I dare. Her bones feel more fragile than I remember. Her skin more papery. I know she's got a long time ahead of her yet, God willing. But I can't help but curse being away from her for so long. It wasn't worth it.

"He was a no-good, two-bit son of a gun," Grandma mutters darkly, stroking the back of my hand with her thumb. "Never treated you right, sweetheart, no sir-ee. He was as wanted as a woodpecker in a church. Don't you cry no more tears over him. You're a firecracker, you hear me?"

Even after several decades in Indiana, she still has that southern Louisiana drawl from her childhood. It seems stronger to me in this moment. We've spoken on the phone and video calls plenty, but there's something about hearing it in person that resonates more with me. It's comforting. Her voice is my home.

I bite my lip and avoid her gaze for a moment. She's right. I know she's right. But she was always so kind when I was with Lowell, with endless patience for my tearful rants and hysterical insecurities. She never once told me to leave him, just talked through everything calmly with me and tried to make me see just how insanely unreasonable my ex-boyfriend truly was.

She knew I had to realize myself that running for the hills was the only option. And damn, I took my sweet time.

"I'll need to get a job," I blurt out. It's not something I really want to think about, but it's better than focusing too much on my disastrous failed relationship.

Grandma blows a raspberry. "Don't you be worrying yourself about all that," she admonishes me. "Give yourself a hot second to breathe."

"I'm not just going to freeload off you," I grumble, making her laugh again.

"Always such a thoughtful boy," she says, shaking her head and bouncing my hand in hers against my knee. "But I paid the house off years ago. Your grandpa set me up sweet before he passed, and my pension keeps me ticking over. The last thing you need to be concerning yourself about is money. It's uncouth."

I chuckle. That's her lowest insult, so I know not to push the matter further just now. But I've been a kept man—a kept boy, technically—for almost five years. It seemed incredible to start with, but I don't want to feel guilty anytime I buy my own groceries or want to go out.

Huh. That's a point. I remember one of the only things Paddle Creek had going for it back in the day was a thriving queer bar. I never tried to go. I was underage and too little to fool anyone otherwise. Besides, I didn't have anyone to go *with* either, and as a newly-out teen the prospect of going alone, not to mention illegally, was terrifying. But checking out The Ice Cream Parlor suddenly gives me something to look forward to for the first time in ages.

Oh, hang on. What if they're hiring? That would be even

better! The only couple of jobs I had before I met Lowell were bartending. If there's any luck in the world, I'd be able to get ahold of some of my old managers for referrals. Yeah, the thought of working somewhere where I'd be surrounded by hot gay guys feels like the perfect antidote to a terrible breakup.

I keep my plans to myself so as not to worry Grandma, but she picks up on my good mood and grins at me. "You got skinny, Harper," she says as we continue to hurtle down the road. "Don't you worry, though. I'll fatten you up real good by the end of the summer."

She's always shown her love through her cooking, so I laugh and again don't argue. But I also hope that Paddle Creek has a halfway decent gym that'll help me keep the pounds off. Nothing against bigger guys, of course. And chubby boys can be twinks, too. It's just part of my kink. I like to be smaller than whoever's on top of me. It makes me feel more submissive. Easier to be controlled.

I sigh, trying not to let my improved mood slip. After everything I've been through, perhaps I should attempt to find myself a new kink. I've only been one Daddy's boy, but it didn't exactly work out the way I'd hoped, to put it mildly.

"How are you going to fatten me up?" I ask instead of dwelling on that painful topic. If there's one thing Grandma can talk about for hours, it's food. "Stuffed zucchini boats?"

Her face lights up. She does this thing with bacon, macaroni and cheese, and maple syrup that she pours into halved zucchinis that immediately brings me back to my childhood. "Oh, I haven't made those in forever!" she cries. "Shall I whip that up for supper?"

"That would be wonderful," I tell her sincerely.

I spend the rest of the drive listening to her rattle off her favorite dishes that she hasn't had the chance to make in a while, aside from church picnics and the like. "There's no point gettin' all fancy for just one," she says ruefully.

I want to tell her that life is too fucking short and that she should absolutely treat herself like a queen every damned day. But I don't want to let her know how much turmoil is raging inside me, so instead, I give her my signature cheeky grin.

"Well, now you have me again. We can be as fancy as we like."

She hums and pats my thigh. "We sure can," she agrees.

Traffic is kind to us, so we come into town just as the afternoon is creeping into evening, and manage to skip rush hour. Grandma naturally falls silent, and I quietly look out of the passenger side window at the all-too-familiar sights that somehow also feel totally alien to me now. I guess a lot has changed since I left.

This wasn't always my home. I was actually born in Chicago and lived just outside the city until I was twelve. But my mom's addictions and stints in and out of rehab pushed my parents' marriage apart. She just wanted to party, and my dad just wanted to work. He's a lawyer, and I suspect only married my mom because he got her pregnant. I doubt he ever wanted kids.

Luckily, I'm an only child, and Grandma stepped up for me when her own daughter couldn't. I came to live with her and honestly never looked back since. We hear from my mom very occasionally. It's good to know she's still alive. Grandma will say "She always was a wild one" in that sad voice before bustling off to bake enough muffins to feed an army.

My dad diligently paid his child support up until the day I turned eighteen, and even offered to help me with college, but I didn't want that from him.

I never heard from him again.

So, no. Paddle Creek might not be a hub of exciting adventures or—for better or worse—filled with a ton of smoking hot gay guys eager to pummel my ass into next week. But I feel safe here. I can get back on my feet and work out what the hell I'm doing with my life. And most importantly, as we pull into the driveway of a one-story house absolutely teeming with flowers in every color of the rainbow, I know my grandma loves me. She always will.

Even if she's the only person on this whole entire planet who does.

CHAPTER 4

Trey

"I KNEW I'D FIND YOU HERE."

I grin as I wipe my hands on a nearby rag and look out over the bike I've been tinkering with for the better part of eighteen months. I watch my husband saunter into the wide garage, past his Jag, my BMW, and the spot where Brady's Chevrolet Bolt usually sits. The empty space has been practically yelling at me the whole time I've been down here this evening.

Rick must have come straight from work. He looks sinful in his suit pants and shirt, the top couple of buttons undone, no doubt because he's already thrown the tie he feels he has to wear into the hamper with disdain.

He's still as handsome to me as the day we met. He could be wearing camo gear or a tux. It doesn't matter. He smiles as he approaches, and I love the crinkles that are around his eyes these days as much as the salt-and-pepper in his hair. He's aging like fine wine, and there are still days I can't quite believe he's mine.

"Hey, gorgeous," he says as he leans down to kiss me, apparently not caring I'm mucky from a day working on other people's cars at Horowitz's, and now from pulling apart the engine on my bike, Ariana.

"Hey," I reply softly. I try to hold his gaze, but it seems I can't stop my eyes from flicking again to where the Bolt is missing. Rick sighs and goes from crouching to dropping his ass down on the concrete beside the soft mat I've been sitting on. "Your clothes!" I protest.

He snickers at me. "You know, there's this fancy machine they have these days that wash clothes *for* you."

I lightly punch his shoulder, only feeling vaguely guilty about the smear of grease my knuckles leave behind.

He arches an eyebrow at it, then at me. I try not to laugh but fail.

"I also have *other* shirts as well, I guess," my husband mutters grumpily, but he doesn't fool me. He's a teddy bear at heart.

I pick up a wrench and go to start fiddling with the front suspension again, but Rick reaches out and gently removes the tool from my hand.

"I'm fine with it," I say before he can open his mouth.

He grins, places the wrench down, then takes my grubby hand in his. "I know you are," he says kindly.

"I want Brady to be free and explore himself," I say, repeating the same things out loud that I've been telling myself ever since I waved him off that afternoon. "He's our baby. I don't think he's going to leave us. I want him to have fun. Relationships evolve."

"I know all that, too," Rick says in that same patient tone of voice.

I huff. "Then why am I tying myself up in knots, replacing a perfectly good fender for the second time?"

Rick lifts my hand up and kisses the back of it. "Would you like me to tell you?" I roll my eyes but nod all the same. Rick kisses my knuckles again. "You're worried about him.

We're devoted to protecting him and loving him, but we're not used to letting our little pup fend for himself."

I chew my lower lip and try and think of something to say in protest, but I realize Rick is right as usual and has called me out. I growl as I exhale. "I mean...what trouble can he possibly get up to in Paddle Creek? He's safe here, right?"

"Exactly," Rick agrees. "He's got a good head on his shoulders. His family raised him right. And he knows his Daddies love him more than anything and are just a phone call away if anything gets out of hand. But I trust him to make good decisions. If he finds someone to play with tonight, I have no doubt he'll take good care of them."

I let out another breath and really think about what Rick's saying before eventually nodding. "You're right. I'm being stupid and acting like he doesn't know right from wrong. He'd never be reckless or do anything dangerous, either for himself or anyone else."

Rick uses his other hand to hold the side of my face. "You're not stupid, dummy," he says, making me laugh. "You care. A lot. It's one of the many reasons I married you."

I snort. "You married me because you proposed when I was high on a serious amount of painkillers, and then I felt bad backing out once my head cleared."

He smirks before crawling into my lap and cupping both hands around my jaw, then kissing me deeply. I get a whiff of his spicy aftershave. I like it, but I prefer it when he smells like sweat and sunshine.

"Well, I hate to break it to you, champ," he says playfully as he rubs our noses together, "but either way, you're stuck with me now, and I'm not ever letting you go. You're mine."

"Damn straight," I mumble against his lips.

We kiss for a little longer before he sighs and looks into my eyes. "Brady is mine, too. Ours. He knows that. He'll come home to us in one piece and tell us all about his adventures." He grins. "If he has any luck finding someone in this tiny town. Chances are he'll come home eager for a good fucking from us to ease his disappointment."

I hum and run my hands up my husband's back. As fun as that sounds, I don't want my baby boy to be sad. "He will come home with stories, though," I insist. "If not today, then someday, and they'll be sexy as fuck."

"We'll get to enjoy them together," Rick agrees with a nod. "Our little wolf pack."

He touches the tattoo on my bicep of a wolf howling at the moon. We all have some kind of lupine ink on our bodies. We got them done last year in place of actually being able to marry Brady legally. We wanted to show our commitment somehow. We'd only been together a year, but there was no point in denying it. We're bound to one another, now and forever.

I know I'm not only being ridiculous but selfish. All of us are non-monogamous, and quite frankly, that's how we thrive. Rick and I have been devoted to each other since the day we met, even when we were too chicken shit to admit it to ourselves. But we also get sparks from connecting with other guys. Rick never bottoms, but I like to switch, so that's always been a consideration. We like play parties and group sex. And when Brady came into our lives, he fell perfectly in sync with that mentality.

But this is the first time he's ventured out on his own since we got together with the specific intent of topping and dominating. Usually, he's our sweet little pup to care for. Ours to fuck senseless, then dotingly put back together once his tears have dried.

This turmoil of feelings within me is unsettling. I want to see him grow and thrive. I know firsthand how kind he is and have no doubt he'll take care of anyone he connects with.

I just…miss him. I'm sad not to be experiencing this with him. Which definitely is selfish.

But I guess maybe this is a bit like having *actual* children. My sister has four awesome kids, and she's mentioned several times how hard it is to watch every one of them turn their backs on her and run off into their first day of school. She's been terrified at times to release them into the wild. But at some point, we have to let those we love go so they can fly off and become the best versions of themselves they can possibly be.

And just trust that they will come home again.

"Talk to me," Rick says, bringing me back to the here and now.

I appreciate that he allowed me a few minutes for my mind to wander, but I don't think there's anything more left to say. I know logically that everything about this situation is fine. Excellent, actually. It means that we've done a good job in helping Brady to flourish. So I just have to sit with my anxiety.

I'm not an idiot, despite my earlier protests. I've done some serious therapy since leaving active duty, and I'm fully aware that I have control issues that stem from my trauma. That's what my fears regarding Brady are really about. It helps to soothe my mind when I keep my hands busy, hence working on Ariana for all this time. The point isn't necessarily to fix her—although I do love riding her when she's fit for it. The point is to know that I always have a project I can fall back on.

Rick also knows very well about my need for physical activity when I'm spiraling. Which is probably why he's currently kissing along my jaw and skimming his fingers under my tank top.

"You going to talk to me?" he asks again, a teasing tone in his words.

I shake my head and dig my fingers into his side. "Done talking," I grunt.

He grins before capturing my mouth. "Good," he mumbles against my lips.

I took my prosthetic off when I sat down to work earlier so I'd be more comfortable resting on the mat. Even after all these years, there are still times when I have to remember to compensate for it and readjust my balance. But that's another thing Rick knows as much about, if not more, than me. As he guides me onto my back, he's aware enough to help steady me as I go down, never letting me fall.

He'll always be there for me and Brady, no matter what.

I'll never get tired of the feeling of his body pressing against mine. And—if I'm really going to go all in with being selfish right now—it's kind of nice to be dominated by him again and have him all to myself. I adore being Brady's Papa...but sometimes I like being submissive as much as I live to hunt and conquer our little pup. I'm very lucky to be in a relationship that gives me such an incredible amount of freedom and versatility.

Rick grinds down on top of me, his hard cock stimulating mine through our clothes. I'm not in the mood to be teased, and he knows that. So it doesn't take long for him to hover over me as he shoves my sweatpants down and unzips his pants.

It's raw and basic, especially on the dirty floor of our garage, but that's exactly what I need in this moment. He spits on his palm then wraps it around our leaking shafts, stroking them together.

"I love you," he murmurs into my mouth. He makes it sound like an order that I dare not defy. He's like a mountain, unmovable and inevitable. I claw at his back through his damp shirt and thrust my pelvis up into his grip.

"Love you, too," I manage to say before he bites my lip, his hand speeding up as we chase our orgasms. I knew it wouldn't take me long as I was so wound up previously. I was like a tightly sprung coil just begging for release.

There's no point worrying about anyone's clothes as I grit my teeth and start spurting all over his hand and my chest. I just drop my head back and bellow as pure pleasure rushes through me. I tremble and pant until the room stops spinning. Then I lean up and kiss Rick as hard as I can, urging him toward his climax.

"I love you," I rasp again, running my hands up and down his back, wanting to feel as close to him as I can without him actually being inside me. "I love you so much."

He drops his face against my neck and cries out as he begins to spill all over me as well. I cling to him like a life raft, feeling his hot, hard body against mine in a reassuring way.

We're a team. We've literally fought side by side in what felt like the depths of hell. We've survived my catastrophic injury and recovery, let alone all the usual ups and downs you get in relationships. There's no one else I would want by myself in this world.

And then Brady came into our lives and somehow made us closer, stronger. That boy is pure sunshine. He brings out the best in both of us.

As Rick and I hold each other tightly in our post-orgasm glow, I know that the three of us are unbreakable. Tonight will probably just be the first of many of Brady's adventures. Nothing or no-one is going to pull us apart. No one could compare to these two men I love.

Everything is fine, and honestly, nothing is likely to change all that much, really, is it?

CHAPTER 5

Harper

I ALWAYS THOUGHT STREET CARS WERE PRETTY NORMAL growing up. After all, I come from Chicago, where public transport is abundant. It wasn't until I left school and went to go see a little more of the world that I realized Paddle Creek's rickety old tram system is actually quite unusual.

As I hop off at the stop by Creams, I feel a pang of nostalgia. I've told myself over and over for the past few years that this place was a dump and I didn't miss it at all. But the truth is, despite the fact that nothing in this town works properly and it's all just a bit shabby, it's still *home*.

And that's the other thing. The people here are different from the big city. As illustrated when I approach the club and the person at the door gives me a kilowatt smile. From their attire, I'm not sure of their pronouns, but they certainly come across as friendly as I near the door. They have dark skin and a slim but extremely muscular form that they're showing off in fishnets, hot pants, and a cinched corset, not to mention the six-inch platform heels and waist-length braids. It feels like they are being so outrageously themselves just by standing there, and it gives me a little spring in my step.

I can do this. I can walk through that door. There is absolutely no reason why I shouldn't, after all.

"Hey there, cutie," they say with a wink. "You joining us tonight?"

"Yeah," I say with what I hope is an air of confidence that suggests that I belong there, not that I'm figuratively quaking in my boots. "I heard this was the place to be round here."

The host preens—fluttering their fake eyelashes and patting over their heart. "Oh, darling. Flattery will get you *everywhere.* I'm Dijon. Welcome. If you don't have a bag, just say hi to Juan over there and get a lil' stamp, and then you can head right on in!"

I nod and greet the bouncer, who is a lot less douche-baggy than pretty much all the guys I dealt with in Indianapolis. "Have a great night," he says with a wink as I head into the club.

"I'll try," I find myself answering.

As its name would suggest, The Ice Cream Parlor looks like a 1950s throwback, with a big neon sign out front displaying its name and more neon as I walk through the door. The walls are minty green, and the booths and stools are upholstered with shiny red leather. The dance floor is made of large black-and-white checkered tiles that make it look like a chess board. In one corner stands a jukebox that I'm pretty sure is just for show, as is the mint green Cadillac that's been repurposed into a VIP seating area.

It's kind of how I've imagined it all these years, but I still feel a little stunned that I'm finally here. If I could go back and tell my seventeen-year-old self that I just walked into Creams all by myself, I never would have believed it.

The place is reasonably busy, considering it's a Tuesday night. The crowd is mostly male, but I don't allow myself to look around just yet. I'm here with a purpose, after all. So I head straight over to the bar and wait for a member of staff to become available.

"Hey," I say brightly when a slim guy with several piercings wearing a baggy muscle tank catches my eye. "I was wondering if you guys were hiring?"

The twink flashes me a smile. "We're always on the lookout for hot young things to encourage people to part with their money." He laughs and winks at me, then grabs a napkin and a pen and starts scribbling. "Here's the main email address. Drop a message to Diego. He's the manager. Tell him Skylar—that's me—told you to message him. It probably won't be tonight, but he'll get back to you quickly."

He hands over the napkin with a flourish, and I take it with a relieved smile. I was bracing myself for a flat-out refusal, but this is a promising start.

"Thanks," I say genuinely as I pocket the napkin for safekeeping.

"No problem, sugar," replies the twink. "Can I get you a drink while you're here?"

I nod, starting to relax a little. "Vodka, lemon, and lime, please."

Skylar winks again. "Coming right up."

I'm sure he's flirting, which is a nice confidence boost, but sadly he's not my type. I like them big so they can throw me around a bit. Speaking of which, I can feel someone watching me, and I glance over to see a guy with broad shoulders and a sweet face sitting a couple of stools down. He's got dark hair and eyes that suggest a little Asian heritage. He nods once and raises his glass at me.

I bite my lip and look away. *Shit.* Maybe I'm not ready for this. I've only been with Lowell for the past few years. I hooked up with a couple of guys before him, but they were one-time things. He's basically been my whole sexual experience, and toward the end, being with him was more something I endured than enjoyed...

Well...that's over. I have to start moving forward some time, so it might as well be now. Besides, I don't have to jump this guy. I can just say hello. There doesn't need to be anything more if I don't feel comfortable.

I pay for my drink and look back around, pleased but also a little nervous that the guy is still glancing my way. His face lights up, though, as I move across and slide onto the stool next to him.

"Come here often?" I say, arching an eyebrow.

I'm so relieved when the guy laughs at my cheesy pick-up line. And not just politely, it's a proper belly laugh. "This is my first time in a while, actually. You?"

"First time ever," I admit.

"Cool," he says with genuine enthusiasm. He picks up his drink and taps it against mine. He reminds me a bit of a big Labrador puppy. I'd guess he's maybe a few years older than me, but he's got an adorable himbo vibe. Like a himbo in training or a baby himbo.

He feels safe, which is the complete opposite of Lowell. I find I'm drawn to this different kind of energy, however.

"You new in town then?" he asks. "I hope you don't mind, but I overheard you asking about a job."

I shrug and glance back at the bartender who gave me the email address. "It's not like it's a secret," I say with a grin. "I actually just moved back home. I spent most of my teen years here."

"Neat," the baby himbo says, his eyes twinkling. "I grew up here, too. You go to Paddle Creek High? I had my ten-year reunion last summer, which was kind of wild. Where did that time even go?"

He laughs, and I join in. There's something pure about him. I doubt he'd play games with me or try and fuck with my head. So what if he doesn't give off Daddy Dom vibes? I think I like him anyway.

"You'd have left before I started my junior year, then," I say, which is a shame. If I'd had a friend like this guy at school, or even just knew there was another gay kid at all, I might have felt less alone.

"Aww, too bad," he says and seems to actually mean it. "You go to college here after? I went on a football scholarship and now I'm an assistant coach, so I might have seen you around maybe."

I shake my head, trying not to feel defensive. He's just being nice, after all. "Nah, college wasn't really my thing," I say as I run my finger around the rim of my glass. Then I give him a flirty look and change the subject. "But if I get a job here, maybe we'll see each other around in the future."

"I'd like that," he says in a breathy voice. He shoves his hand forward. "I'm Brady, by the way."

"Harper," I say as I accept the shake, grinning at the formality of it.

This guy is very cute. Perhaps I *would* be interested in getting back on the horse tonight, after all. Or rather, getting on the himbo. He might not be as old as my usual type, but he's certainly big enough to climb.

"So, are you here all alone, Brady?" I ask, leaning a little closer and giving him a look up and down. If I'm really interested in him, he needs to know that.

I'm rewarded as his cheeks go slightly pink. "Uh, yeah," he says as he shifts in his seat. "I'm sort of conducting an experiment."

"Ooh, that sounds intriguing," I say, amping up the flirtiness. I know what I'm doing. I'm putting on an act to protect myself. But that's fine just for one evening, right? I can be the sassy, confident boy I wish I really was for a few hours.

Being myself wasn't good enough for Lowell, so I'll just hide that part away for now behind alcohol and bravado.

"I guess, yeah," Brady says. He sounds nervous but also kind of excited. "I, well…you see, I actually have two partners. But I wanted to try topping for a change. So they said I could go and find someone to play with."

I blink as I feel my eyebrows raise. Now that *is* intriguing. "You have two tops?" I say, slipping my hand over his knee. This is incredibly sexy. My cock is definitely plumping up in my jeans. "Two guys who usually dominate you?"

He licks his lips. They're such a pretty shade of pink. "Yeah," he says hoarsely.

"And they don't mind you going out to have fun on your own?"

He shakes his head. "We're polyam but non-monogamous. So we're definitely a throuple, but when I said I wanted to try, uh, topping, they encouraged me."

I don't have to pretend anything now or convince myself that hooking up with someone would be a good start to getting over Lowell. This is seriously turning me on. If baby himbo wants to experiment with being the Dom for a night, I will happily be his guinea pig.

I glance around the bar and happen to see a group of people vacating a booth. I don't think. I just grab my glass and Brady's hand. "Come on," I urge him.

We manage to nab the booth before anyone else does, and now we have a lot more privacy. I slide my hand over his thigh and grin at him. He's got a bit of a deer-in-headlights look as he stares at me, but that just makes me hornier. Damn, I want this sweet jock so badly.

But first, I want to have a little fun. After the past five years of slowly sinking into misery, I feel the need to live vicariously through this guy.

"Tell me about your partners," I say, stroking my fingers against his leg. "Is it kinky?"

"Y-yeah," he stammers, his eyes wide as he nods.

He glances down as my hand creeps closer to his groin. I love that he's getting flustered, but he doesn't make any attempt to stop me. I have a feeling baby himbo is a bit of an exhibitionist.

"Go on," I encourage him.

I feel like I'm letting something out of myself I didn't know was there. I've always had this contradiction in me. Lowell wanted me to be a good little sub and tried drilling it into me. But I think the truth is that secretly...I'm a bit of a brat. I've only just met this guy, but perhaps that's part of what makes him feel so safe. I can conduct my own experiment and have a go at letting my sassy brat loose. Like trying on shoes for size. There's no harm if I don't like it.

So far, though, that doesn't appear to be the case.

"Tell me the good stuff," I purr into his ear. "Are they your Doms? What's your pleasure?"

He swallows and jumps a little as my hand caresses over the bulge in his pants. He moans and leans a bit closer to me. Yeah, I can see how submissive he really is. I'm curious what's led him to come out on his own with the mission of topping.

"They're, uh, my Daddies," he says, licking his lips and looking at me through his dark eyelashes.

I tilt my head, my interest even more piqued. "I had a Daddy," I say softly. A little sadness creeps into the words, but I smile and shake it off. In the end, Lowell was never what I imagined a Daddy would be. It was just a name he used. "And you have two, you lucky thing. Are they soft or hard?"

On the word 'hard,' I deliberately give his shaft a squeeze. He gasps then bites his lip, his gaze never leaving mine.

"It depends," he rasps. "Daddy's in charge. He makes the rules. Sometimes he's mean. He laughs at me and makes me do whatever he wants. Papa is softer, but he does it too in the heat of things."

"But you like it?" I clarify, still stroking him through his jeans.

He nods hastily. "I love it. I love submitting to them. Once they catch me, they can do whatever they want to me. It's so freeing and, uh…"

"And?" I prompt. I'm guessing what made him falter was me popping the button on his jeans and dragging his zipper down. I wait for him to tell me to stop, but he doesn't.

"And I f-feel important, special." He gulps as I reach through his open fly and slip my hand through the front of his briefs. His eyes roll into the back of his head for a second as my fingers encircle his hot, pulsing shaft.

Fuck. I feel so alive! I know this is probably a result of all those years slowly feeling more and more worthless. Lowell always wanted things his way, and as time wore on, I just went along with it. Even if I didn't feel like it, I'd fake it. I honestly kind of forgot what it was like to have someone else make you feel horny. I guess all I needed was the right sweet guy to come along. Seeing Brady respond to my touch is intoxicating.

"So your Daddies chase you?" I ask.

He nods again. "Primal play," he utters. I love that he's struggling to speak. "It's our kink. One of our kinks, I mean. They're my…wolves. I'm their pup."

I lick my lips and consider that as I continue to fondle him under the table where no one else can see in our dark little corner. My adrenaline spikes just thinking about what he's saying. The idea of being hunted down and then submitting to whatever my pursuer wanted to do with my body once he pinned me down does sound fucking hot. Which is weird, because letting Lowell do whatever he wanted in the end was the opposite of hot. But the way Brady is describing it makes me want to know more.

"Tell me how they fuck you," I whisper in his ear. His chest is rising and falling rapidly as he pants. I can smell the musky hint of perspiration as I get him all flustered. I nip at his earlobe, getting another satisfying moan from his throat. I hardly recognize myself right now, but I can't deny that I'm having a lot of fun.

"All kinds of ways," Brady utters. "Daddy likes to fuck me while I suck Papa's cock. Sometimes they make me ride them one after another or DP me. Sometimes they tie me up or pin me to the wall. I like kneeling for them and worshiping both of their cocks at the same time."

Jesus, my dick is like iron in my pants. I could hear him talk about getting used like that for hours. "What else?" I grunt, rubbing my thumb over his leaking slit.

"We-we go to parties," he says breathlessly. "They like to give me to strangers and watch them use me to pleasure themselves. I like spanking and being told I'm a good, *good* boy. I like bukkake."

"You like to feel special," I say, repeating his words from earlier. "Adored. You like having the decisions all taken away from you." He nods fervently. "I like that, too," I admit.

I realize that's true. It's what I got out of my relationship with Lowell at the start. He just took over my life, and in the beginning, that felt so freeing and comforting. It's as if hearing Brady describe it is bringing all those old feelings of mine out of hibernation. God damn it, I just want to be taken care of.

I think Brady could do that for me tonight.

"But now the puppy wants to have a little chase of his own?" I clarify.

I wasn't far off with my first impression of him as a

Labrador. Thinking of him as a wolf pup is even cuter, though.

He grips onto the leather seat and nods slowly. "I want to try hunting. And I want to take care of them afterward like my Daddies do for me."

I'm keeping the movement of my hand deliberately slow and tortuous. "And what would you do to me if you caught me?" I whisper in his ear. He smells delicious, so I give his neck a little lick. He squeaks adorably, and I grin, proud of myself.

"I-I'd push you against a wall," he says, his cheeks going red as if he's shocked by his own audacity. "I'd rip your clothes off, spread your legs open, and eat you out until you were ready to take my cock."

I hum deeply, high on this lust with him, all my worries from before just melting away. "Is it a big cock?"

He nods, managing a punch-drunk grin. "Pretty damn big," he says with a chuckle.

I do my best not to squirm in my seat. Of course the baby himbo has a giant dick. I can't wait for him to split me open with it.

"And you'd fuck me against the wall?" I suggest.

"Yeah. Or on the bed. Or in the shower. Wherever I wanted."

"Because you'd be in charge," I say.

"Yeah," he says again.

He's thrusting his hips up, trying to get more friction from me as I play with his length. He hasn't even touched me yet, and I feel all tingly and light.

I squeeze his cock and make him hiss. "Are you going to fuck me like an animal, little wolf?" I goad him. "Are you going to have your way with me no matter how much I fight and try and get away?"

He swallows, something feral and dark flashing in his

51

eyes. "Yes," he says with much more conviction than before. "Because you're mine. If I catch you, then I own you."

"You better catch me, then."

Without warning, I release his dick and slide out of the booth. I get one fleeting glimpse of his shocked and confused face before I make a beeline for the door. Then I'm gone, out into the warm summer night, my heart hammering in my chest as I rush down the street, waiting to see if my wolf is going to catch up. I hope he does.

I want him to *devour* me.

CHAPTER 6

Brady

IT TAKES ME A SECOND TO WORK OUT WHAT THE HELL JUST happened. Harper flashes me a mischievous grin before he bolts from the club, and I have to physically shake my head to bring myself back to my senses.

The obvious first issue is that my dick is literally sticking out of my pants. Hastily, I shove it back in, trying to ignore the tenderness and blue balls. I wasn't really close to coming, but his little stunt has certainly got my blood pumping and my mouth watering.

I knock back the rest of my Coke. I'm not drinking anything stronger tonight, because I drove here, but mainly because if anything happened, I wanted to make sure I was sober and in control. I am really, really glad I made that decision now.

I feel like I'm drunk off Harper anyway. Where the hell did he come from? I thought he looked interesting when he came into the bar, but I didn't realize he'd be such a firecracker. The white-blond hair and beautiful face make him look innocent when it seems like he's anything but.

I double-check that my jeans are done up properly and

that I'm decent before hurrying out of the booth and pushing my way through the crowd to follow Harper out of Creams. I was worrying that he might have actually run off and I'd lose him without getting his number. But as I look right, I see him leaning against a lamp post. He flicks his eyebrows at me before spinning around and dashing down the street.

I don't exactly run after him. I don't want anyone to think there's something wrong or—worse—that I'm chasing him with malicious intent. But there's no mistaking that this is a hunt, and my heart is beating like crazy from the thrill of it all.

This. This is *exactly* what I was hoping to find, even though I wasn't entirely sure what I was looking for. I want to be the one with the power for a change. But I also want to make someone—*Harper*—feel the way I do when my Daddies chase me down. He's the sole focus of all my attention. He's my world, my purpose.

I hope he feels special, because he is.

I weave my way past the other pedestrians, never letting Harper out of my sight. We're on the outskirts of the town center, and most of the businesses are closed. But it dawns on me where he's heading.

The motel.

My heart skips a beat. I guess he was serious about getting ravaged and not just teasing. I lick my lips as I speed up, nerves fluttering through my body. I'm in charge now. His happiness, pleasure, and submission are my responsibility.

I can't help but think of our meeting as some sort of sign, though. Before he arrived at Creams, I'd looked around but hadn't felt a spark with anyone, and I'd actually been working on a Collr profile to see if I could widen the net and find someone interesting in the surrounding areas.

But then Harper walked in, and it felt like the universe

was highlighting him for me. As if the clouds had parted and he was illuminated by brilliant sunshine.

I can't let him down.

To be honest, I'm hoping that won't be an issue as he gets nearer to the motel. He got me so fucking turned on just now it feels pretty natural to me to track him down and jump him. I'm still a little anxious about doing a good job, but I feel like that's probably quite normal when doing anything new.

Harper wants me. I can tell that from a mile away. And I want him so badly. I want to make him feel amazing and let him float. Surely, if I just follow my instincts, we'll have a good time, right?

Sunken Treasure is a nautical-themed establishment that no doubt found its inspiration from the bright lights of Vegas and might have been kind of cool back in the day—by which, I mean a time before I was born. Now the plastic seagulls, crabs, and tropical fish that decorate the front of the building are cracked and faded. I've never seen inside, but I know it has a pool out back and the place is more of a cheap family vacation spot than a seedy hookup site.

Tonight, however, my intentions are definitely of a more mature nature.

I'm not sure if Harper slowed down or if he's genuinely not as fast a runner as me. I suppose I am in pretty good shape. But whatever the case, I put on a burst of speed, managing to catch him just before he reaches the front door of the motel. I grab his arm and spin him around, slamming him against the brick wall as we both gulp for air. In the darkness, I study his face in the glow from the flickering yellow neon light of the busted old sign above our heads.

"You caught me," he rasps, his eyes wide and shining.

I grin and lean in so I can drag my nose up his neck and the side of his face, inhaling deeply. He's wearing a pretty, sweet cologne, but I can also taste his musk on the tip of my tongue.

"I did," I growl, squeezing his arm tighter. "Now what am I going to do with you?"

He bites his lip and looks at me through his eyelashes. "Well, I've never been here before, either." He jerks his thumb behind him. "Fancy showing me around?"

It's kind of presumptuous of him that I'd spring for a motel room for us, but the truth is, I actually kind of love it. He's a naughty little brat. I've known subs and boys like that before, but I've never dallied with one personally.

I think he's going to be a whole lot of fun.

Besides, I have my credit card for Daddy's 'treats' bank account. He told me I was absolutely allowed to use it when I came out if I needed it for me and a date. I'd imagined using it to pay for dinner or drinks, but I'm sure he won't mind me using it on a room. I'd thought about playing in the woods, but for my first time taking charge, being protected by four walls and a locked door seems safer.

"Stay by my side," I rumble into his ear, loving the feeling of him shivering against my body. It's not cold out at all. That's pure anticipation. "Don't try and wander off, understand? You're mine now."

I lean back and look into his eyes. He smirks. "Yes, baby wolf," he says, his voice like silk.

Until that moment, I'd planned on asking anyone I played with to call me 'Daddy.' But I already have one of those, and Harper is right. I am the baby wolf, venturing out on my own. And I've captured myself a little...

I look him up and down, his skin and hair so pale, almost white...

Like lamb's wool. A fleece as white as snow. That's it! I've caught myself a little lamb.

"Are you ever going to kiss me?" my little lamb asks cheekily.

I huff and shake my head. I know I'm supposed to be in charge, but I've definitely picked someone to play with who is going to push me on that.

"Naughty boy," I mumble as I press my mouth to his, tasting the citrus from his drink on his lips and then his tongue as I push mine against his. He makes fists with the material of my T-shirt and grinds his groin against my thigh. I can feel all of his lean body pressing against mine.

Fuck. I need him now.

Without warning, I break the kiss and swat his ass. "Get inside," I hiss.

He takes a couple of breaths before wiping spit off his chin and sauntering through the door that has a life buoy attached to it. I also drag the back of my hand over my mouth, adjust myself in my pants, then follow him into the lobby.

The carpet is threadbare, and the lightbulbs are dim, but there's a cheerful mural that's been painted on the wall of a blonde mermaid wearing a seashell bra, surrounded by her animal friends in what must have once been a colorful underwater tableau. It's faded now, but I still like the spirit of the illustration.

In the corner by a vending machine is a very plastic-looking wooden chest on a table filled with fake gold doubloons, diamonds, pearls, and other treasures. There's a big sign saying 'DON'T TOUCH!' but I have a feeling that almost everyone who passes through here sneaks a little tacky memento from the display.

The guy behind the desk raises his gaze from the battered sci-fi paperback he's reading. "One room or two?" he asks, sounding decidedly disinterested in the answer.

"One," I say firmly, offering the credit card I've just pulled from my wallet. The rates are clearly listed on the board. It's not as cheap as I'd assumed it would be, so I really hope that means the sheets will at least be clean.

He puts his book down and snags the card from my fingers, already tapping away on the computer in front of him. When he silently offers the card back along with an actual key on a large fob shaped like an anchor, I'm startled when Harper snatches the key before I can touch it.

I look at him as I take back my credit card. The guy is already ignoring us, his nose between the pages again, so I don't feel self-conscious when a grinning Harper starts moving away from me backward, heading in the direction of the room that matches the number on the fob.

I take a step forward, and he instantly spins and breaks into a run, shoving his way through the fire door.

My heart jumps in my chest as I dash after him, my whole body vibrating. The motel is a single story, so I just chase him down the one long corridor, anticipation growing with every thud of my sneakers.

He skids to a halt in front of a room about ten feet away from me, grinning as he uses shaky hands to jab the key into the lock. Just before I reach him, the door gives, and he tumbles across the threshold. Immediately, he tries to slam the door behind him, but I lurch forward and slap my hands against the wood, forcing my way in.

I'm trembling with excitement as Harper squeaks and almost trips over himself as he stumbles backward into the small room. I yank the key from the other side, then shove the door shut behind me, locking it firmly. I throw the key onto the nightstand with a loud clatter, loving how Harper jumps. He's smiling, but he's also panting and sweating, his eyes darting back and forth.

Of course he's trapped. That's kind of the point of coming

to a room like this. But the look on his face tells me he's only just realizing that in this moment.

"What's your color, little lamb?" I ask.

His eyes widen at my question. We should have discussed safe words and limits more before, but he ran off on me. "Huh?" he says.

Aw, shit. My bad. I assumed because he talked about having a Daddy and from the fact that he immediately got on board with the idea of primal play that he'd be familiar with the traffic light system. I wonder why he's not, but now isn't the time to have that discussion.

"Green is good to go," I explain. "Yellow means you need to pause and think. Red means stop immediately."

"Ohh," he says, nodding thoughtfully. But then he flashes me a cocky grin. "Green, you fucker," he replies sassily. "That doesn't mean you don't have to work for it, though."

He grabs a pillow and throws it at me. I bat it away and step closer. The bed is between us, but there really isn't anywhere for him to hide in here. It's perfect for both our first times at this. At least I assume it's his first time trying primal play, from the way he reacted earlier when I explained it. He's clearly enjoying himself, however, from the way his face is shining and his pants are bulging at the crotch. But it was worth checking his color just in case. I desperately don't want to make any mistakes tonight.

I'm aware of exactly what it's like to be in his position, and I know how thrilling it is to feel trapped. He needs to accept that he's not in charge anymore. I am. He doesn't get to make any decisions now—unless of course he needs to use his colors.

He backs away from the bed, clearly trying to get me to move around it.

So I jump onto the mattress in a single bound.

He gasps and hits against the dresser, making it rattle. My

arms are spread out for balance and my fingers are curled like claws. I feel every bit the apex predator in that moment —big and scary.

"Fuck off," he says nervously, doing his best to run around the bed. But I jump down in front of him and make a grab for his wrist. He twists and scrambles away, a fluttering laugh escaping his throat as he tries to make it to the locked door. This time when I reach for him, though, I snag his hips and throw my body against his.

"Gotcha," I snarl as I pin his front against the wood. He slams his palms against the door and attempts to shove me off, but I'm larger and stronger than him. "Now, now, little lamb," I admonish him before kissing the side of his neck.

I love feeling him shiver at the touch, but he's still trying to push me away. Good. That's what I do with my Daddies. I want to feel him struggle because I know it'll make it that much better when he submits to me.

"I'm not a goddamned sheep," he snaps.

I chuckle against his skin. "No, you're not," I agree, squeezing my arms around his chest. "You're a little baby lamb, sweet and succulent. I'm going to eat you whole." He groans and goes a bit limp against me. I laugh again. "You want that, don't you? Sweet boy."

He appears to remember himself and starts trying to pull at my arms. "I'm not sweet. You've got to *earn* it, you shit," he says.

He kicks back, and the pain in my shin is sharp. He pauses, probably unsure if that's allowed. But just because I'm topping here doesn't mean I no longer get off on that. The adrenaline spikes through me, making my cock throb. It's different from getting spanked or my nipples clamped, but I like it all the same. I feel powerful.

"I don't have to earn a single thing," I say softly. I grab the collar of his open shirt and strip it from his shoulders in one hard tug. Luckily it's short-sleeved, so I didn't have to contend with the cuffs.

He gasps as I scrunch it into a ball and throw it onto the floor. He uses the brief moment I haven't got my hands on him to dart to the left, but I'm too fast for him. I spin him around and get my leg between his, then yank his T-shirt over his head.

"Stop me," I dare him.

He lurches forward and kisses me instead. I grab his face with both my hands, but he surprises me when he bites my lip.

"Call me a lamb again, baby wolf," he dares.

I throw my arms under his ass and pick him up. He squeals in shock and almost tumbles out of my grip, but I turn us instead and drop him on the bed, watching in satisfaction as he bounces on the mattress. His eyes are wide as he looks back up at me.

Before he can regain his wits, I make short work of the button and zipper on his jeans, then yank them and his underwear down, releasing his hard, leaking cock. I'm grateful that his sneakers each come off with just one pull, and then my work is done. I have my conquest completely naked in front of me.

I crawl on top of him, loving how ragged his breathing is and how he doesn't take his hazel eyes off me. "So pretty," I murmur as I lean down to kiss his mouth again. I find his cock with my hand to stroke and squeeze it. I want to taste him everywhere.

And I can, because I caught him, so he's now mine.

I throw his hands over his head before scooting down the bed a little. I wish I had rope or cuffs to keep him restrained, but I hope he'll stay where I put him. I want him to understand that I'm in charge, not him. He needs to let go.

He yells out as I wrap my lips around his reddened shaft

and take him deep. I absolutely love sucking cock, and I employ all my favorite tricks to drive him wild. I'm not going to let him come like this, however. Not a chance. He'll get to come when I'm done with him. When he's a shivering, weeping mess.

The fact that he's kept his hands stretched above him has made me extremely happy. I pop off his cock and wipe my mouth before smacking the side of his thigh. He jumps and blinks at me.

"Up you get, little lamb. Hands against the wall and spread your legs so your wolf can eat you up."

It's almost comical how fast he scrambles off the bed and throws himself at the wall. No—not the wall. He's got his hands on either side of the full-length mirror. *Naughty boy*, I think with high approval. He wants to *watch* me fuck him.

I want that, too.

He's trembling slightly as I take my time getting off the bed. The floor is carpeted, and I'm wearing jeans, so I don't bother getting myself a pillow like I would if I were naked. I just sink to my knees one at a time and use my hands to pull apart his cute little butt. I don't waste any time burying my face against his musky crack.

He wails as I kiss and lick his puckered hole, but he stays still against the wall. "Good boy," I mumble against his entrance. "Touch your cock. Watch yourself. But don't even think about coming. Your big bad wolf will tell you when you're allowed."

His breathing is labored as he wordlessly does as he's told. I peek over his hip to see his hand wrap around his cock. He drops his head back, but he's watching his reflection through those golden eyelashes.

"Good boy," I say again. "You look so pretty. Stay like that for me now."

He whimpers and gasps as he fondles his dick, and I use

my tongue to begin stretching him out. I lose myself in the task, feeding off his mewling and feeling powerful. When my jaw starts to ache, I pull back, cleaning my face off, then reach into my back pocket for the sachet of lube and condom I packed in my wallet earlier. I really wasn't convinced I'd be using them at all this evening. The fact that I am gives me a thrill and a surge of confidence.

I only use a small amount of the gel on my fingers as his crease is dripping with my saliva. But I wanted a bit of extra help as I go ahead and force two fingers inside him, loving how he bucks at the intrusion.

"Stay still, little lamb," I warn him.

He curls the hand against the wall into a fist, but he otherwise remains in place. I stand, giving my legs some relief after kneeling for a while, and continue to pulse my digits inside him.

Our eyes meet briefly in the mirror before I drop my head and sink my teeth into the fleshy part where his neck meets his shoulder. "Fucker!" he yells, but I ignore him. Instead, I take my hand and wrap it around the one he's got over his cock, squeezing tight.

"Mine," I growl in between sucking and licking at the tender spot. "Mine."

He takes a few shuddery breaths before I look up and meet his gaze again. "Yours," he agrees hoarsely.

That's what I wanted to hear. I've had enough of playing, and I want to claim my prize.

I pull my fingers out of his ass, making him hiss. "Both hands on the wall again," I tell him, making sure he does as he's told. His cock belongs to me now.

I make short work of undoing my pants and shoving them and my underwear down to my thighs. I grab the condom and rip the foil open with my teeth so I can hastily roll it down my cock, then use up the rest of the lube over my length and his hole.

We just watch our reflections wordlessly as I start pushing the blunt head of my dick past his fluttering ring of muscle. I've got one hand on his hip, the other guiding my cock as it sinks farther and farther inside him. His mouth is hanging open as he pants, and his skin is dripping with sweat. His white-blond hair is beautifully damp as well. I want to jam my fingers through it while he sucks my cock, but there's no time for that tonight.

Maybe next time.

God, I hope there's a next time.

"Take it," I grunt. "Good boy. Like that. Pretty lamb."

"Fuck me, you beast," he sneers with a laugh. I don't waste my time.

Now I've got both hands digging against his pelvis as I thrust into him, bending him over even more so I can really slam his prostate. He meets my every move with equal vigor. I'm not even pretending to draw it out. I'm just chasing the bliss that I've discovered between these gorgeous cheeks.

Our eyes are locked as I pummel him. I wasn't lying about the size of my cock, but he's taking me so well. His own length jumps and spits against his belly like it's waving for attention.

"Fuck, yes, FUCK," Harper yells as I speed up even more, feeling my climax rushing up to greet me. I know we have the protection of the condom, but the animal in me wants to fill him with my seed. To breed him and claim him as my own and no one else's.

"Mine," I growl again before I drop my head back and bellow, my load shooting hard and fast. I use his deliciously tight hole to milk every last drop from my throbbing cock. Then, while I'm still hard, I reach around and take his dick in my hand. "Watch," I tell him firmly.

I can see him trying to close his eyes as the pleasure builds inside him, but under all that bravado and brattiness, he's a good boy. He manages to keep his eyes on us through his lashes, gasping for breath and quivering his body against mine.

"Please," he begs, starting to thrash. "Please, baby, *please.*" I know what he's asking me for, and after he's done so well, I don't want to tease him anymore.

"Come, little lamb," I tell him, my post-orgasm voice warm and syrupy.

He explodes all over the mirror, the noises escaping from his throat primal and raw. He sags against me, even as he's still spurting, and I hold him fiercely, protecting him now that the climax has hit us both.

"Good boy," I keep murmuring softly as he shakes and leans against me. "I've got you. Good boy. You were so perfect. Well done."

He gulps down air into his lungs, his fingers flexing and curling against the slightly peeling wallpaper of the motel room. I kiss his shoulders and stroke his arms and torso. After a while, we both seem recovered enough for me to withdraw from inside him.

My plan was to pull him over to the bed to snuggle and bask in our glow. But as I'm disposing of the condom, he stumbles toward the bathroom, and I hear the rumble of toilet paper as he presumably tugs several sheets off. I hear the flush, and assume he's mopped up the mess from his ass. I'm a little hurt. I was going to do that, but he didn't give me a chance. I'm not sure why, but after I throw the trash away, I tuck myself back into my pants and zip up, not wanting to feel exposed.

Harper reemerges with a grin and a skip in his step. "That was great," he says brightly, darting over to where his clothes were discarded and putting his briefs back on in a flash. "We should do it again sometime."

"Uh, yeah," I say uncertainly. This isn't how I imagined this moment would go. He's already got his jeans back on and is shoving his feet back into his shoes. He snatches up his T-shirt and button-down with a grin, then glances at the desk next to the mirror.

"Oh," he says, seizing upon the only thing there aside from the phone. A pen and a small pad of paper with the Sunken Treasure logo at the top. "Here's my number. I'll be around over most of the summer—probably. Hit me up."

Once he's scribbled down the digits, he hauls his T-shirt over his head and winks at me. "Thanks for the fuck, baby wolf Brady."

And just like that, he's out the door, leaving me all alone to wipe off his drying cum from the mirror.

CHAPTER 7

Rick

I wasn't asleep anyway when I hear the faint click of the front door. I've been twitching at every slight noise since we came to bed, hoping to listen out for Brady's return. For all I comforted Trey earlier with his worries, I do completely understand where he was coming from. I want to make sure our baby boy is all right, so when I'm certain I detect him quietly moving around downstairs, I carefully untangle myself from Trey. He's out cold and doesn't stir, but I smile and kiss his cheek gently anyway.

"I'll be back shortly, darling. I'll bring our little wolf with me."

I'm only wearing briefs, so I shuffle my feet into my slippers and retrieve my robe from the back of our bedroom door before heading down the stairs. Trey and I left a few lamps on when we retired for the night, as well as the under-cabinet lights in the kitchen in case Brady was hungry or thirsty when he came home.

I grin as I pad softly from one room to the next, eager to hear all about his evening. It's after midnight, so I assume he's had some fun, even if it was just dancing at that club he likes in town.

But when I finally come upon him, he's curled up on one of the sofas in the living room. His face is shadowy as there's only one lamp on, but he's hunched over a glass of water, and I can see enough to tell that he's nibbling at his lower lip. Our two British shorthairs—Merlot and Chardonnay—are hanging out with him like fat, fluffy gray sentinels. One is on the rug, and the other is perched on the armchair.

Practically snuggling as far as cats go. They can tell something's wrong.

"Baby?" I say uncertainly, fear and anger already trying to claw their way up from my belly.

He glances up and gives a tiny sigh of relief. "Daddy."

"What's wrong?" I ask urgently as I rush to sit beside him and wrap my arm around his shoulders. "Did someone hurt you? Are you all right?"

He laughs and shakes his head. "Daddy, I'm fine," he says firmly.

Well, excuse me if I arch an eyebrow at that bullshit, because he's clearly been crying. "You want to tell your face that?" I ask skeptically.

He sighs again, much heavier this time, and wipes under his eyes. He drinks a gulp of water before placing the glass down, then puts his arms around me to snuggle in closer. "I'm fine," he mumbles once more.

I resist the urge to punish him for lying to me. This isn't the time...but I might remind him of it later when he's in a better headspace. He's not supposed to keep anything important from me. Perhaps a cock cage or a butt plug might jog his memory of that tomorrow.

Instead, I put my finger under his chin and force him to look at me. "Do I need to hunt somebody down?" I ask in all seriousness. If anyone has laid a finger on my baby boy, I won't be going to the police. I'll be dealing with it myself.

He shakes his head and frowns, though. "No, Daddy. I swear. I think...I think maybe *I* messed up."

His lip wobbles, and tears spring in his eyes. I know he's obviously distressed, but I can't help but feel relieved. "I doubt that very much, sweetheart."

He shakes his head once more, however. I don't like being contradicted, especially when I know that this sweet boy doesn't have a malicious bone in his body. But I hold my tongue for a moment, giving him a chance to explain.

"I met someone," he begins, fiddling with the cuff of my robe. If not looking at me makes it easier for him to tell me what happened, I'll allow it. "At Creams. He was...oh, Daddy. He walked in, and it was like the whole room lit up."

I stroke the backs of my fingers very lightly against his cheek. "He was handsome?"

"More like pretty," he says thoughtfully. "His name is Harper. He was sassy and teasing, and he looked at me like I was the whole world. I thought we clicked so well."

"But?" I prompt as tactfully as I can. I want him to tell me right now what this fucker did to him so I can go wring his neck. I need to be patient, though, and let Brady tell the story.

"He'd never tried primal play before," he continues. "I'm not sure he'd even heard of it. But he ran away from me at the club, and I tracked him down to the Sunken Treasure. He was an absolute natural at it all. I paid for a room, and we had such a good time. I pinned him down and fucked him, just like a real wolf."

I frown. "You are a real wolf," I insist with a kiss on the top of his head.

He huffs. "A real...*toppy* wolf," he elaborates, making me laugh.

I do know what he means. I just don't want him feeling like he doesn't belong in our little pack. I know we don't talk about it, but he is acutely aware that Trey and I are married to each other and not to him. I wish we could make it legal. We've done everything financially that we can to ensure we're all protected. But there's something so romantic about being officially husbands. We made it as permanent as we could with our set of wolf tattoos, but recently Trey and I have been talking about having some kind of ceremony with Brady, perhaps for his thirtieth birthday, which is coming up.

That's something to think about for another day, though. For now, Brady is one thousand percent mine, and I need to take care of him, however I can.

"It was everything I wanted," Brady continues. "I felt just like I hoped I would—like how I imagine you and Papa feel when you catch me. It was fun and exhilarating and powerful."

"So the sex was good?" I ask, not quite seeing where the issue is.

He shakes his head, and I'm almost ready to get angry again. "It was *amazing*," he says, and I cool down. "But...we'd barely finished. I was still trying to get rid of the condom, and he was already dressed and running out the door. I didn't get to give him any aftercare, and I feel so *shitty*."

"Oh, baby," I say, cuddling him tighter and tucking his head under my chin. Trust my little wolf to be tying himself up in knots because he didn't get to look after this ungrateful brat to his satisfaction. "It's okay."

"What if he has a sub drop?" he asks tearfully. "I let him down. I told him he was good and perfect, but it was like he couldn't get out of there fast enough."

I hum thoughtfully, stroking my boy's hair. "Perhaps he's just a jerk?"

Brady shrugs and leans back to look at me. "I really don't

think so, Daddy. I know I only just met him, but...the rest of the night felt so real to me. It was raw and honest and electric. That bit right at the end felt completely false. Like he was a store dummy putting on a big plastic smile to pretend everything was okay. I'm worried I hurt him or that he didn't enjoy it like he said he was. I checked his traffic lights, I swear!"

"Hey, shh, shh, okay?" I soothe him, forcing him back against my chest and holding him tightly until I feel him start to relax again. "Kink isn't absolute. There isn't one right way to do everything and all else is wrong and dangerous. You know that, sweetheart."

"I do, Daddy," he admits begrudgingly.

I chuckle lightly. "Every person is different. Maybe he loved it. Maybe he freaked himself out by just *how much* he loved it. Maybe he didn't enjoy it as much as he hoped he would and needed alone time to process that. Maybe he's a sociopath who got his kicks, then really didn't need any aftercare?"

That gets a small laugh out of him, and I reward him with another kiss on his thick black hair. He doesn't smell like sweat and sex. In fact, his scent is one I don't recognize.

"What did you do after he left?"

Brady shrugs. "I cleaned up after us, but I was all hyped up and jittery, you know?" I do know. Aftercare is for the Doms as much as it is for the subs. My poor baby was filled with all that unspent energy and needed to put it somewhere. "So I had a shower there and just played everything over and over in my head, trying to work out what went wrong. In the end, I just wanted to get home. So that's what I did."

"Good boy," I murmur as I think over what he's told me. "I'm sorry your first try wasn't so great. But I'm sure you've got lots of exciting experiences ahead of you."

He huffs, and I can't help but grin a little where he can't

see me. "No, Daddy," he says, getting a tad bratty himself. It's unusual for him, but it's very adorable when he gets stubborn like this.

"No, what?"

"Until that moment, it was amazing. I want to understand what I did wrong."

"What if you didn't do anything wrong?"

He blinks up at me like that thought hadn't occurred to him. "Really?"

I shrug. "It sounds like you were in command and took care of your sub's needs. It's not your fault if something was off on his end. It takes two to tango, baby boy."

He chews on his lip, even though he knows that's against the rules. This is a slightly out-of-the-ordinary situation, though, so I allow it for once. "I guess," he admits.

"And unless you run into him again, I'd say you'll just have to chalk this one up to experience and see what happens next time with someone else."

His face brightens. "Oh, no," he says, sounding light for the first time since he came home. "He left me his number. He said he wanted to play again."

I laugh a little too loudly and hope I haven't woken Trey up. But honestly, this boy is too much sometimes.

"So you're worrying yourself into fits, yet you have his number and can just *ask* him how he feels?" I clarify. "In fact, he already *told* you how he felt, and he wants to meet up again."

Brady looks sheepish. It's adorable. "But the aftercare," he insists. I happen to agree with him that what this other guy did wasn't cool, but he's making all this out to be so much more hopeless than it actually is.

"Perhaps next time he wants to play, you lay out better ground rules and tell him exactly who's in charge and that you *will* expect him to stick around and let you fuss over him until you're happy."

He gives me just a small smile, but it's there, like sunshine breaking through the clouds. "I told him I was in charge several times," he says thoughtfully. "And he submitted to me so nicely. But I didn't *actually* tell him he had to stay or anything."

The lead balloon in my chest is becoming more and more like helium, ready to float away with my rage and concern from earlier. "I think maybe this boy just isn't very experienced in kink, baby."

"He said he used to have a Daddy," Brady protests, and I have to admit it's adorable how much *he* still doesn't know about kink.

"And do you know anything more about that relationship than that?" I ask. He shakes his head. "It might have been very vanilla in the bedroom for all you know. But you're right about one thing. This boy—"

"Harper," Brady supplies, his eyes shining. Oh, he really likes this little brat of his, doesn't he?

"Harper," I repeat. "He might need aftercare and not even know it. Have you messaged him yet?"

Brady shakes his head. "I didn't know what to say," he admits.

"That's easy," I tell him truthfully. "Just text him what you would have said if he hadn't run out. It's not the same as a warm bath, cuddles, and a snack, but it's the best you can do without physically being there with him."

Brady takes a deep breath. "You're right, Daddy."

I snicker and tickle his side, making him wiggle and squeal. "I'm always right," I remind him.

I'm not surprised to look up and see Trey has come downstairs as well. Our noise has finally woken him up.

Yawning and in his robe as well, he's picked up his crutches rather than bothering to attach a prosthetic.

"What's going on here?" he asks, amused.

I pat the sofa beside me. "We're going to sit with our baby wolf while he writes a text."

Trey raises his eyebrows but comes over anyway, dropping beside me. He angles the crutches on the arm of the couch so he can reach them easily when he wants to get up. "A text, huh?"

"I'll explain later," I tell him softly.

Brady has already gotten his phone out of his pocket as well as a scrap of paper with the local motel's logo on it. He diligently types in the number with his tongue between his teeth. Trey and I watch him, and I can't help but feel proud. I knew he would want to take care of whoever he found to play with. He could have easily just forgotten about this Harper guy after he blew my baby off like that.

But I have to say that I'm intrigued. Brady is clearly captivated by this boy he only just met tonight, and I must admit that I'm curious to see what kind of guy would have that kind of thrall over him.

For now, though, this is Brady's show. I'll have to step back and see if Harper even wants to meet up again—and if he does, if he'll consent to actually being taken care of properly. But if they do see each other again or if this even becomes a regular thing...

Then Daddy wants to meet him, too. And I won't take no for an answer.

CHAPTER 8

Harper

WELL, I FEEL LIKE SHIT.

I roll over in bed, wondering if I should just give up and haul my ass out into the shower. I had one when I got in last night, but I feel so uncomfortable and sweaty that another one wouldn't go amiss.

I managed a couple of hours sleep after my *very* exciting encounter with the gorgeous baby himbo, Brady, last night. But I've basically been staring at my ceiling since around three o'clock, and I'm seriously over it.

I don't understand what the problem is. We had fun—*so* much fun. And I made sure to hightail it before I was in any danger of catching feels. So why am I curled up in bed feeling like garbage right now? This sucks. I want my money back.

Except...I really don't. I can't stop thinking of what Brady and I shared. It makes me feel shaky and afraid but also like I'm soaring through the sky like an eagle. I just...

I want him to text.

I want to text him.

But I can't, because I only gave him my number. And I shouldn't be texting any fucking men anyway. I went to that bar to get a job, not a hookup. Yet it was like sweet, gorgeous Brady cast a spell over me. I haven't dared check my phone in all these hours I've been tossing and turning, choosing instead to check the time on the ancient digital alarm clock I have in my grandma's guest bedroom.

This way, it's like the cat that is or isn't in the box. Both statements are true so long as you don't check, right? In this moment, he both has and hasn't texted me. And if he hasn't— which he won't have—I can still pretend that he has.

I screw up my hands and eyes, rubbing my fists against my forehead. Why do I feel so hollow? That was literally the best sex *I've ever had.* I shouldn't feel like the barnacles on the bottom of a pirate ship.

Urgh. Even my metaphors keep dragging me back to his dark eyes and strong arms and sinful fucking lips. That motel was cheesy AF, and yet I'm finding myself craving rewatches of both The Little Mermaid and Pirates of the Caribbean just to try and recreate some of that magic we found in a silly underwater-themed room.

It's past seven, so Grandma will be up. If I wander out like a zombie soon, she'll likely jump at the chance to make me bacon and pancakes and eggs and all that good stuff. I'd feel vaguely guilty, but I honestly don't think anything makes her happier than cooking for people she cares about. We'll both win. And perhaps I'll feel less hollow if my stomach is full of hot food.

With a frustrated grunt, I roll over and finally unplug my phone from its charger. I take a brief moment to enjoy how deliciously sore my ass feels, then I push the feeling away. It's too complicated.

That's nothing to how I feel when I realize that a message from an unknown number has been sitting on my phone since just before two in the morning.

"Please be Brady," I whisper without knowing if I really

mean it. I thought I was swearing off men and recovering from Lowell.

What if the message is *from* Lowell?

I drop the phone before I even get to the text, my heart lurching horribly in my chest and my insides cramping. I know I blocked his number and his accounts on all my socials, but he's fucking loaded. He wouldn't think twice about buying a whole new phone just to hunt me down. Not to mention all it takes is a different email address to set up different social accounts.

I take a deep breath in and let it out again. "I can either live like a hermit," I repeat to myself. "Or I can hope that he read and understood my good-bye letter and chooses to leave me alone."

I desperately hope that it's the latter. That he'll realize what we had wasn't a real relationship or *love*. He didn't see me for who I really was. He just wanted to control me. And while I wouldn't wish that on anyone else *ever*, I do kind of hope he'll move on and find someone who maybe thrives on that kind of co-dependency.

Even if I think that person would be better off with real, serious therapy, that's not my business. I can't fix everyone. I can only protect myself, and I need to stay far, *far* away from that asshole.

I decide I need to know if the cat is in the box or not. I grab my phone and jab at the message from the unknown number, ripping off the proverbial Band-Aid.

Then my heart melts all the way into my toes. It's not just one message but several.

UNKNOWN: Little lamb. You left so fast that I didn't get a chance to properly tell you how beautiful you were for me tonight. You took everything I gave you so perfectly and I wanted to hold you tight and make sure you knew that. Next time, I don't want you to leave like that.

Next time? He's added an emoji of a devil's face grinning, and I squirm in my bed, burrowing farther under the covers. But I make sure to bring the phone with me and keep reading.

UNKNOWN: There will be a next time, even if it's just to safely close what we experienced last night. I like you, Harper, and it's my job to take care of you. Please message me back so we can arrange coffee, a stroll in the park, or something more private. Whatever you want. But I'll be very disappointed if you leave me hanging.

UNKNOWN: You are a very special boy. Even if last night was our only time together, I want you to know that. Much respect, your baby wolf, Brady.

I clamp my teeth and screw up my eyes as I clutch the phone to my chest. "Holy fuck," I whisper out loud. Is this real? How can it be real? Why has all that hollowness just evaporated like rain after a storm on a hot summer's day?

I read through all the messages about ten times before it finally occurs to me to save Brady's number. Now all I have to do is compose a reply.

That requires pancakes. And probably a grandma.

I choose to forfeit the second shower and instead scramble around my room for shorts and a T-shirt. Sure enough, as soon as I open my door, I smell freshly brewing coffee, and inhale deeply.

"Good mornin', sunshine," my grandma greets me from the kitchen table as I bound into the room. She looks up from the crossword she's doing on her tablet. "You're up early, considerin' how late you got in."

I pause as I'm reaching for a mug in the cupboard, looking sheepishly over at her. "Sorry," I say with a grimace. "I tried to be quiet."

She hums and pushes her glasses back up her nose. "Oh, you were. I just couldn't sleep until I knew you were home. I know, I know," she says, waving her hand at me. "You're all grown and don't need me fussin'. I just can't help it, is all."

I grab my favorite rainbow mug and close the door before going over and bending down to kiss her cheek. "I love that you care," I say genuinely. "I just don't want you worrying or losing sleep over me."

She chuckles and shakes her head. "If you ever have babies, you'll understand that you never stop worrying about them."

I scoff and pour myself some hot caffeinated goodness. "I will *always* be the baby, Grandma."

She chuckles again and sensibly doesn't disagree. I tip both cream and several sugars into my coffee. "So, what's cookin'?" she asks slyly.

I don't attempt to hide my grin as I slide into one of the other chairs at the table, but I do build up anticipation by taking a sip of my drink first. "I met a boy," I say in a sing-song voice.

She arches an eyebrow. "I thought you were on the hunt for a real *man* after that nasty business in the city."

I shake my head. "I am. But...this guy is sweet. He's a nice boy, I promise, Grandma."

Her expression softens and she picks up her own flower-patterned mug to take a drink herself. "Good. You deserve 'nice' and 'sweet' after everythin' you've been through."

I pull my phone from my pocket and fiddle with it, thinking about what Brady said in his messages. I was so ridiculously happy to hear from him and to see that he wants to meet again, but he was clearly miffed that I left so fast. I was only trying to protect myself, but I'm not an idiot. I know Lowell fucked me up in the head. What if I transfer that fuckery over to Brady if we keep seeing each other?

"What if I don't deserve it?" I ask my grandma softly.

She peers at me over her glasses, and I can't help but

shrink away from her scorn. "You are a *good* boy who met a *bad* man. You just have to make sure this fella from last night is the good sort, and then you treat him right. Your grand-daddy treated me right for over forty-five years, God rest his soul."

I sigh and rub my thumb over one of the slightly raised rainbows on my mug. "I think maybe I didn't treat him so right. I was afraid of getting hurt, so I sort of ran off. But," I say, talking myself around before she can even get a chance, "I did leave him my number, and he sent me some cute messages already."

She flicks her eyebrow at me again. "Did he call you out for your bad manners?"

I blush and slide down a little farther in my seat. "Yes," I mumble.

She preens. "Then he does sound like a good sort. Are you gonna make it up to him and behave better next time?"

I nod. "Yeah, I think so," I say. "I'm only staying here for the summer anyway until I can get back on my feet. What's the worst that can happen if we go on a few dates?"

"You know you're welcome here as long as you need," Grandma tells me with a pat on my hand. "Now, how about some breakfast? I could make waffles or pancakes."

"As long as there's maple syrup, I'll eat whatever's put in front of me," I say with a grin.

"Don't I know it," she says with a wink, rising to her feet. "All-righty. Let's see what this old bird can whip up on this fine mornin'."

I switch between watching her puttering about at the stove and re-reading Brady's messages. I am scared, there's no denying it. Lowell held my heart captive in a cage for years, making me feel like I was small and worthless. I can put on a front of sass and brattiness, but what Brady and I shared last night was raw and honest, even if it was role-playing.

It was also world-rockingly good fucking. My fear isn't enough to quell my thirst to feel that way again.

Fine. I can do better and not brush him off next time. I don't want to make *him* feel unimportant or insignificant, either. Hell no. But I can keep my guard up and have some fun at the same time, surely? Then once I've saved up some money and come up with a plan—any plan—of what I want to do with my life, I'm sure I'll be heading back to somewhere with a population of more than ten thousand people. I've always thought about going back to Chicago, or maybe even trying New York.

But in the meantime, it might be nice to see Brady a few more times. When I think of his adorable smile and the way he took charge of me in the bedroom, my insides get all light and fluttery.

Nobody has to catch feels. That doesn't mean I can't have a little fun. Who knows? This might be exactly what I need to wash Lowell out of my hair for good. A summer fling before I head back to the bright lights of the big city could very well be the cure I need for this bruised and battered little heart of mine.

I unlock my phone and think about what I can text Brady back.

CHAPTER 9

Brady

I TOOK IT AS A SIGN FROM THE UNIVERSE THAT WHEN I CALLED up Toe Beans to ask if they had any tables available, they'd just had a cancellation for the very next day. Usually, I don't even try to make a reservation there, as it's typically booked up weeks in advance. But I knew I wanted to take Harper somewhere special for our little chat, and so I'm thrilled this has worked out for me.

Our resident cat café is probably the closest thing this town has to a tourist attraction. It's run by this—I'll be honest—mildly-terrifying looking dude with almost military-grade short hair, a dark beard, a shit ton of tattoos, and a permanent scowl on his face. But while he might not do much more than grunt around the customers at his café, I always see him with a tray of freshly baked goods from his own hands and some sort of tiny feline hiding on his person.

Today, there's a silver tabby kitten perched right on top of his head. He doesn't even seem to notice his companion as he wordlessly points me to a small round table covered in white, frilly doilies and a cluster of glossy succulents in little pots.

I'm here early, but as there's a sign holding the table for

me, no one is sitting there, so I don't have to kick anyone off, which is nice. Once I'm seated, a young woman with a tumble of shoulder-length blonde curls cheerfully bounds over to me. "Hi, there," she says, notepad in hand. "Would you like a minute to look at the menu, or are you ready to order?"

"I'm meeting someone," I say, intending to delay our order.

But then I stop myself. This is my opportunity to show Harper that I'm serious about taking care of him. Even if it's just for this one coffee date and then we part ways. He didn't let me provide him with aftercare when we last met, so this is my chance now.

"We can order extra if necessary," I continue to the bubbly server. "Can I get two cappuccinos and one of those cake stands with all the little bite-sized treats?"

She beams at me as she jots down my request. "Perfect," she tells me.

I figure if we have a selection of things to eat, hopefully, there will be something Harper likes. And that's a pretty safe coffee order, but I can just get him something different if he prefers. I asked him when we were making arrangements if he had any food allergies, and he said he didn't.

Once the blonde waitress walks away, I'm left alone with my nerves. I try my best to shake them off, though. I've talked to Daddy and Papa a lot about what happened at the Sunken Treasure the other night, and they have both insisted over and over again that I didn't do anything wrong. I still can't shake the feeling that I did fuck up some-how, so I'm eager to see Harper this afternoon and set things right.

Luckily, I'm not short of things to look at while I wait for both my order and Harper to arrive. The café is teeming with people, almost all of them in couples or groups, chatting noisily away over a soundtrack of smooth jazzy cover versions of what I'm pretty sure are metal songs.

Across the room, I see Papa's boss from the garage, Ruben Ward. Papa and Daddy mentioned he had a new boyfriend, and I guess that's the sweet-looking dark-haired guy sitting across from him. He's wearing the uniform from that kids' dinosaur place, complete with a baseball cap adorned with T-Rex teeth. He's waving his hands around happily as he talks, and Ruben is looking at him like he hung the moon. It warms my heart. Papa said the younger man had some awful trouble with his family, so I'm glad he has a Daddy like Ruben to take care of him now.

It makes me grateful for my Daddies, who would never let anything bad happen to me, I'm certain. But it also makes me even more determined to make sure that Harper is okay. I don't know much at all about his life, but I'd hate to be any source of uncertainty or sadness for him.

There are cats everywhere in the café except the kitchen, coming and going as they please while people do their best to pet them or take photos and videos. A little girl squeals in delight as a massive orange monster jumps onto her table. She claps her hands while her parents grab up their coffees for safety.

I'm too busy chuckling at the sight that I don't notice someone approaching the table. As a shadow falls on me, I glance around, expecting it to be the nice blonde waitress back again. But to my absolute delight, it's Harper.

"Hi!" I yelp, leaping to my feet and almost knocking the spindly chair I've been perched on into the couple at the next table. Fate is on my side, though, and it teeters for a second before landing on all fours again. "You're here. I mean, you came."

I laugh, aware I'm babbling, and try and regain my composure as I run my hand through my hair. Harper smiles bashfully at me and bites his lip. He's about my height but has a slender frame, which he's dressed in jeans and a T-shirt with a burgundy blazer. The lightweight cream top clings to his torso. I can practically see his nipples through it, and the urge to run my hands over his chest is strong.

Instead, I open my arms and am immensely grateful that he leans in for an easy hug. Okay, good. Things can't be too weird between us if he's doing that.

"Of course I came," he says flirtatiously as he slips into the other seat. "You invited me."

It's funny how I can feel the Dom side of me rise up. I'd never feel like this with my Daddies because they take care of me. But as I retake my own seat, I fix him with a stern look that I'm utterly thrilled to see makes him squirm.

"You also bailed on me the other night before I even got the chance to give you a hug," I say firmly. "We shared a scene. It's my responsibility to give you aftercare."

"Oh, I don't need anything like that," he starts to say flippantly. But he catches my eye and immediately becomes sheepish, looking at the tablecloth as he fiddles with the hem of a doily. "Um, yeah. Sorry, Baby. You're right. I took off. I was, um, just trying to keep things casual."

I won't lie, I feel myself puff up like a self-righteous pigeon. I love that he's shortened 'baby wolf' like that. My Daddies call me baby boy, but I can practically hear the title in the way Harper says it. I've never felt more like a switch in my life, and for some reason, I'm stupidly proud. Perhaps because it's a true feeling? Honest and authentic. Like I'm achieving my full potential.

I also love that he cut the bullshit with me immediately and recognized my authority. Yes, I'm in charge here, and I'm not happy with what happened. But...like Daddy said, it takes two to tango.

I reach my hand out, offering my palm up so he can take

it. He does, much to my delight. Even better is that's the moment our drinks and pastries arrive, so we have a few moments to just feel our hands resting against each other while the nice blonde girl sets everything down.

"I got you a cappuccino," I say. "I hope that's okay."

He smiles and nods. "Absolutely. I'll just add some sugar." I'm sad to let his hand go, but I watch on in amusement as he uses the tongs to pick up three cubes from the flowery pot and plop them in his coffee one by one.

I'm thrilled I got his order well enough that he'll drink it. I want to ask what his actual preference is, but that's getting ahead of myself. Today is firstly about wrapping up last time. Then we can consider if we want there to be a next time.

"I'm sorry, too," I say, picking up our previous thread of conversation. He raises his eyebrows at me in question before taking a sip of his drink, so I elaborate. "I'm sorry I didn't make things clear the other night. I wanted you to stay. I should have asked you to."

"Or *told* me to," he suggests sassily. But he then places his cup down and sighs. "No, I think this is mostly on me. Regardless of who's the Dom or sub or whatever, it was rude of me to run out of there like my ass was on fire. I...I got out of a bad relationship recently—*very* recently. I don't think I know what I'm looking for right now."

I offer him a genuine smile. "And that's absolutely *fine*," I assure him. "What matters is that we talk about it and make sure we both know where we stand. I don't need this to be a serious thing. We're both taking baby steps toward different things, it seems. But we also have to ensure our needs are being met. I felt...hollow after you left."

He visibly sags and looks relieved. "Me, too," he admits like he's not certain if he should be ashamed or not. "Which made no sense because the sex was *epic*."

He leans in to deliver that last word quietly, making me

chuckle. "It was," I agree, pleased to see his face light up. "But what you probably felt was sub drop. We had a scene, and I overpowered you. I degraded you. Which was all delicious in the moment, but afterward, your brain can play tricks on you if you're not careful."

Harper frowns and chews his lip, apparently considering my words carefully. I wonder yet again what kind of Daddy he had previously if he doesn't know about this stuff. He's clearly kinky. He also just said he was fresh out of a bad relationship, and I wonder if it was the same guy.

I have to laugh at myself as I feel my protective hackles rise. Is this what Daddy feels like *all the time* with Papa and me? I suspect so.

I choose my next words carefully. "If we play again," I say slowly as I catch his eye. "I'd expect you to stick around and let me fuss over you."

He licks his lips and rubs his thumb against his coffee cup. "Fuss over me how?" he asks curiously.

I feel myself getting excited. As far as I'm concerned, aftercare is the best part of kink. Sure, in the moment, all the super sexy stuff is thrilling. But for me, nothing compares to the gentle healing that comes afterward.

I reach out for his hand again, and he accepts it. I rub my thumb across his knuckles and look him directly in the eyes. "I would hold you, little lamb," I explain, painting a picture. "I would tell you how good you were for me, how perfectly you took whatever I'd given you, and how gorgeous you are. Then I'd run us a bath or take you into the shower with me. If there wasn't much mess, I'd maybe just clean you up, but submerging in hot water is definitely the best remedy after playing rough, I find. I'd make sure you had something to eat or drink, and if you'd be okay with it, I'd take you back to bed, snuggle you in my arms, and watch over you until you fell asleep."

His mouth has fallen open and he's looking at me with wide, almost confused eyes. "Whoa. Really? You wanted to do all...that? The other night, I mean?"

I nod. "If we'd done any kind of impact play, I would have rubbed lotion on your skin to soothe it. I'd give you a massage if your muscles were tense. The whole point—I think—of breaking someone is that you *have* to put them back together again." I shrug. "At least, that's what my Daddies always do for me."

He shakes his head with a kind of wondrous look on his face. "This is really your first time as a Dom?" he asks, to which I nod. He chuckles. "Well, I think you're kind of nailing it already."

I feel myself blush. I'm not sure if that's true or not, but it gives my confidence a nice boost. "Thank you."

He looks away and seems to consider everything I've said for a long time. "Brady, I'm really sorry," he says, shaking his head. "I didn't understand any of that. I feel like I ruined our amazing night."

I lift his hand up and kiss his fingers. He looks back at me. "Hey, no. You didn't ruin anything. We're here, aren't we? I'm just making it clear that if we play again, that's how I'd want it to end."

Harper swallows and looks like he thinks carefully about what he wants to say. "I like you, Brady," he says, which I think is a good start. But sure enough...there's a 'but.' "But I'm probably only here for the summer. I don't know what I'm doing with my life, honestly. I don't want to hurt you."

"Oh, sweetheart," I say, kissing his fingers again. "There's no pressure, I swear. All I ask is that if we do a scene, we treat the experience with the respect it deserves." I roll my eyes and grin. "I already *have* two boyfriends. It's okay if we just have some fun. It doesn't need a big commitment. But if you'd like, I'd definitely be up for some more scenes. Maybe some dates like this, too, if that's not asking too much."

He purses his lips, seemingly fighting back a grin. "And what do they think of all this?" he asks. "Your boyfriends—your *Daddies*. Of me?" he adds in a quieter voice.

"They're intrigued," I admit. "In fact, I think they'd like to meet you. Only if you wanted to make a couple more friends in town. I'm not saying that in a 'meet my family' kind of way."

I laugh, but I am aware that it is a sort of significant step if I suggest that. But I can't help it. Daddy is obviously insanely curious, Papa is trying not to be protective, and I strongly feel they'd both be more at ease if they met Harper in person. I know I didn't give the best first impression of him after our last meeting, and I want to fix that.

I want them to like him. I want him to like them.

I know I'm probably getting ahead of myself. I meant what I said just now. This doesn't have to be anything serious or long term. But I *like* Harper. This coffee date is only proving that further. Even if he disappears in a couple of months, I want our time together to mean something significant. If there's anything I've learned from being polyam, it's that the briefest of encounters can have important meanings that linger in your heart and your soul.

He tilts his head and gives me a curious look. "Your Daddies want to meet me? Seriously?"

I shrug but can't contain my grin. "What can I say? They like having a little control in my life."

That gets a genuine, knowing laugh from him that we both share. That's the other thing, I guess. I want my Daddies to be proud of me. I want them to see the pretty little lamb I caught all by myself and for them to tell me that he's as sweet as I say he is. To tell me that I've done a good job being his

Dom—even if I am just a baby wolf fumbling my way through.

If Harper says he's not up for it, though, that's totally fine. I'll keep this just between the two of us if it means we can see each other again. But I watch as he selects a tiny strawberry tart and holds it delectably by his lips. "What did you have in mind?" he asks. "If I did want to meet them?"

I can't contain my excitement. "Well," I say as I pluck a mini blueberry muffin up myself. I hold it up, and he touches his own pastry to it like we're clinking glasses. "I have an idea."

"I can't wait," Harper purrs.

Neither can I.

CHAPTER 10

Trey

"YOU SURE ABOUT THIS?" I ASK RICK, GIVING THE BUILDING we're standing in front of the side-eye before looking back at my grinning husband.

"Nope," he says, popping his 'p' and generally looking excited. "Why? You not feeling in the mood for a game today?"

I sigh and rub the back of my neck. "That's not it," I say truthfully. The three of us often go paintballing in the summer. It's a fun way to feel adrenaline outside of a bedroom scenario, and I find it gives me a chance to exercise a number of the skills I learned in the Army without being realistic enough to trigger my PTSD.

It's not getting shot at that I'm worried about.

"I thought Brady said he and the Harper kid weren't taking things seriously?"

Rick shrugs in that infuriatingly calm way that I can't help but love...most of the time. "They're not. But Brady wanted us all to meet, and his friend was up for it, so what's the harm?"

I narrow my eyes at Rick, even though he's cheerfully

ignoring me. "*You* just want to meet this kid and get the measure of him," I say.

Rick squints against the sun and looks at me. "Would it be so bad if I did?"

I huff. "Brady is supposed to be venturing out on his own to try new things. Isn't that what you told me? So how," I plow on when he tries to interrupt me, "is he going to do that with you meddling?"

Rick is still grinning. "I'm not doing anything of the sort. Brady is proud of this little lamb he's caught, and he wants to show him off. Besides…if I want to vet this new boy, it's only because I'm looking out for *our* boy. What's so wrong with that?"

Reluctantly, I realize I'm not going to win this, so I just laugh. It's too late to back out now, anyway. "You are such a control freak," I mutter.

"Why, thank you," Rick replies, flashing me a shark-like smile. "Oh, look. Here they come."

I'll be honest. I've had some choice thoughts about this young man after the way he messed with Brady's head on their first encounter. But following their coffee date earlier this week, it seems like they've talked things through and want to keep seeing each other.

Begrudgingly, I was impressed that they've met a couple of times since and haven't tried to mix things up with sex again. They went for a walk by the creek one time and then saw a movie another. Perhaps there is something more between them than just lust.

Not that there's anything wrong with that, but I know what Brady's like. Once someone steals his heart, he's too sweet to ask for it back. Luckily, that worked out just great with Rick and me, and I haven't seen him fall for anyone else since we met. But when he talks about Harper, his eyes light up, and he gets all breathless and giddy. I can see he's falling for him.

It's my job to make sure that Harper is worthy of that.

And Rick's job as well, of course. I watch him pull off his sunglasses as Brady and Harper head over from the parking lot, walking hand in hand. Rick seems genuinely enthusiastic about the situation—probably because he knows he can end it without a second thought if he doesn't like what he sees—so I try and borrow some of his positive energy. Brady is still mine to love and protect, and as I resolved to myself before, part of that is letting him go and be free.

Harper is around the same height as Brady, which makes them both a little shorter than Rick and another couple of inches shorter than me. But where Brady is stocky, Harper is slim and willowy. His skin is pale, and the straight hair that's swept over to one side is almost white blond. I can see why Brady calls him his little lamb.

I'm also immediately struck by the way Harper is looking at my boy as they approach us, laughing and wrapped up in conversation. Harper yanks on Brady's hand to pull him against his side, close enough to plant a big kiss on his cheek. He says something that I can't make out, but I can see it makes Brady blush.

Okay. There's clearly chemistry there. That's a good start. The cynical part of me wonders if he's doing that to put on a show, but as far as I can tell, neither of them realizes Rick and I are watching them.

"Hey!" Brady cries as they get closer and he does finally see us. "Harper, these are my boyfriends, Rick Bryant and Treyvon Caldwell. Guys, this is my friend, Harper Kendall."

"I thought they were Daddy and Papa," Harper whispers loudly in Brady's ear, making him blush again.

"Only to Brady," Rick says with a raised eyebrow.

HJ WELCH

Harper bites his lip as a grin spreads over his face. "Yes, sir," he says in a sultry tone. Oh, he's a firecracker, all right.

I stick out my hand. "You can call me Trey, though."

He shakes it, his eyes only darting very briefly to my prosthetic foot. I'm wearing a tank top due to the heat, so my burn scars are clearly on display on my left arm as well. But he just blinks before meeting my eyes and smiling again.

"You better not be thinking of taking it easy on me," I say, calling him out.

Rather than look sheepish, he just gives me that devilish look he also offered up to Rick. "No, Sir," he says in that same flirty tone.

Rick claps him on the shoulder, making Harper's head snap around. "Shall we?" Rick asks, jutting his head toward the entrance building. That's just the area where we register and get our gear. The outdoor course spreads out behind it.

"Uh, yeah," Harper says, and it's kind of nice to see his cocky demeanor shaken a bit. We're in charge here, not him. If he's going to play with us—even in a non-sexual way —he needs to realize that he's the prey and we're the predators.

As we walk toward the front door (Rick with his hand still squeezing Harper's shoulder), I glance at Brady. It'll be interesting to see how he behaves in this scenario. He's always been our sub, even in group dynamics. He said he still wants to get chased by us and to keep a lot of what we have. But I'm not sure what having the boy he's claimed as his own in the mix will do to the dynamic.

Once we're through the doors, Rick releases Harper to go pay for our tickets. There's another ten minutes or so until they bring the people already out on the course in and let us start our fun. Plenty of time to change into the boiler suits and clear goggles that the venue provides.

And to have a little interrogation.

"So, Harper," I say as casually as I can as I unzip the suit I've been handed. "What do you do?"

He freezes up for a second, and my protective instincts immediately kick in. But then the boy smiles like nothing even happened. "I work at The Ice Cream Parlor. You know? The gay bar in town."

"I do know it," I say. I'm not sure what he felt defensive about, but if he's going to brush over it, I will too. For now. "You just moved from Indianapolis, right?"

"Papa," Brady says in a warning tone.

"I'm just making conversation," I say innocently.

Brady narrows his eyes at me. "Fine. Just no water-boarding."

Harper's eyes widen at the dark humor. I give his arm a reassuring squeeze. "It's okay," I tell him. "When you've seen some of the shit Rick and I have, you kind of have to make light of certain thing. Otherwise, you'll lose your mind. I was never involved in anything like that."

"Oh, no," Brady says, earnestly shaking his head. "Sorry, I wasn't thinking. That was a tasteless joke."

"It's fine," Harper says, sounding sincere. "Thanks for explaining. I've, um, never really talked to anyone who saw active combat about what it was like. Thank you for your ser—"

"Nuh-uh," I cut him off loudly with a wag of my finger. I hate when people say that, especially when they notice my foot or my burn scars. Harper doesn't mean it in a pitying way, but I still don't want to hear it. After the millionth time, it loses its significance. "I'm just Trey."

Harper nods and looks at me for a second. "Sure thing, Trey," he says with a small smile. "And yeah, I did just move. I left a shitty relationship in a hurry." He looks warmly over at Brady. "And then I ran straight into this troublemaker who helped me forget all about it."

Pride warms my heart, and I pull Brady to me to kiss the top of his head. "That sounds like my boy."

"All right, are we doing this?" Rick asks as he walks over, zipping up the front of his boiler suit. I don't know how he still looks so sexy when I feel like a dork, but he does.

"You're on," I say, my heart starting to beat a little harder in my chest. I've fought by this man's side too many times to count. It's a long time since there were any real stakes, but still.

I'd trust him with my life.

Harper looks like he's unsure of what to do or where to go. But before I can step in, Brady's already handing him the silly toy gun and explaining how to load the little paint pellets. "You can keep the spares in your pocket, like this. Just don't forget and crush them. You'll end up with a wet leg, and not in a fun way."

Watching the two boys giggling together as they make their way outside gives me a fuzzy feeling. Brady is a natural caretaker. That's why he stuck around with his former foot-ball team at the college so he could guide the next generation of players. But he also thrives under Rick's and my ministra-tions. I thought what he needed was another cat to look after.

Turns out a little lamb seems to be doing the trick quite nicely.

"See," Rick whispers in my ear in a teasing tone. "Aren't you glad you've now seen them together?"

I roll my eyes at him. "We haven't seen anything yet, old man. The real fun's just getting started."

"Ain't that the truth," he agrees with a wink, already running backward toward cover. The siren is blaring. The game is about to begin.

It's time to see what side all the players are on.

The course itself is pretty basic. Just an open space filled with empty oil barrels and bales of straw like we have in our barn at home. There's also a crude fort in the middle where someone has cut out and painted plywood to make it look like a European castle. There's even a two-dimensional dragon standing up beside it, breathing cartoon flames. Everything has traces of paint in all the colors of the rainbow from previous skirmishes over the years that can only be cleaned off so much.

There are a couple dozen other people also playing around us in our time slot. The whole arrangement is pretty casual. Guests can organize into big teams if they want. I even hired the whole place out for an hour once just for all the guys at work to blow off steam by firing ruthlessly at one another. That's how our team shows love. But usually, people just run around in their own little groups.

I watch as Harper sprints away from Brady, grinning like a maniac. Brady doesn't run after him, however. He just starts slowly stalking to the bale where Harper has taken cover, his gun raised. There's a different kind of energy around him. It's pretty damn sexy to see this confidence emanating from him.

That pride surfaces in me again. Whether or not it's justified, I can't help but feel like Rick and I have done a good job helping him flourish. He'd never have had the faith in himself to be like this when we first met him.

Our baby wolf is growing up.

I look around for Rick, who—as much as it pains me to admit it out loud—is the alpha of our little pack and always calls the shots. But instead, I find him approaching Brady by the oil drum where he's crouched. I jog over to join them, although my blade makes it difficult for me to drop down. It's good for moving fast, however, which is what I generally want in this scenario. My other more foot-shaped prosthetic is back in the car.

"What's the plan?" I ask. Harper is still hiding and definitely not trying to get us just yet. Sweet lamb.

I look at Rick, but Rick shakes his head and juts his chin at Brady. "You're calling the shots, little pup. What's the plan?"

For a second, Brady's eyes go wide. I imagine he's feeling a little intimidated at the prospect of telling his Daddies what they should do. But then he nods, a grin spreading over his face. "Follow me," he says.

And that's what we do. For the first time, we're hunting together as a pack. My blood is pumping, and my dick is already hard.

"Let's go have some fun," I growl.

CHAPTER 11

Harper

MY HEART IS BEATING STUPIDLY FAST AS I CROUCH DOWN OUT of sight. It's not like this straw bale is going to hide me indefinitely, but it's giving me a chance to catch my breath as the game starts.

This is ridiculous! Why am I so amped up? It's just pretend. No one's really trying to hurt me.

But they are hunting me.

I've got that same all-consuming feeling I had from the moment I fled Brady the other night and he chased me down to the motel room. I knew I wasn't really helpless. He even checked my color, which sort of annoyed me in the moment, but since our talk on consent and aftercare, I actually deeply appreciate it. I can stop this pursuit anytime I want.

But I don't want to. I want Brady and his Daddies to catch me. However, the fear I'm feeling is still very real. My body thinks it's under attack, and no amount of logic from my brain is going to tell it otherwise.

I've been sheltering here for around a minute, so I peek my head over the hay to work out where Brady's gotten to. I almost fall over in shock when I see that he's running toward me at full speed. I shriek loudly and nearly trip over my feet as I move to get away from him. Holy fuck, my adrenaline has spiked. I'm short of breath and dizzy as I make a run for it. Everything's made that bit more difficult because my cock is already rock hard and chafing against my jeans.

I'm so focused on looking between where I'm running and back at Brady, I don't even see the attack come from the side. Either of them. I'm suddenly getting blasted left and right with different colored paintballs from both Rick and Trey, making me squeal and throw my arms up, automatically trying to defend myself. It doesn't even occur to me to fight back.

The next thing I know, Rick has seized me around the waist and is spinning me around as I scream. "Got you, little lamb," he snarls in my ear, sending delicious shivers all over my body.

I thrash my limbs and find myself freed, probably because that's the way Rick wanted it rather than me actually getting loose, but it doesn't matter. I still make a run for the castle, even as I look around and see Brady firing at me. The paintballs sting when they strike, but it's the good kind of pain. Like when Brady spanked me and bit me when we were having sex.

Not the bad kind. Not like Lowell.

No. Absolutely fucking *not*. I'm having fun. I refuse to think of that asshole. Instead, I focus on the bursts of pain that jolt through my body like electric shocks. God, I feel so *alive*.

I run around the basic wooden castle structure, darting past other patrons who are playing in their own groups. I don't know where any of the wolf pack is, but I'm already covered in paint, and I'm pretty sure they haven't got a drop on them. I don't know if there are any real rules to this game, but my bratty side is rearing, and I don't want to make this easy for them.

Like I told Brady before, they have to *earn* it if they're going to capture me.

I nip around the cartoon dragon, raising my gun as I look back over the wood. Brady is charging toward me, so I take my shaking hand and fire.

"YES!" I bellow as I get him square on the chest, thrusting my hands up in the air in victory.

The pretty pink color has exploded like a flower blooming on his body, turning him into a walking work of art. I guess that's what I am, too, with these three men as my artists. It occurs to me that this is the first time in years that I've even touched any paint. But that memory also feels a little raw, so I push it down along with everything else.

I know that me marking Brady is only one hit compared to the many splatters on my boiler suit, but it makes me feel like I'm not just lying down and taking it. I do, however, let Brady barrel me over onto the ground and kiss me senseless.

In that moment, I realize what the starkest contrast is between Brady and his Daddies, and Lowell. I just told myself not to dwell on that piece of shit, but fuck it. This is a good thing.

Even though we're engaging in primal play, Brady—and now his Daddy wolves—actually make me feel powerful. Important. All three of them are chasing after me. I'm their goal, their prize.

I matter.

In the end, Lowell's only goal seemed to me to make me understand how powerless I really was against him. That I didn't matter and that if I dared to leave him, nobody else would want me.

Well, fuck him, seriously. He couldn't have been more wrong.

And that really is it. I banish him from my mind and let myself be fully absorbed in the cat-and-mouse chase between me and my wolves for the rest of the session. I know Brady and I talked about keeping things casual, and I meant it. I'm not ready to commit to anything aside from this game. But right now, in this moment, that feels like enough. It feels significant. I've never felt this way before. So vital and spirited and fucking horny. It's exhilarating, and I just want to have a good time.

I deserve that after the last few years.

Our hour time slot goes by in a blur. By the time the sirens go off announcing that we need to come back to the entrance building and give back our gear, I'm completely out of breath, in quite a desperate need of water, and trembling with adrenaline. Brady hugs me to his side, propping me up as we walk back with his arm around my waist. When he kisses the top of my head despite all the paint in my hair, I melt a little more into him.

"You did good, kid," Rick says from my other side. He punches my arm lightly, and I wince. I'm sure once the adrenaline wears off, I'm going to be sore all over. But I don't care. In fact, I'm really hoping I'll have several colorful bruises that I can keep with me for the next few days, like little trophies of just how well I did. I want to look at them and remember how it felt to belong to a pack. To be hunted and wanted.

After getting changed, we walk back out into the parking lot together. Brady picked me up from my grandma's house in his car. It took all my tricks to keep her in the house, but she still waved at him from the window as we left. Although I was pretty mortified, a part of me was also kind of pleased in that moment. She never met Lowell, and yet I know she always hated him, no matter how well she tried to conceal it. This thing with Brady might be only a summer fling, but Grandma seems determined to like him anyway.

I know the feeling.

I'm prepared for him and me to get back into his little light blue Chevy Bolt. What I'm not prepared for is Rick getting his key fob out and the fucking cherry-red Jaguar a few cars down beeping to show it's now unlocked.

"That's yours?" I splutter, not even caring when all three of them laugh at me.

"Yep. He's subtle, my husband," Trey says, squeezing Rick's shoulders. "Modest, too."

"Psh," Rick scoffs. "I did my time in the dirt eating slop and sleeping on camp beds. I earned a few luxuries."

Trey kisses his cheek as they head over to the Jag. "You guys going to join us at the house for a bit?"

I look to Brady for guidance. He raises his eyebrows at me and shrugs. "You wanna come over for some dinner or something?"

Or something. I do my best not to smirk. After the last hour of being chased around a field by him, if he doesn't fuck me, I'm going to combust. But that's something we can do in a room in his house, I assume. Besides, dinner sounds kind of...nice. Cute. And I really do like Rick and Trey. It would be cool to talk with them more now that they're unarmed.

"Hell yeah," I say, flashing a grin at him and then his Daddies. "Count me in."

I slide into the passenger side of Brady's car, and he starts the engine, wasting no time in pulling out of his space. He lets Rick go first, and I muse again on the dynamic between the three wolves.

I've just seen him as the guy topping me. I love that he always buys me coffee and now he's made sure to learn my specific order so he can get it right in the future. I like it when he takes charge and makes decisions. Unlike Lowell, who was a control freak, I know Brady's doing it to show that he cares.

But he's also fucking adorable. My baby himbo. So it's not really a surprise to see his more submissive side around his two Doms.

I won't lie, I've fantasized about watching them fuck him on several occasions where I've then had to relieve myself with my own hand. In fact, in a few of these imagined scenarios, I've pictured us both there, being topped by the previously unknown Daddies together.

Now that I know what they look like, the sound of their voices, how Rick's eyes narrow when he's giving commands, those daydreams are going to get so much more vivid.

I try not to let my imagination run away with me as we drive out of Paddle Creek, presumably toward their house. They just invited me for dinner. Nothing else is going to happen. Well, not with Rick and Trey. Something better happen with Brady. If not, I'll just brat at him until he gives in and jumps my bones. The desperation is getting out of hand now.

Probably for the best, I'm pulled from my overenthusiastic thoughts as we turn down what I assumed was a dirt track but it's actually a private driveway, a long one. My mouth drops open as I look around and see one massive house at the end. There's also a large barn, a little bridge crossing over a stream, and woodland that surrounds the grounds.

"I-is this your home?" I stammer.

When I glance over at Brady, he's grinning. "Daddy inherited it, but yeah, this is where we live. It's called The Vineyard, even though it's never been one." He chuckles to himself.

I feel a thousand times better about letting Brady pay for the motel room that first night. I worried afterward that he was putting himself out to show off in front of me, but clearly, these guys aren't lying awake at night worrying about their finances.

It does give me pause, though, as we get closer. Part of the problematic power imbalance between Lowell and me was that he was filthy rich and I had nothing. I relied totally on him for everything. I don't want to get into that situation again.

I mentally slap myself. I've not *moving in.* I'm here for dinner. And hopefully, some explosive sex. Besides, I'm *poor.* Even with Grandma insisting that I don't pay her any rent, I'm still not making much from the bar. I kind of like the idea of being spoiled by a sugar daddy so long as it doesn't come with giant strings attached.

The house looks more like a ranch or something. It's all wooden pillars and slanted roofs with a massive porch and a wraparound balcony on the entire second floor. I briefly wonder if I'll ever inherit anything like this from my own rich father, then I decide that's not worth dwelling on. The scenario is highly unlikely and anyway, I wouldn't want that from him.

I'd rather have had a father.

My mind wanders, though, as Brady pulls into the garage that's the size of my grandma's whole house. I hope Rick inherited this place under better circumstances than I was just envisioning.

My eye is caught by a Harley-Davidson motorcycle that's standing by the wall with several parts laid out around it. There's a poster hanging on the wall above it of the logo surrounded by big black wings. I feel like I could fly away just looking at it.

"That's Trey's," Brady says with a fond smile. "Her name is Ariana, after his mom. He's always tinkering with her. Sometimes he even rides her."

"Very cool," I say genuinely. I know Grandma calls them death traps, but to me, they look like freedom on two wheels.

Rick and Trey are already getting out as Brady locks up his Bolt. Rick salutes to us as we exit our vehicle. Brady looked like he was heading toward a closed door, but now that he's stopped, I have as well. He smiles, but I feel like I can detect an air of impatience.

"Welcome to our home," Rick says as he uses another fob to close the garage door, stopping the A/C from leaking out.

Trey is maneuvering on the other side of the Jaguar. I don't want to be an asshole in any way, but it seems impressive to me how much mobility he has with his prosthetic foot. Brady warned me he lost it in combat and made me promise not to be weird. It hurts my heart to think people would be. I just think it's badass that he doesn't let something like that slow him down. He'd be well within his right to hide away from a world that hurt him.

In a funny way, it makes me feel braver about getting over my situation with Lowell. If this man can overcome losing a whole fucking appendage, I can get through losing one douchebag of an ex-boyfriend.

"It's beautiful," I say in response to Rick's comment about their home. But he smirks and indicates the garage, which, to be fair, is all I've seen of the inside.

"This is Trey's man cave," he says, flicking an eyebrow at his husband as he comes around the car. "Why don't you let me give you the *grand* tour?"

There's something flirtatious in his tone that makes my body shiver. Am I interested in him like that? Group sex is very different from group paintball, although I can't deny I fucking loved having all three of them chase after me this afternoon. But I've never been with more than one guy at once. The idea is a little intimidating.

Brady makes the decision for me, however. He comes up

behind me and presses his chest against my back as he wraps his hand around my arm. I can feel his cock against my ass cheek.

"I think after all that exertion, Harper needs a shower—don't you?"

Rick snorts, clearly seeing through Brady's weak story, but he seems amused regardless. "Sure thing. Why don't you boys make sure you're back down for dinner by five, hmm?"

"We will, Daddy," Brady says breathlessly, already pulling me through the door.

I don't know which I like more. The fact that Brady felt confident enough to call Rick 'Daddy' in front of me or the fact that Rick sort of called me his boy.

Both. Both seem pretty hot.

"Bye," I manage to call out before Brady pulls me through the garage door into the main house. I catch glimpses of wooden floors and walls, as well as a lot of houseplants as we rush through, heading toward the stairs. I hope later I can get that tour from Rick. I'm genuinely interested to see where this throuple live and how they operate. But for now, I have other priorities, and I'm glad to see that Brady seems to share them.

I'm not sure what room exactly he pulls me into upstairs, but it's definitely a bedroom. It's perfectly well kept and doesn't seem to have any personal touches, so I guess it's a guest room. But then he tugs me into the en suite, and I realize he wasn't actually lying about the shower idea.

He was just maybe a little misleading as to how many people he insinuated were going to be in said shower at once.

He's laughing as he kisses me, pulling at my clothes, which only got a little paint on them thanks to the boiler suit. They got hella sweaty, though, so I'm very glad to be rid of them, helping Brady to throw them to the floor.

"It's like that, is it?" I say.

"Shut up and get in," he rasps, pushing me into the cubicle, yanking the door shut, and turning the dial on the wall. Water spays all over us, cold at first and making me yelp. Brady doesn't seem to care, though. He shoves me against the tiles, kissing the shit out of me and rubbing our thickening cocks against our bellies.

"Hello," I mumble against his mouth. "Someone's eager."

"You were so fucking hot out there," he says as he kisses down my neck, his fingers digging into my hips. "So helpless. All mine. I caught you."

I laugh throatily and don't resist at all as he spins me around, his fingers probing my hole as the water cascades down our bodies. "You did," I assure him. "My baby wolf. You were so fierce."

I look over my shoulder as he captures my mouth. I've realized too late that we can't really fuck in here without a condom, but then I remember that it's not my place to be making decisions right now. I've given myself over to Brady, and he appears to have a plan.

A fruity scent fills the air as he uses some kind of gel to help lubricate his fingers. I moan wantonly as he fucks two inside me, cruelly neglecting my dick as he does, instead shoving it against the cool tiles of the shower. But then he withdraws, using that same gel to hastily wash over my body and lather up my hair, then doing the same to himself. The second the last of the suds and paint runs down the drain, he flicks off the water and hauls me back out of the cubicle.

"Come on," he growls, throwing me a towel. "You've got thirty seconds."

He dries himself at a more leisurely pace as I drag the towel over as much of my body as I can. It's not my bedding —I'm not going to be sleeping there—so I don't really care if it gets damp. But my heart is fluttering again at being given a command by him, and I'm determined to comply.

"Go," he utters.

I drop the towel and flee into the bedroom. I'm not sure if he's expecting me to run or put up a fight, but instead, I scramble onto the bed and stick my ass in the air. I try and steady my breathing as I hear him slowly follow me out, but it's useless. I'm completely buzzed.

"Little lamb?" he says in question.

I turn my head to the side, resting my temple on the mattress. "You caught me, remember?"

He smirks. "I did, didn't I?"

As I was hoping, I watch him go to the bedside cabinet and retrieve both a condom and some lube. He stretched me out a little in the shower, but I kind of want it rough and raw, so I'm pleased when he just squeezes out some of the cold gel onto my entrance, then starts forcing the blunt head of his suited cock against it.

"Yesss," I hiss, thrusting back and encouraging him. He doesn't disappoint. I keep hissing and the burn gets worse, but I want him in me. I want to feel him, now and tomorrow. There are no guarantees with any of this. It could be the last time we fuck, and I want to emblazon it in my mind.

He sinks all the way inside me with that giant cock of his. It's not monstrous like I've seen in some porn, but it's enough that it feels like it's tickling my tonsils. "Is that good, little lamb?" he asks, his voice so hoarse and sexy with desire.

"Fucking amazing," I tell him honestly. The burn is still very much making my eyes leak, but I don't care. "Take me hard."

He starts sliding in and out of me, tagging my prostate with every thrust. He's not going full pelt yet, obviously, because he's probably worried about hurting me without me consenting to it. I go to tell him he can go ahead and ravage me, but then I change my mind. He's been rough all afternoon—pinning me to the ground and covering me with bruises. He's just forced his way inside my hole. The tenderness in this moment is actually quite lovely.

Besides, I know it won't last. I moan and whimper as he begins to work harder. I get the feeling neither of us wants to drag this out, and I'm thoroughly relieved when he reaches around and jerks me off.

"Who do you belong to, little lamb?" he grunts as I'm balling my fists around the duvet.

"You, Baby Wolf," I manage to utter. And I realize it's true, even if it's only for a short while.

It might just be for the summer, but I think I trust Brady more than I ever did Lowell. He can have my heart if he wants it. I trust him to give it back intact.

There's no more talking after that.

The burn eases, and I'm consumed by so many other sensations as he pounds into me, freeing me from all my cares. I belong to him. He's in charge of everything. He wants to pleasure me and use me to pleasure himself. That's all that matters right now.

"Come for me, sweetheart," he rumbles into my ear, his hand flying over my cock, urging me toward my climax. I'm so close already it doesn't take much. I let go of everything, just listening to his words, following them like chasing a rainbow through a storm.

"Baby," I utter as my climax smashes through me. I explode all over his hand and the bed sheets, shaking and whimpering. He pistons his hips, snapping again and again, until eventually, I feel him pulsing inside me, delivering his load into the condom deep within.

We collapse into a heap, our breathing heavy as the last of our ecstasy fades away. He wraps his arms around me tightly as our chests rise and fall. I feel boneless and beautiful and perfect.

"Stay," he croaks.

My heart drops. I can't believe last time I just ran out on him. Of course he's going to be worried that's what I'm about to do now.

But there's no way.

I twist my head over my shoulder, allowing him to capture my mouth for a kiss. "I'm not going anywhere," I promise him. I don't dare look too closely within myself exactly what I mean by that.

Just how long can I realistically stay in his arms?

CHAPTER 12

Rick

I DROP MY HEAD BACK AND BELLOW AS MY CUM FILLS TREY'S ass. We're both panting and covered in sweat, but he grins as he leans back so I can kiss him over his shoulder.

"You really did jump me back there," he comments with a laugh, and I can't deny it.

"Blame Brady," I say with a shrug as I rub up and down his arms and kiss the side of his neck. "He got me all hot and bothered, then went to go fuck that cute twink without inviting us."

Trey laughs again, then groans as I start to ease my way out from his tender hole. "You really wanted to join them?"

I shrug again, reaching over to the nightstand so I can grab a couple of tissues. "Not really," I admit as I mop us both up a little. "I don't think they're entirely sure what's going on between them yet. I like the kid, though. He's got hard edges, but under all that BS, I think he might be pretty sweet."

"I like the way Brady is around him," Trey admits. "They might have gotten off to a rocky start, but they seem pretty compatible. It's kind of strange seeing that Dom side of Brady."

"But hot, right?" I say, pulling him up off our bed. I let him take my weight and use me as a crutch, seeing as he's taken his prosthetic off.

He slaps my ass as we head to the bathroom. "Totally hot. A fast and dirty orgasm was just what I needed, thank you."

"You're welcome," I say chivalrously with a wink.

I help him to perch on the corner of the tub, then start running the water. We have a little time before five when we said we'd meet the boys. Baths are better for Trey than sitting on the flip-down seat in the shower, even if they take a bit longer.

I sit on the floor beside Trey on the fluffy mat so my ass doesn't get cold on the tiles. I rest my head against his knee, loving when he starts caressing his fingers through my damp hair. "All I care about is Brady's happiness," I say, thinking out loud. "If he wants to keep Harper all to himself, that's fine."

"But," Trey prompts, and I can hear the smile in that one word without even looking up.

"But," I concede, "I got a good vibe out there today. I think we could all play well together. If that's something Harper would be interested in."

I expect Trey to tease me, but instead, he hums thoughtfully. "I got a strong feeling as well," he says. "The boy might be new to kink—at least our kind of kink—but he seemed to revel in it. If he enjoyed being chased by all three of us, perhaps next time he'd like to try that but naked."

I've just come, and my bounce-back isn't what it used to be. But I have to admit that my dick twitches at the idea of playing with Brady's young man like that. We go to parties and often share with others, but usually, Trey and I will watch Brady get fucked and maybe then fuck each other. To add a fourth member to our pack games here at home would be something quite new and a not-so-insignificant change.

Something about the idea feels right to me, though. Especially if Trey is considering it. He was so nervous about protecting Brady's heart when this whole thing began. Now it seems like he's all in.

I quietly muse further on the matter as Trey and I bathe. I wrap him between my legs so I can hug and kiss him as I wash him off. He's quiet as well. I assume he's also considering the matter of Harper Kendall. That, or he's just hungry and wondering what's for dinner.

"How does a big pot of carbonara sound?" I rasp into his ear. He grins as he turns around to face me.

"Heavenly."

I help him out of the tub, and we dry off before moisturizing. Trey swaps the blade he had on previously for his more sturdy prosthetic. For clothes, he sticks with a fresh pair of jeans and a fitted T-shirt, but I feel just as comfortable in slacks and a button-down with an open collar. And yeah, okay, perhaps I feel like impressing Harper a little. He's special to Brady and I want him to know that we're making a bit of an effort for him. Besides, I know I'm dapper. After all those years in uniform, I like it when I get the chance to show off a little style.

Trey hums and kisses the side of my neck as I give myself a couple of spritzes of cologne. "You're divine. I'd let you fuck me all over again if we didn't have a guest."

I turn and capture his mouth. "There's always later, darling. Maybe Brady can join us then."

He nods and licks his lips. "It's a promise."

I'm glad we beat the boys downstairs. It gives me a chance to open up a bottle of red and put out a couple of bowls of olives and pretzels. I've poured Trey and me a glass each when we hear the thud of footsteps and the low murmur of chatter. I wink at my husband.

"Showtime."

It's funny. I'm perfectly confident in my relationship with both Trey and Brady. Yet I feel a flutter of nerves. Like this is a first date. I suppose I want to take care of everyone, and now there are three men putting their trust in me.

I need to prove I'm up to the challenge, whatever form the evening takes.

I'm grating cheese when they enter, freshly showered and both wearing Brady's clothes. They're more casual in sweats and tees, like Trey, but that's okay. I'm the alpha of the pack. Sometimes it's good to remind everyone of that fact with a little power move.

"You boys want a drink?" I ask.

Harper is looking around the kitchen, his mouth hanging slightly open. Brady's holding his hand, sweetly watching him.

I'm not a fool. I know it's gorgeous, even though I maybe don't stop and marvel at it anymore after all these years. The counters are dark marble, and there's a stone hearth at the other end of the sturdy oak dining table where Trey is currently sitting. It's rustic but grand. Almost medieval in style, especially with the circular wrought-iron chandelier above our heads.

"Uh, yes, please, sir," Harper stammers, as if only just realizing he hadn't answered my question. "I mean Rick. Uh, thank you."

I chuckle and wink at him. "Rick is fine, but I don't hate being called 'sir,' I'll admit. What do you fancy? We have wine, spirits, soft drinks, or I can make you coffee or tea. Anything you want, really."

Brady juts his chin toward the open bottle. "Is that your favorite?"

I nod, brushing my hands clean on a dish towel. "It sure is. The French pinot noir."

"I'll have that as well, if that's all right?"

HJ WELCH

"Of course, baby boy," I say in amusement. He's obviously got his manners on for Harper.

Speaking of which, Brady leans in and whispers loudly to his new friend. "Do you want to try some, too? Daddy has *really* good taste in wine."

"I know a thing or two," I admit as I fetch a couple more glasses.

"Uh, sure," Harper says.

He's looking a little like a deer in headlights, which I find appealing. His bratty side was certainly attractive earlier, but I'm not really into arrogance. I think under his bravado, he's actually quite sweet.

"Daddy runs an import/export wine company," Brady explains as he and Harper sit down. "He's got connections to vineyards all over the world, and sometimes we get to go visit them."

"Ohh, that's why this place is called The Vineyard. Wait. I thought you were in the army," Harper says as I pour, then looks abashed. "Sorry, that was rude."

"Not at all," I tell him, sharing a warm look with Trey. It's strange sometimes thinking about our time in service. That's like a completely different life to us now. "Trey and I both toured in Afghanistan with the armed forces. That's where we met. But after Trey's accident, I knew I was done, too. I saw out that tour and left with an honorable discharge."

"And then he made an honorable man out of me," Trey says cheekily. His wedding ring catches in the light as he takes a sip of wine, and my heart expands.

"That I did," I murmur.

"I always knew I wanted to stick with mechanics," Trey continues to explain. "It's what I specialized in anyway. So once my rehab was over, I was pretty confident I could get a job."

"I, on the other hand, had no clue what I wanted to do," I

116

say as I dice up the pancetta. "All I knew was that I was pretty good at bossing people around. Luckily, I had nepotism on my side."

Trey and Brady both laugh, but Harper frowns. "What does that mean?" he asks innocently.

"It's when you get ahead because of who your family are," I explain without a single drop of bashfulness.

I don't give a shit what anyone thinks. I paid my dues out in the desert with blood and tears. I almost lost the man I love in the blink of an eye. When life handed me a golden opportunity, you bet I grabbed it.

"My mother created the company from the ground up. My dad comes from old money and helped her make it a global success. We moved into this house when I was a teenager, and they always said it would be mine someday if I wanted it. When my military career ended sooner than anticipated, they said if I was interested in taking over the business, they were more than ready for early retirement by the ocean. And here we are."

"Wow, that's awesome," Harper says, sounding sincere. I wonder what his family's background is but decide that's a little too personal a question for right now.

Brady rubs his thumb over Harper's hand, which he's still holding. "Daddy doesn't just sit on his laurels, though," he says proudly, and warmth spreads through my chest. My sweet little pup. "One of the first things he did when he took over was strike up a deal with Intrepid Atlantic. You know? The airline. So anyone who gets wine on one of their flights, now gets one of Daddy's reds or whites."

I grin from where I'm getting the pasta boiling on the stove. "I just really like the idea of accompanying people when they're excited and off on their travels."

"That's such a nice way of thinking about it," Harper says as he sips from his glass. I'm not sure that he's usually a

117

wine drinker, but it's clear that he's trying, and I think maybe he's warming up to the pinot noir. He laughs and shakes his head. "I'm also glad to hear you had no clue what to do with yourself for a while. That's where I am right now."

"Oh, yeah?" I gently probe.

He nods. "I was, um, with someone who had a lot of money. He said I didn't need to work and that he'd take care of me."

There's something in his tone that puts my hackles on edge. Brady mentioned something about a bad relationship, and I immediately jump to conclusions. Not working means that Harper would have been financially dependent on this other guy, and that can very easily lead to control and manipulation issues, not to mention how isolating it can be not going out and working. But Harper smiles and moves on, so I don't dwell on the subject either.

However, I won't forget that potential red flag. This young man might not be mine, technically, but I hate the thought of him being abused, even if it was in the past.

"Anyway, so I have a bar job now, but it's just while I figure out what the hell to do with myself. I don't know where I want to live, what kind of career I want, or anything."

"There's no rush," I assure him with a one-armed shrug. "Trust me. You might not feel it, but you're still so young. In the meantime, don't be afraid to live your life. Have some fun."

I wink at Brady and am very pleased to be rewarded with a blush. Yeah, they're having fun. I can tell.

"Did you go to college?" Trey asks.

"Oh, no," Harper says with a laugh, shaking his head aggressively. "No, that wasn't for me. I don't have that kind of money."

I raise an eyebrow. "But you would have gone if you could?"

He fiddles with the stem of his wine glass. "I mean...like I said. I don't even know what I want to do with myself. If I had a burning desire to be a doctor or something, maybe it'd make sense. But it just seems like a waste of money to go for the sake of getting a few letters after my name."

I hum noncommittally. College isn't necessarily about getting a degree that will guarantee you a job afterward. It's where a lot of people go to find themselves precisely so they can work out who they want to be once they're done. But he's right. It's also a lot of money, and plenty of people don't have that privilege.

"Do you like sports?" I ask, changing the subject. "Brady's an assistant coach for the college football team, the Panthers. He used to play himself."

"Yeah, I knew that," Harper says in a flirty tone as he squeezes Brady's arm. "It doesn't surprise me. You still look like a jock."

It's adorable how flustered Brady gets. He looks between Trey and me, seemingly unsure if he should be proud or embarrassed.

"Uh, yeah. I mean, thanks. I mean, you should come watch a game sometime. We'll be starting the new season in August."

Harper grins, looking genuinely delighted by the invitation. "Sounds like fun. I'll bring my pom-poms and everything."

The conversation moves on as I continue cooking a vat of delicious creamy pasta for us all. The wine flows, and my bones feel warm. I like this kid. It's clear Brady is besotted and Trey is enamored, too.

But there's definitely a little darkness lurking there. Maybe some demons. Lord knows I've got those as well.

Most people do in this life. But it's something I make a note of to just be cautious of.

In that moment, though, I know I want to spend more time with this young man, especially if Brady intends to keep seeing him. As the evening stretches on, the dynamic of the group is light but sincere. It's almost like I can see the threads in the air of how we all slot nicely together. They glimmer and shine between us. This is good energy, and if possible, I'd like to explore it. The three of us have played with a lot of guys before, but it's very rare I feel a connection like this.

Harper says he doesn't know what he wants, and I respect that. But I'm *really* good at figuring out not what people want but what they *need*.

And I have a feeling that what this little lamb needs is a wolf pack to keep him safe and sound.

CHAPTER 13

Brady

"Are you sure about this?" I ask yet again as we pull up to the driveway. "If it's too much too soon, we can just turn around and leave right now."

Harper laughs at me from the passenger seat of my Bolt and gives me a fond look. "We've already survived dinner with your Daddies. My grandma is dying to meet you. What's a cup of coffee with your mom? Are you worried she's going to crack out the baby pictures?"

I snort and shake my head as I park the car and kill the ignition. "Yes, actually. I give her five minutes, maximum."

"I bet you were a chubby baby," he says gleefully as he unbuckles his seat belt. "And big, like a bowling ball."

I jab a finger at him. "We will not be asking my mother how many stitches she had to get because of me," I warn him, but he just laughs harder.

My heart does a slow roll in my chest. I'm trying not to get confused here. He was very clear that he doesn't know what's going on in his life and that he might up and leave for Chicago any day now. But then he goes and agrees to meet my family. My Daddies really liked him and have even brought up the possibility of us all doing a scene together.

This feels like a real relationship to me. One that's moving not exactly slowly. I know it was all very fast with Rick and Trey, so it wouldn't surprise me if that's my MO. But is it really what Harper wants?

Am I falling for him, only to get my heart broken down the line?

All relationships are a risk. Nobody really goes into one hoping for it to end badly, right? If they do, they need a better therapist. We all have hope. I just don't know how tightly to cling to mine when it comes to Harper.

What do I want from him?

I'm not exactly sure. So all I can do is keep going with it and take each day as it comes.

"Your grandma really wants to meet me, huh?" I ask as we approach the front door to my parents' place.

Harper grins. "Oh, man. So badly. I think she's already a big fan."

My chest puffs out a little at that. I might not know precisely what's going on between us, but it does make me happy to think that Harper's only real family approves of me.

He's skirted around the issue of his parents, but basically, I reckon all I really need to be aware of is they're not in the picture. He's an only child like me, and I can't imagine what it must be like not to be close with your mom and dad. I love my folks more than anything. But some people have no one at all, so I'm grateful that his grandma sounds like an awesome woman. A real Southern belle, the way he tells it.

My mom is...not that. But I still think she's the best mom in the whole world.

The door crashes open, and there she is, covered in bits of different colored yarn with a pair of scissors sticking out of her shirt pocket. Her glasses are smudged, her nails chipped, and her jeans have streaks of butter on them.

I wouldn't expect anything else.

"Pie!" she cries, using my childhood nickname despite the fact that I'm approaching my thirties. She throws her arms around me, and I congratulate myself on not getting stabbed by the scissors.

"Hey, Mom," I say, squeezing her tightly before letting her go. "You remember I said I was bringing a friend over? This is Harper Kendall. Harper, this is my mom, Mindy Ritter."

She blows a raspberry and bats me aside so she can also hug Harper. "Of course I remembered. That's why I made bungeo-ppang. Come in! Come in!"

She waves us over the threshold, bouncing excitedly. I used to bring friends over as a teen, but the only 'special someone' I've ever had over has been Rick and Trey. Basically so they could assure her that me moving in with them wasn't total insanity.

So, yeah. Me bringing Harper over is not a small thing, and I'm still not entirely convinced how it happened. I guess I mentioned that I always try and make it over for lunch on Sundays during the off-season, and it just slipped out of my mouth to ask Harper if he wanted to come along. Otherwise, because of our schedules we wouldn't be able to see much of each other for several days.

I was surprised he said yes at all, let alone so enthusiastically, but now I'm glad I did. He might not be sticking around, but whatever happens, I think he's going to be an important chapter in my life, and I'll be glad that my mom and dad met him.

"Your dad's out in the yard, Pie," Mom says as she bustles down the hall toward the kitchen. "Mowing the lawn. He'll be in shortly. Can I get you boys some lemonade? It's homemade!"

"That sounds lovely," Harper calls after her before leaning into me. "Pie?" he asks with a raised eyebrow.

I snort. "Mom called me her pumpkin pie when I was born. That got shortened to Pie and it stuck. Be nice."

He grins and raises his hands. "No judgment here. It's adorable, which isn't surprising when it comes to you. Everything about you is so cute."

I pinch his side and make him giggle and squeal. "I think the word you were searching for was 'sexy,' right?"

"Sure," he says, practically skipping into the kitchen.

My mom is pouring lemonade from a pitcher into four glasses at our kitchen table. I can see my dad out in the back yard, fighting with the lawnmower in the heat. He's not so great with small talk and meeting new people, but hopefully he'll come inside soon enough and at least shake hands with Harper.

I'm so lucky that my parents have never been fazed by me. Gay? No problem. College football? Just try not to get injured. *Two* boyfriends? Sure! Why not? They've always just wanted me to be successful in whatever way makes me happy. So when I told my mom that I'd made a new sort of 'special' friend, she didn't bat an eyelid. I told her we were just trying to keep it casual—only a little more than friends— but she's my mom, and I think she knows even better than I do when I'm lying to myself.

"Wow, these look amazing," Harper says as he takes a seat. He's looking at the plate of fish-shaped pastries that my mom has placed in the center of the table. They're about four inches long and have a sweet bean paste filling inside. As I reach out for one, I can tell they're still warm, just like they're supposed to be.

"Korean street food," I say proudly as Mom quickly nips around and slips small plates and napkins in front of us for all the flakes that are about to get on the table.

"Is that where you guys are from?" Harper asks.

My mom smiles proudly as she spins around looking for her phone which she's left on the counter. She grabs it with a flourish before sitting down with us. No doubt it's preloaded with baby photos that will soon make an appearance. She lets out a happy huff and gives Harper her full attention.

"Yes, I was born in South Korea. But my parents brought me and my sister here when I was three. And Brady's dad is Indiana born and bred. So he's had a mix of both cultures."

She reaches out and squeezes my hand. When I questioned her a couple of years ago about whether or not she was truly all right with me being in a throuple, she held my hand tightly, just like she is now, and told me that no one should be judged for living their lives differently simply because it's not what folks are used to. I think she suffered a lot of racism growing up, unsurprisingly for a small town in middle America. And she and Dad got it from both their families because they're an interracial couple.

It made her fiercely protective of me. She's such a happy person, but sometimes I'd catch her crying. She'd hug me to her and wag her finger, saying, "Promise me you'll always chase your dreams, Pumpkin Pie!" I'll admit it did get a little suffocating when I was growing up. I didn't always have big dreams. Sometimes I just wanted to eat pizza and play video games with my buddies. But I never had any doubt I was loved dearly.

Even so, there have also definitely been many occasions where I struggled with straddling the two cultures. I went to Korean school on weekends to learn the language and customs, and I still wear a hanbok for New Year and the few weddings we've been to back in Korea. I'm proud of my heritage and everything my mom has been through. But like most multiracial kids, I'm sure I'm never Korean enough for my relatives in Asia and still not quite American enough for

125

some people here, even though this has literally been my home my whole life.

And then realizing I was gay on top of that! Not to mention polyamorous. For all the times I told my mom to quit fussing over me as a kid, I appreciate now how deeply she understands what it's like to be ostracized for being different and never let me feel alone.

But Harper probably doesn't realize any of that. His eyes just light up as he carefully takes one of the bungeo-ppang. "I've seen these in anime," he says as he gently places the pastry onto his plate, then delicately licks his fingers. "I didn't appreciate they were real! My grandma absolutely loves baking. I bet she'd think these were so cool."

Sometimes I forget how things have changed recently in terms of media representation—even since I was at school. Anime has always been a thing, but it seems to have gotten super popular lately with so many new shows out every month. Then there's K-pop and K-dramas as well, even boy love stories showing gay characters. I know some of it is western ideals of what they think my mom's home country is like rather than the actual reality, but anything that makes kids more accepting of children that look different from them is really okay in my book.

Harper's never looked at me like I'm different. Just like he took Trey's prosthetic and burn scars in his stride. For all that I'm worried he's still got some walls up, I do think he's a genuine sort of person.

And more often than not, the way he looks at me makes me feel like a snack. Sometimes it's a little tricky to remember just who's the top between us.

"Well, you can take your grandma one back home if you'd like," my mom says earnestly. Of course she remembered that I'd said that Harper lives with his grandma and not his parents. See, I'm here thinking about my own interesting life journey, and I don't really know what he's been through. I bet we have a lot to learn from each other.

He beams. "Could I? That's so kind of you."

My mom waves her hands dismissively. "No trouble at all. Let me get you a box. Oh, actually, I'll go fetch Brady's dad before he gets himself too hot and bothered, and I'll bring a box back with us. You boys sit tight!"

She bustles out of the kitchen, and I watch Harper as he nibbles the golden fish talc. "What?" he asks, licking crumbs off his lips.

"It's just pretty cool seeing you in my family home," I say honestly.

He rubs his foot against my calf under the table. "You just like seeing me anytime," he says flirtatiously.

Heat spreads over my cheeks, and I feel my cock twitch in my pants. "True," I admit.

After this, we've got plans to go back home and play. He's been over a couple of times since we all went paintballing, and I know Papa and especially Daddy are getting more and more eager to try something as a group. I've been enjoying keeping Harper to myself as it's felt like I never know if—or more likely *when*—he's going to up and vanish on me.

But he's here, right now, meeting my parents. He wants me to meet his grandma. Maybe it's time to see about taking it to the next level. Even if this affair is going to be short-lived, it doesn't mean it can't be deep and meaningful.

"You still want to stay at my place tonight?" I ask, warming up the subject.

To my delight, he nods earnestly. "I've packed my sleep-over bag," he says in a devilish tone.

Ever since we had that chat after our first encounter, he listened to what I said about aftercare. He always lets me hold him and fuss over him now, but he's also started staying over and allowing me to fix him breakfast before he leaves.

Sometimes my Daddies join us for food or just to hang out a little while.

But I want to take it further now.

I reach out to slip my hand over his, glancing out of the window. I don't want my folks walking back inside when we're right in the middle of a delicate conversation, but they look to be engrossed in discussing my dad's delphiniums for the time being.

All right, then. Now or never.

"I thought maybe we could try the barn tonight," I say. I've told him about our assault course and shown him around on his last visit. But we've never seriously discussed doing a scene there before.

"Ohh," he says and visibly shivers, which I take as a good sign. "That sounds fun."

I lick my lips and choose my words carefully. "I know we'll have a lot of fun. But if you felt like it, I think my Daddies would be very interested in playing with us as well. Is that something you'd consider?"

He looks away, clearly thinking it through, which makes me happy. This isn't a decision I want him rushing into. "Would you all chase me, like with the paintball?"

"It's up to you," I say sincerely. "I love hunting you, little lamb. But I still love being my Daddies' wolf pup, too. So we could track you down as a pack, or if you wanted to ease into it slightly, maybe you and I could stick together and let Rick and Trey do the chasing?"

He nods and obviously thinks that over as well. But then his phone pings, making him jump. We both laugh as he pulls it from his pocket, but then my stomach drops as his face goes slack and the little color he has in his cheeks drains away.

"Harper?" I say, my hackles immediately rising. "What's wrong?"

For a second, he just stares at the phone, his chest moving rapidly as he breathes hard. But then he aggressively swipes at the screen and presses the button to lock it before shoving it back into his pocket.

"Nothing. Everything's fine. Yes, that sounds super hot, and I'm super into it."

I blink, not sure how to handle this. I don't want to pry, but whatever he just saw blatantly upset him. However, we really don't have that kind of relationship. He doesn't have to tell me everything, or in fact, anything. All I can do is check in with him and ask if he's okay, and just trust that he's going to be honest with me.

"Are you sure? We can keep it just the two of us. Or we can even just watch a movie or something—"

He cuts me off by leaning forward and smashing his lips against mine for a possessive kiss. *"Hot,"* he repeats. "I want all three of you chasing me like you said. Make me feel special."

My heart expands, and I squeeze the back of his neck while looking into his eyes. Now *that* I can do.

Because he is special. He might not realize it himself, but he is *so* special.

"Of course," I murmur. "We'll take good care of you."

He squirms in his seat. "If by that you mean 'fuck my brains out,' then—yes, please."

He gives me a naughty grin, but I see what he's doing. He's putting up those walls I feel stronger at times than others. It's like he keeps remembering that he has to keep his guard up to protect himself.

I'm not exactly happy about that, but I sense there's only so much probing I can do right now. I just bookmark it for later in case we want to—or *need* to—come back to it.

I laugh and draw him into a hug. Out of the corner of my eye, I've seen my parents are coming inside, so we need to

129

wrap this up anyway. "Who's in charge?" I say in a low rumble.

He draws back and looks at me through his eyelashes. "You are, Baby Wolf," he says softly.

"That's right." I skim my hand up his thigh, just grazing over his crotch and making him moan quietly. "So if I say we're going to take care of you, then that's what's going to happen. All right?"

"Yes, Baby," he says just as my parents reach the screen door.

"Good boy."

There's still more going on here than I understand, I'm certain. But I just have to hold on to what's important.

I want to spend more time with Harper, and for that to happen, he needs to let me look after him. So long as that's the case, we can work everything else out, I'm sure.

While he's still here, he's still mine, and that's all that really matters.

CHAPTER 14

Harper

FUCKING LOWELL. I *KNEW* HE'D BEEN SNOOPING AROUND MY socials, so in a way, it's a relief to finally get a message from him. In the same way, I imagine it's a relief to get bitten by a snake that's been cornering you. It's over. In theory, the most painful moment has passed.

Much like I'd have to tend to a swollen, venomous bite, I'm now soothing my wounded and fractured heart in the only way I can think of.

I'm going to let Brady and his Daddies destroy me.

Sex with Brady is like nothing else. Even when we go light on the primal stuff, it still utterly drowns anything else out that I might be thinking or worrying about. I've been contemplating whether or not I'd want to try a group scenario, and tonight seems like the perfect opportunity.

Lowell's message made my skin crawl.

You belong to me, it had read. *You're my property, and I don't appreciate it when people take from me. Enjoy your little stunt. I'm going to punish you when I get you back home. I'll lock you up forever, and you'll never steal from me again.*

That's fucked up, right?

It doesn't actually *say* it's him. I checked, and that account doesn't have any posts and has only been following me for a week. But I have no doubt. I knew he'd create sock-puppet handles just to creep on me. I've been careful not to tag any locations of anything and keep things vague, but I refuse to live like a hermit just because I dated a psycho.

I deleted that message and blocked the account. He probably already has others following me, but I can't do anything about that. I can just give myself the satisfaction of not rising to his bait.

Besides, it just confirms everything I've come to realize about him. He doesn't love me. He never did. He just gets his kicks from trying to control me and make me feel small.

Not like Brady at all.

When Brady tells me that I'm his, I feel warm and cherished. That's why I'm jumping into this group scene between the four of us, even though I'm a bit scared of what it's actually going to be like. The paintballing was exhilarating. Rick and Trey were laser-focused on me with Brady taking the lead as my pursuer. It was electric. My heart has never beaten so fast, and even though it was quick and dirty in the shower, the orgasm in the bed afterward was earth-shattering.

Even if I'm not entirely sure how it would even work. Like…would they all try and stick it in me at once? Take turns? That sounds…like a lot. I really would be overwhelmed and overpowered. But it's going to be hot, right? Just like the paintballing.

I want to feel like that again. The world exists beyond Lowell. There are more than those four walls that at first seemed so liberating with their floor-to-ceiling windows looking out so high over Indianapolis. But it didn't matter that they were transparent. It was still a prison.

The truly saddest part was that I wasn't even locked inside. In the end, all I had to do was find the courage to walk out the door and not look back. He just ground me down to the point where I felt like I couldn't leave—that I couldn't do *anything* without him. But that's not who I am. It's not my nature. I'm a fighter, a firecracker, as Grandma sometimes calls me. That fierce little creature has always been inside me, trying his best to get out.

So while I love that Brady calls me his little lamb, I need to prove to myself tonight that I've still got spunk. I'm not just going to roll over and take it. I'll bite and scratch and claw my way to freedom. And if they conquer me, it'll be because *I've* allowed it. Because it makes me feel good and desired. If they want to claim me, they have to work hard and prove it to me.

I'm done being small and worthless. I am *important*, and what better way to show that to myself than having three hot guys hunt me down and mate me?

My heart is like a battering ram in my chest as we drive up to Brady's house. I enjoyed meeting his parents, but I must admit that after seeing Lowell's message and agreeing to the group scene, everything became a bit foggy. I found it difficult to concentrate on what was being said, although I tried my hardest because I really liked Mindy and was genuinely so interested in her stories about Brady.

But it's like I've got a fever, and only coming my brains out can break it. If Lowell was the venom, then Brady and his Daddies are the antidote. I need it—them—inside me as soon as possible.

I'm not prepared for Rick and Trey to be waiting for us at the front door. Rick has his arm wrapped around his husband, but he's watching me carefully as I exit the vehicle. We're parked in the drive out front today rather than the garage out back. I'm not sure why, but something tells me it's to do with pomp and ceremony.

Good. Like I told Brady—I'm special. I want them to

make a fuss over me. I'm a treasure, a prize, something to be celebrated. Not a moldy old antique to be hidden away from the sunlight so it doesn't get damaged.

I'm the star of this show.

"Harper," Rick says warmly as Brady and I make our way up the stairs. Rick opens his free arm out, drawing me to him, and I drift against his side like a moon being pulled into a planet's orbit. Rick kisses my cheek—by far the most intimate thing we've done so far—and heat rushes through my body. "We're so glad you could join us," he murmurs into my ear.

I gulp. These guys fuck strangers all the time. They do crazy, kinky things and then never speak to those men again. This must be easy for them. So I use that to push my fear down and try and think like them. I don't need to know them all that well, really. I might not know much about kink, but I've been reading more on the internet lately. Not knowing about the traffic lights system freaked me out a bit. It's super common, but Lowell never once mentioned it to me.

Of course he didn't.

But I now know as the sub at the bottom of this food chain, I'm *technically* the one with the most power. They might be 'in charge,' but all this is only happening because I want it to.

I'm the super star. The guest of honor.

Still, I don't expect Trey to lean around and hug me as well, nuzzling his nose against my neck as he inhales deeply.

"Beautiful little lamb. Are you ready for this?"

I feel myself tremble but shove those feelings away. "Are you?" I ask snarkily instead.

That gets a dark laugh out of both of them, and I'm already feeling cornered. *That's the point, dumbass,* I snap at myself. This isn't Lowell backing me into the bedroom and telling me I have to suck his cock whether I like it or not. I lied to myself back then and told myself I was into that.

This is different.

They're going to chase me, and they're going to *earn* it, and anything that happens will be because I want it to. I banish Lowell from my head. He has no right to be there. This is my new happy, sexy place. And it's going to be fun! And there's no pressure to commit. We can play some games —tonight, the next few weeks, whatever—and then I'll walk away from it all because I *can.*

That's the power I have.

Brady slips his arm around my waist so now they're all touching me. "Remember, Harper," he says seriously. "You can back out at any time."

I don't like him putting doubts in my head. Instead of answering him, I lean over and kiss him hard. Then I kiss Trey, who tastes fresh and clean, his lips as soft as pillows. Finally, I claim Rick. I sense he's amused that I'm doing this, but he still lets me, and that feels exhilarating in and of itself. He tastes the spiciest of the three, his mouth the hardest.

"I'm ready," I tell Brady, looking him dead in the eye.

"You know what to do," Rick growls to him. Brady looks excitedly at me.

"Come on, this way."

He takes me by the hand and leads me through the house that I'm becoming familiar with. We hurry to the kitchen, where he stops us by the back door. I see one of their cats— I've got no hope of telling them apart—watching us from the floor as she swishes her fluffy tail. She's gray with yellow eyes that feel like they're looking into my soul.

Do you know what you're doing? I imagine her asking me.

Of course I do, I tell her back firmly. Honestly, I'm not letting a *cat* give me cold feet.

Brady pulls me back to him. He kisses me with a grinning

mouth, then slips his fingers under the hem of my T-shirt, pulling it upward.

"You're okay being chased by yourself?" he asks as he drops my shirt on the floor where I've also placed my overnight bag down. "I can still join you."

I shake my head, watching him unbuckle my belt and slide it through the loops. "I want you to hunt me," I rasp, my throat already tight. "My Baby Wolf and his pack."

We've undressed each other before, and he's certainly yanked my pants down and such. But this is the first time I've just stood there and allowed him to divest me of all my clothing with the lights on. It's strangely intimate in a different kind of way. I feel extremely vulnerable. As he crouches down and carefully unties my sneakers and slides them off my feet, I can feel myself trembling.

"We'll take care of you, little lamb," he promises, unzipping my jeans before tugging them and my briefs down. His head is right by my already half-hard cock, but he's just looking up at me with those beautiful dark eyes.

I'm completely naked in a stranger's house with a gorgeous man at my feet. It's kind of intoxicating. I reach out and cup the side of his face. "I know you will," I say.

He's not like Lowell, and neither are his Daddies.

I need to stop thinking of that mother fucker right now. Screw him. I bet I'm about to have the best sex of my young life.

Brady stands and opens the back door into the darkening evening. My heart skips a beat, and I swallow down a gulp. This is it.

"Run, little lamb," my wolf says, his voice dropping low and dangerous.

I sprint out into the night. My feet slap on the patio, but then I'm on the cool grass, little twigs and stones biting into my soles. My blood is pumping so hard I can barely hear myself think, especially over the sound of my heavy breathing. My cock and balls bounce almost painfully against my thighs.

I can't believe I'm really doing this.

Brady told me in the car that I should run for the barn door that will have been left open for me. The softly glowing light is like a beacon to me, but I know that inside I won't find safety from my pursuers.

But perhaps I'll find salvation.

I crash through the door, wincing as the ground under my feet switches to concrete strewn with straw. It looked completely different in the daytime when Brady and I wandered around here before, kind of like the paintball course. Now there's atmospheric lighting and a soundtrack playing like I'm in a forest. The straw bales and various farm equipment cast deep shadows as I run around them. I look at the first mattress I pass. It's made up with a fresh sheet, pillows, and a basket of all kinds of sexy things next to it.

Is that where they'll catch me? Where they'll pin me down and fuck me however they want?

Genuine fear spikes through me as I spin on my heels, bouncing off the side of a stack of bales that's acting like a wall, dividing the space up into a small maze. This is completely different from being cornered in a tacky motel room or using the spare room that I've started thinking of as 'Brady's room.' This is a proper hunt.

I need to hide.

Darting around another corner, I look for a good spot. My heart skips a beat, and I don't know if I heard a noise or not. I should probably try and be quieter, but all I can think about is getting away.

I'm having trouble in this moment remembering that this is supposed to be fun and that I volunteered for this shit.

I turn yet another corner and suddenly shriek, jumping

several inches into the air. Brady's right there, totally naked, and running at me like a linebacker. I pivot and sprint away, but Trey is waiting for me, his teeth bared as he snarls like a wild animal, his fingers curled as if they were really claws. I've seen Brady naked several times before. But seeing his Papa without any clothes on makes me gasp, the reality of the situation truly dawning on me.

Three men are planning on fucking me if they get their hands on me, and all of them are much bigger and stronger than I am.

I feel dizzy as I fumble against the straw bales, trying to get to the next turn away from them both. Trey lunges and snatches me around the waist. He might have a prosthetic, but he's still damned fast and nimble. I cry out as I struggle, trying to get away, but then Brady is on me as well, grabbing my shoulders and sucking on my neck.

"Hello, little lamb," Trey growls, and I can't help it. I whimper as if I really were prey.

"Fuck off!" I yell, lashing out at both of them. I don't think about Trey's foot or if I could really hurt either of them. I just think about getting away.

They laugh at me as I scramble to freedom, and I can't stop the sob that escapes my chest. My head is spinning, and I'm not sure what I'm supposed to be doing, but all I can think of is getting to the door and fleeing into the night.

That's before Rick comes stalking out of the shadows, his hand wrapping around my throat as he shoves me against the barn wall. I've somehow managed to corner myself, and now he's here, looming over me with a vicious smirk on his face.

He's undoubtedly older than all of us, and the hair on his torso might be graying like on his temples. But even as the terror shoots through my body, I can appreciate his stunning physique. The man looks like some kind of god, for fuck's sake. All chiseled, gleaming muscles that if I wasn't busy trying not to piss myself, I'd probably want to lick all over.

But his fingers squeeze around my neck, and I'm yanked back to the here and now. My hands scramble against his wrist and bang on his chest, but he doesn't even flinch. He just grins maniacally at me, leaning in closer and forcing me to look into his blue eyes.

"You're *mine* now, little lamb," he sneers. "Don't try and escape. Otherwise, Daddy will have to punish you."

It all happens so fast.

I hear Rick accidentally echoing Lowell's words, and it's like I've suddenly dropped underwater. Everything's muffled to my ears except the blood that's rushing through my veins. It's as if I've found myself caught naked and alone in a hurricane, with nothing to protect me at all. My knees give out from under me. Rick seizes my shoulder, but he's still mostly keeping me up by the grip he has around my throat.

No escape. None.

You're going to be punished, boy.

Choke on Daddy's cock. It's all you're good for.

I can hear Lowell's words as clear as day as the light dims from my vision. I feel like I'm falling down a well or being sucked under by the tide. There isn't enough oxygen in my lungs.

But I have breath enough for one tiny, desperate word that ghosts over my lips.

"*Red.*"

Everything stops. I still can't really hear properly, but the pressure on my neck vanishes, and I'm finally dropping to the ground. I don't hit it, however. Instead, I find myself being held incredibly tightly. Rick's arms. His chest. Yes. I'm being rocked. The light in my blurry vision gets much brighter, and I can sense frantic movement around me.

"*Harper?*" a voice calls, sounding exactly as if it's being

139

shouted through water, and I wonder if I really did fall down a well.

"Harper, breathe for me," another echoey voice says. But there's such an iron-hard commanding tone to the words, that I manage to blink and look at the man who spoke them. "Harper," Rick shouts again, his voice becoming clearer. "Harper, you've got to take deeper breaths. Do it with me."

He inhales long and slow, and I realize that I've been taking such teeny gasps like a panicked bunny rabbit. He grips my hand and nods at me, and I manage to copy him, finally getting some proper air into my system again. My vision starts to clear.

Brady is crouching next to me, holding my leg so tightly that his fingers are digging into my thigh. There are tears in his eyes. He's still naked—we all are—but then Trey comes running back into my view, holding a blanket that he swiftly wraps around my front.

"No," I moan, the realization dawning on me of what I've done. I've ruined the scene. I was stupid and a baby and couldn't cope, so I spoiled everyone's fun, and I can't have that. "No, stop," I mumble.

"Stop what, little lamb?" Rick asks. He brushes a lock of my hair out of my eyes.

I shake my head. "Keep going," I mutter. "I'm fine."

Rick chuckles darkly. "Okay, champ. You just safe-worded. We're taking it easy tonight. Come on."

I grumble as he hugs me to his chest, but I don't try and get free of him as he stands, holding me in a bridal carry. He jostles me until I've got my arms around his shoulders and my face buried against his neck. I feel hands on me, tucking the blanket around my body tightly, and I assume it's Brady.

He trusted me, and I spoiled his fun. He let me play with his Daddies. I know how big a deal that is, and I've gone and blown it.

I don't want Brady to be mad at me.

I protest and keep telling them 'no,' but Rick ignores me, carrying me all the way back to the house. I'm vaguely aware of Trey and Brady behind us. Trey has his arm around Brady's back and keeps kissing the top of his head. Brady looks upset.

I did that. This is all my fault.

"No, stop," I sob as Rick puts me down. I don't know how, but we've made it to a bedroom. We must be upstairs. The bed is enormous. Is this their *actual* bed?

Before I can try and wrestle myself away, Brady is in front of me. Somewhere along the way, he's put pajama pants on. He wraps his arms and legs around me like he's trying to cocoon me. "It's okay, Harper," he's saying over and over. "We've got you."

"No," I mumble, getting mad. I don't want this. This is all wrong. "Get off. Go."

"We've got you," Brady says, ignoring me.

"Here," Trey's voice floats from somewhere above.

"Thanks, babe," Rick replies.

The bed dips. Through my tear-laden eyelashes, I see Trey get on the bed behind Brady, curling up behind him. He's also now wearing pants, one leg shorter than the other, so I can see he's removed his prosthetic. Brady's head is still tucked against my chest like he's a small animal trying to burrow inside me. But Trey strokes his hair and then leans over to gently kiss my forehead. "It's okay, sweetheart," he tells me.

I want to shake him off. I want to push them all away. But Brady's like an aggressive koala, keeping me in place.

The bed dips again, and I feel Rick spooning up behind me. "Drink some of this, little lamb," he instructs, holding a sports drink up to my mouth. I assume that's what Trey gave him. He went and got that for me.

"Don't need it," I mumble petulantly.

"Who's in charge here?" Rick asks in a dangerous tone.

I gulp. I don't have *that* much fight in me. I don't answer, but when he presses the top of the bottle to my lips, I swallow obediently.

"There we go, good boy," he says after several seconds of me drinking, apparently satisfied that I've had enough. I try and reject his words, but I can't help the warm and fuzzy glow I get from being told that I'm good.

I'm not good, though. I'm *bad*.

Rick puts the bottle down and then spoons up tighter behind me. I can feel he's also wearing pants now, and with the blanket that's still over me, the body heat between us all is like a radiating oven. It's too much. I want to get out, run, go anywhere but here.

Anywhere I can escape from my shame.

"No," I whine again, screwing up my face and trying to struggle against all the arms holding me in place. "Let me go. Fuck off, fuck *off.*"

Rick just gives me that dark chuckle again. "Are you using your safe word again, little lamb? Do you *actually* want us to fuck off?"

I grit my teeth, hot tears spilling down my face, but no words escape my throat.

"I thought so," Rick says smugly.

I thrash again, but it's like I'm covered in tightening vines that won't set me free. This wolf pack has turned into a puppy pile, and they're suffocating me.

I don't want this. I don't deserve it. Fuck off, *fuck off!*

"It's okay, Harper," Brady whispers against my chest, stroking my skin where he can and pressing little kisses against my clavicle. "It's okay. We've got you."

I start to cry harder. I cry until I finally fall asleep.

CHAPTER 15

Brady

I wake up completely disoriented. For several seconds, I can't remember where I am or what was going on.

Then it slowly comes back to me.

I fucked up.

I knew Harper wasn't in the right frame of mind to be doing a big scene like that. Whatever that notification on his phone was spooked him badly. But he seemed so keen, and I was so eager for him to play with my Daddies that I ignored my gut instinct.

And he had a complete breakdown.

It was like he became catatonic. His eyes were open, but there wasn't anything behind them for the longest time. He scared the shit out of me. Thank fuck Daddy was there to take charge and look after him. I don't know what I would have done if I'd been by myself.

I wasn't there in the moment, so I don't know what triggered him exactly. Daddy was with him, but he's fast asleep now, as is Papa.

It's taken me this long to realize that among the tangle of

limbs I'm in, somehow Harper has slipped away. He's no longer in the bed.

Panic grips me, and I extract myself from my Daddies without waking them, for which I'm glad. This is my mess. I'm responsible for Harper. It's me who needs to go find him.

My first thought as I dash out of the bedroom wearing only sweatpants is that he might have left the house altogether. But that's one advantage of living out in the middle of nowhere. Unless he found a set of keys and liberated one of our cars, he can't really have gone far.

Still, my heart is in my mouth as I hurry downstairs. I should have maybe looked in the spare room where Harper and I have slept a few times now, but my instinct tells me to head for the living room. I ignored it earlier. I'm not making that mistake again.

Sure enough, as I rush down into the lobby, I see the faint glow of a lamp in the front room of the house. Papa and I turned pretty much everything off when we followed Daddy and Harper up to bed a few hours ago, so I'm not surprised when I quietly pad into the room and see Harper curled up on the sofa.

Thank goodness. I didn't really think he'd run off into the woods, but he was in such a fractious state of mind earlier I couldn't be totally sure.

"Hey," I say softly to make him aware of my presence.

He looks up and blinks at me from whatever he's got in his lap. But he doesn't really react much more than that, and I worry that he's still in shock from the panic attack he had earlier. I know I haven't been on the scene nearly as long as my Daddies, but I've never seen someone safe-word out so completely as that before.

"Mind if I come sit with you?" I ask.

He stares at me a moment, then he nods, curling up his legs tighter so there's more room for me on the couch. I notice he's dressed once more in the clothes I took off him and left at the back door. I grab a blanket that's laid over the back of the couch, toss it around my shoulders, then drop down onto the cushions beside him.

"Are you okay?" I ask. He shrugs and goes back to looking at his lap. I realize he's got a sketch pad out from somewhere and is working on something colorful I can't really make out from this angle. "Oh, wow," I say, craning my neck. I stop when he hugs the pad to himself, but I still smile at him. "I didn't know you liked to draw."

He shrugs again. "It's stupid."

I frown and feel my Dom rising pretty fast. "No, it's not. It's actually very cool. Let me see, little lamb."

His eyes go wide at my tone, but he wordlessly hands over the pad regardless.

"Oh, fuck," I say in genuine surprise.

It's not just cool. It's actually *amazing*. He's been capturing the fireplace in front of us, complete with one of our elusive cats. I can tell even from this rough sketch that it's Merlot. He's only using a palette of about a dozen colors from what it looks like, but the range of tones is remarkable, let alone the detail of his pencil strokes.

"You're really good," I say, shaking my head.

"Not really," he says flippantly, looking away from me, but that just makes me cross.

"Stop that," I say, letting my Dom come out again. "You're allowed to take a compliment. I wouldn't lie to you, Harper. Not ever. I think this is really beautiful and that you have talent. Other people must have told you that before."

He bites his lip, looking at the sketch pad rather than at me. But then he gives a tiny nod. "Yeah. It's a silly hobby, but...thank you."

"Good boy," I say, not missing the flush that appears on his cheeks. Oh, he wants to be good for me, all right. I don't

145

like that he dismissed his creative talent as something silly, but it's more important right now that he accepts some praise. I glance down at the pad in my hands. It's about halfway full. "May I look at some of the others?"

He licks his lips, and just when I think the pause has stretched out so long he's going to decline, he nods his head. Carefully, I start flicking backward through the pages.

"Wow," I say as I take in all the amazingly colorful scenes. There are fountains, bus stops, flowers, bridges—all views I guess from Indianapolis, where he was living. Each page is dated, and I can tell he hasn't drawn anything in a couple of years. Moving backward, the dates start far apart, but then they get closer and closer.

Over the past five years—since he graduated—he's slowly sketched less and less.

Until tonight.

I go to hand it back, and he surprises me by speaking up as I pass the pad over. "This and the box of pastels are some of the only things I took with me from my ex's place. I forgot they were still in my backpack, but I found them when I pulled my clothes out. I guess one of you put them in there after…earlier."

"Yeah, I did that," I say softly. I did it before I even started hunting him. I wanted to make sure he didn't lose a sock or anything.

"It's like a visual diary," he whispers, closing the book and clutching it to his chest. "One of my teachers suggested it at school."

"It's gorgeous," I tell him. He nibbles his lip and shrugs again, but he doesn't tell me it's stupid, at least.

"It's cheaper than therapy."

Oh, wow. That's a statement.

"Have you been to therapy?" I ask. I haven't myself, but Papa has seen both a private psychiatrist and is part of a few different groups. Even Daddy goes along to see a group of retired vets sometimes. They've both drilled it into me that there's absolutely zero shame in talking to someone about your problems, but not everyone sees it like that.

Sure enough, Harper shrugs again, not properly answering me. But he seems so fragile right now, I don't push it. I have other questions I want to ask that are most likely going to be tough enough to tackle—if he opens up to me at all.

"What happened tonight, sweetheart?" I ask.

His face darkens like a thundercloud. "I ruined everything," he spits out.

I grip his knee and glower at him. "Absolutely not," I say sternly, waiting until he peeks at me through his golden lashes. I let my expression soften. "You did exactly what you were supposed to do. You didn't feel okay, so you used your safe word. I'm proud of you."

"I *should* have been okay, though," he protests, getting agitated. "I wanted it! If I'd have just sucked it up—"

"Hey, hey, no," I insist. "That would have been awful if you'd done that. I would have been really upset. Please listen to me when I tell you that you were a very good boy and did exactly the right thing. Harper? Say it back to me."

He looks like he wants to cry again as he stares at me for a few seconds, but then he takes a shaky breath. "I was a good boy," he manages to whisper.

"Yes, yes!" I say happily. I carefully take the pad and pack of pastels, putting them on the coffee table. Then I draw him into a hug, wrapping the blanket around us both. "Is this okay?"

"Yes, Baby," he mumbles sadly, but he clings to me in a way that lets me know he means it.

"Good boy," I say again.

For a while, I just hold him, feeling his heart beating

through his chest and stroking his blond hair. My sweet little lamb.

For him to have a reaction like he did, someone must have hurt him quite badly. It makes me want to hurt whoever that person is quite badly as well. But they're not here. Harper is. He's all I really care about.

"Do you want to talk about it?" I ask after a while.

He laughs ruefully. "Which part?"

It's my turn to shrug. "Was there something that triggered you? Were you really into the scene, or were you just going along with it to please me? Is there anything I can do to help?"

He turns his head to look into my eyes, his expression serious. "I really thought I wanted to do it, I promise. I love playing with you. But it all got too much. I…"

He falls silent for a while, chewing on his lip. It takes some restraint on my part, but I manage to wait without saying anything. He'll speak when he's ready. Sure enough, after a minute or two, he takes a deep breath.

"Something Rick said reminded me of my ex. He messaged me earlier. I think it scrambled my brain."

I still want about a million more details, but that's a really great start for now. I knew that message he got before was significant. If anything's taught me to trust my gut instincts after this, it'll be that.

"Good boy," I say emphatically, almost like I'm talking to a dog. "Thank you. That means so much that you would tell me that. I'm so sorry that happened. How do you feel now?"

"Calmer," he says slowly. "Like I cried a lot of it out. But so tired, even though I can't sleep."

I nod, hugging him tighter. "That all sounds like a pretty standard reaction to shock from what I know. What you said helps me understand so much. We can carry on discussing it now if you want, or I can just keep holding you if you'd like?"

He nods and snuggles in closer to me. "Thank you, Brady," he says so quietly I almost miss it. "I want to just cuddle."

"You're welcome, little lamb," I say before I kiss his temple. "I'm here for you, I promise. Whatever you need."

He nods again but doesn't reply. We shift a bit on the sofa, getting comfier, and after a while, I can feel his breathing even out as he's fallen asleep.

I'm ridiculously proud. That's probably stupid, but I am. I love that he's comfortable enough now that he can be so vulnerable as to fall asleep in my arms. My sweet boy.

I know there's still a lot going on in that head of his that I don't understand. I wonder if I ever will. But tonight, it's almost like I can feel those walls of his starting to crumble a little as he tries to let me in. I want that. I want to support him and be there when he needs someone to lean on. He doesn't have to put on this act all the time. The confidence is sexy, for sure. But my heart actually swells more for him like this. When he's being genuine and letting himself be helpless.

Because he's not helpless. I'm here to protect him.

I'm anxious how my Daddies feel about tonight. I hope they're not mad at me. I'm sure they won't be, and even if I did fuck up, they'll talk through with me what happened and how to avoid it next time.

But I can't help it. I love them so much, and Harper is also becoming very important to me. I want them all to get along so badly. I want to be intimate with all of them. I can feel the electricity between the four of us like it's a physical presence. I hope I'm not being selfish, but I feel so strongly that this energy between all of us is growing into something momentous.

I shouldn't have rushed it tonight. Harper wasn't ready. I just pray that I haven't ruined things and we can try again, slower this time. Gentler. Whatever Harper needs. I know Daddy and Papa want to take care of him as much as I do.

It's just whether or not he'll let us.

I'm not going to give up, though. This boy is special, I know it. I'm pretty sure whoever this ex of his was tried to convince him that he was worthless. So even if Harper doesn't stay long with us, I'm making it my mission that before he goes, I'll at least make him see the truth.

He's extraordinary. And for now, he's still mine. So I'm going to treasure him.

Whether he damn well likes it or not.

CHAPTER 16

Trey

"I CAN SEE YOU," I SAY IN A PLAYFUL TONE, GLANCING OVER the top of Ariana. Harper's hovering by the door that leads from the garage into the house. He's wearing some of Brady's larger clothes again, and he looks adorably small. But I guess he only packed for one night, and it's been a couple of days now.

I know it's happened for less-than-ideal reasons, but I kind of like that he's hanging around.

"Sorry," he mumbles. "Brady's asleep. I was exploring."

I grin, reaching over for a rag so I can get the worst of the grease off my hands. "Don't be sorry. How about you come sit?" I clear some tools from the mat beside me before patting it, showing him that he's welcome.

He nibbles his lower lip, but then he silently comes down the steps and pads over the hard floor to join me. "This is your bike?" he says, even though I'm pretty sure he knows the answer to that. We've talked about it over dinner, I know. But it's a nice, easy conversation opener, so I give it to him.

"Yep, this is Ariana."

"Brady says you don't drive it. You just pull it apart and put it back together again."

I laugh loudly and lightly punch his arm. For a second, he looks stunned. But then he grins back at me.

"I ride her," I say defensively, but I'm still smiling. "In fact, my buddies and I are planning a little day trip soon, so she'll be purring like a kitten in no time."

He scrunches up his nose as he looks the bike over. "So you're a mechanic, but your hobby is also mechanics," he says. The fact that he's teasing me lights up my heart.

I've been into kink for a while now. Seriously so since Rick and I got back from Afghanistan and committed to each other and the lifestyle, so I've seen a fair bit. What Harper went through the other night was pretty extreme. That panic attack came almost out of nowhere, or so it seemed. Brady's talked to him and gotten a little background from him, but the truth is, I'm worried.

Which is why I'm so thrilled that without anyone really discussing it, he hasn't left the house yet. Brady says he's talked to his grandma, so she knows where he is and isn't concerned. And he managed to do a shift at his work yesterday, which Brady drove him to and from.

But until he opens up and faces what triggered him like that, I figure the next best thing is for us to watch over him. Brady's off work because school's out for the summer. However, he's supposed to be doing some extra training with the team. Coach Drevin insisted he take some personal time off, though, when he realized it was a family matter.

Rick worked from home yesterday as well. However, he had an important meeting today about his upcoming fundraiser, but I spoke to my boss, Ruben, and he okayed a personal day so I could stick around for the boys.

I might not be Harper's official Papa, but I am Brady's, and it's important to me that I look after the both of them.

"We can't all have crazy-talented hobbies," I tease Harper back after his quip about my bike. Unfortunately, though, his face drops.

"Brady told you about that?" he asks uncertainly.

I put down the rag that I've been fiddling with and squeeze Harper's knee. "He said your artwork was incredibly good and that he was glad you shared your sketches with him. I'd love to see them too someday if you feel like it." He shrugs and looks away, but he doesn't flat tell me no. I take the win. "Do you find it helps soothe your mind?" I ask.

I'm not being entirely honest. Brady mentioned that Harper thinks of drawing as therapy, and that's something I feel quite passionately about.

After a few moments, he nods. "It helps me feel connected to the world," he says. His voice is small, but I feel like the words are strong.

I pat the side of my bike. "I totally get that," I say with a small laugh. "Working on Ariana here makes me feel grounded."

"You named your bike after your mom?" he asks playfully. "Brady said so."

I give him a light shove. "You wanna make something of it?" I ask in a poor impression of a New York mobster. Harper just laughs harder, but then his gaze softly trails over the bike once more.

"Could I...um. Could I sketch you and her?"

My heart does a little dance. I feel like this is hugely significant. Brady's been worried that Harper has too many walls up and that he's struggling with being vulnerable. That's a pretty big thing to ask.

"I'd love that," I tell him honestly. We can both do our therapy together, even if we don't use our words.

This time.

He goes off to fetch his stuff, and I resume tightening

bolts on the seat. I don't want to make this a big deal, but it kind of is.

One of the reasons that Rick, Brady, and I work so well together is that even though our personalities are very different, we have similar hearts. We enjoy being physically intimate with other men—strangers, most of the time—but when our hearts fall, they fall hard and fast.

Brady has fallen for Harper. It's been obvious since the moment they met. But the more time Rick and I spend with this sweet young man, the more difficult it is for me to keep my distance and treat this as some kinky fling. It started out as an experiment to see if Brady enjoyed topping and hunting for a change. But it's like Harper is effortlessly carving a space for himself in our three-way relationship, and I want to see where this goes.

I like having him around. He's bright and sassy, but he's also clearly wounded and caring, too. The adoring way he looks at Brady is hard to miss. He tries to act as if nothing fazes him, but that's such an obvious defense mechanism he's developed to protect himself against whomever hurt him in the past. This mysterious ex of his, I assume.

I know I have a bit of a hero complex. A lot of people who join the armed forces and emergency services do. It's not necessarily a bad thing. But I just need to make sure that the person in question actually wants to be saved before I put my own heart on the line.

It feels like a small victory when Harper comes back, sketch pad and box of pastels in hand. Part of me expected him to change his mind, and I'm really glad he didn't. This is the first time we've hung out just the two of us, and I'm not ready for it to end.

For a while, we both work quietly. The only sounds filling the air are the cranking of my wrench and the soft scratching of his pastels. After some time, one of our fat cats comes wandering in to say hello. It's Chardonnay, and I take a second to stop and pet her.

"Good girl," I murmur, loving how loudly she purrs.

When I glance over, Harper is watching me with his lower lip caught between his teeth. "Can I ask you something?" he blurts out.

I give Chardonnay one last pat before giving Harper my full attention. I have a strong feeling where this is going—it's only natural—and I don't mind. But Harper looks nervous.

"Of course," I say lightly. "Is it about my foot?" He drops his gaze bashfully, but I shake my head and laugh. "It's fine, honestly. Do you want to know what happened?"

Harper swallows as he looks back up at me, then gives a one-armed shrug. "Brady said it was an accident and that it ended your military career. I guess…I guess I'm curious how you move on from something like that. From something that almost took everything from you."

I'm pleasantly surprised. People often want the gory details of how I survived, like it was a scene from a movie. Or they think that Rick rescued me and want to get off on that. Sometimes I don't mind talking about it. Other times I'd really rather not. But I get the sense that Harper's looking for advice here. His trauma is probably very different from mine. Most likely, it's far less obvious, but that can often be more insidious in the damage it causes, in my experience.

"I had two choices," I say as if it was just that simple. "Give up or move on. Giving up would have been the easy option." The rueful smile creeps onto my face whether I want it to or not. "Luckily, I had an incredibly stubborn fiancé who would rather die himself than let me quit."

Harper gives a little laugh, but his eyes are still sad. He plays with the black pastel between his colorfully smeared fingers. "That is lucky," he agrees.

I shake my head, realizing I might be giving him the

wrong message. "I still had to fight for myself, though. Every day. If I didn't want it, it wouldn't matter what anyone else thought. Are there times when I wish this didn't happen to me? That I still had my foot? Hell yeah. Sometimes it fucking sucks. But this is my journey, and I own every damned minute of it. It's my life, and I deserve to live it to the fullest, for me. Having someone else invested in me who I care about is just a very nice bonus."

Harper looks back toward the house. "You guys really love each other, huh?"

"Now and forever," I say, repeating our little mantra. "Some people never find that kind of love. I've found it with two men. That's the true luck in my life."

Harper hums. "I guess some people do have a lot of love to give, don't they?"

"They do," I agree.

I don't want to put words in anyone's mouth. But I know Brady. I worship him. So to see him opening his heart out to this young man doesn't threaten me. Like Harper says, some people just have a lot of love in their hearts, and Brady's might as well be the size of that Panthers' stadium. If he's falling in love with Harper, that won't diminish how he feels for me or Rick. It'll only strengthen it.

But I get the feeling it might take some time for Harper to appreciate all of that. It might help that my feelings are growing stronger for him as well the more time we spend together. Perhaps if we smother him with affection, his past won't haunt him quite so badly anymore.

He'll see that he deserves to be loved, no matter what fucked-up shit his ex told him.

"Can I ask *you* a question?" I figure a change of subject might be good to let him ponder what we've just said later in private.

He adds a few lines to his drawing. "Sure," he says casually, but I can feel the barriers he's got up between us.

Nuh-uh. I'm not having that. The only way he's going to start to heal is if he begins letting people in. And Rick, Brady, and I are the kind of assholes who will force him to do that, for his own good.

"Why have you been hiding your art away?"

He freezes, his eyes fixed on his drawing. "I haven't..."

"Brady said according to the dates in that book, you haven't done anything in years until now. It sounds to me like your teachers encouraged you. Why didn't you apply to art school?"

He frowns and scoffs at me. "And waste all that money? On what? Art is just a stupid hobby. I need a real job, something productive to society."

Why do I get the feeling that he's parroting that last sentence from somebody?

"You don't think art is productive to society?" I say, arching an eyebrow. He's not meeting my gaze, though.

"Of course not."

It's my turn to scoff. "Oh, so you never listen to music? Watch a movie? Read a book? All that is just trash you can live without, hmm?"

Now that does cause him to look back over at me. Just a peek through his long blond eyelashes. But I've got his interest. I'm not certain, but I swear I see a tiny flicker of hope in those hazel eyes.

"No, I mean..." he says, chewing on his lip again. "Of course I do. Those things are good for the soul. But how would I earn *money* from art?"

I want to say that not everything is about money, but that's naive and idealistic and I know it. Not everyone can have a filthy rich husband. But I'm not backing down.

"You could work in marketing. Do concept art for movies. Have your own website and sell custom prints. You could teach kids, or you could train in art therapy. That shit is seriously important."

Now his whole goddamn face lights up at that, his eyes as wide as saucers. He looks between me and the pad in his hands. "Art...therapy?"

"Yeah," I say gently. I don't want to get too excited, but holy shit, I think something just happened here.

"What does that mean?"

I lick my lips, trying not to get too enthusiastic and spook him. But after the crap I've been through, I feel very strongly about healing both the body and the mind.

"Sometimes people have emotions that are just too big or too messy to understand all at once. Doing something like art can help someone be physically present but allow what's troubling them to float to the surface. Some people work out or dance." I tap my wrench against Ariana's exhaust. "Some people take bikes apart and put them back together over and over. It's absolutely important to keep working on whatever trauma is hurting us by talking through it, I think. But projects like that could be a healthy coping mechanism. Art therapy helps people safely confront their demons, and that makes them feel safe. Hell, I've heard of old crimes actually being *solved* from things that surface through putting paint on paper."

Harper's looking down at his pad like he's never seen it before. Then he turns the page back one and holds it up for me to see. It's incredibly dark and violent looking, but I *think* what I can see is a cityscape.

"I didn't show Brady this," he mumbles, looking purposefully down at the floor. "But it came to me after I lost my shit in the barn. The next day. I...I think it was something I was feeling. I felt better after drawing it. Like an exorcism."

I reach out and gently wrap my hand around Harper's wrist, encouraging him to lower the picture. I wait until he looks at me, then I smile, feeling so much warmth flowing from inside me toward this young man.

"It is like an exorcism," I agree. "Harper, do you know what PTSD is?"

He nods, but it's in a dismissive sort of way. "Yeah. It's when soldiers get flashbacks or whatever."

I rub my thumb against the sensitive inside of his wrist, pleased when he gives me a little shiver. I want us to feel connected in this moment. "Yes and no," I explain. "It's something that happens to people who have suffered a traumatic incident. Soldiers, yes, or victims of accidents or crimes. And it's not just remembering. To your body, it's time travel. You're flooded with all the chemicals that you felt during that moment or that period of time when you were scared or angry or in pain. As far as your body's concerned, you're right back there in that moment. I think you might have had a PTSD flashback during our scene."

He frowns, clearly thinking my words over for a few moments. "I'm sorry," he rasps.

"Don't be," I say firmly. "Never apologize for that. It's not your fault what happened to you." I lick my lips and choose my next words carefully. "It *is* up to you to own your recovery, though. You need to process what happened to you. This is a very good place to start."

I nod at the dark drawing, and Harper looks at it thoughtfully. "I just…it wasn't trauma, though. There wasn't some big thing that happened. It was just a shitty relationship, and it's over now."

I don't want to contradict him, but I don't think he's seeing the full picture here. "Maybe you've got a lot to untangle," I say kindly. "Perhaps you can't see the forest for the trees. It might be worth talking to someone to help you see what's really going on. Even if that's just a family member or Brady to start with. No one should bottle things up and feel like they're alone."

"I don't want to be selfish," he says. "I don't want to be a burden."

It's like a knife to my heart. I hate that someone's made him feel like that. "You wouldn't be," I assure him. "Hey—seriously. I'm telling you right now, if you want to talk about some of these things, you can always come to me. I'll give you my number. You wouldn't even have to go through Brady."

He takes in a shaky breath, and I rub his wrist again, reminding him that I'm already here for him in this moment. "Really? I wouldn't…be bothering you?"

I chuckle. "I don't do anything unless I want to, kid." I roll my eyes. "Unless Rick makes me, but that's my kink." That gets a laugh out of him, which I enjoy. "Really. I want to be your friend. And part of the way I am still healing from my trauma—and probably always will heal—is being there for others. Brady isn't the only one with a big heart." Harper hums, and I squeeze his arm for reassurance. "What do you say? Can we be friends?"

"I'd like that," he whispers, his eyes shiny.

I smile and open out my arms. To my delight, he moves over to hug me without hesitation.

"I'd like that a lot," I tell him before kissing the top of his head.

I was wary of Harper when Brady initially met him for the way he'd run out on their first scene. Then I was drawn to him because he's beautiful and bratty. But now he's shown me a little of his heart, and it's like there are threads between us that are knitting together.

I have no idea what road this young man is on. But I'm glad his path has crossed with ours, even if it's just for a short while. He's got a bright future ahead of him, of that I'm sure. Just so long as he starts healing now and doesn't self-destruct. If he'd let me, I'd like to help him with that.

I'll just have to wait and see if he's brave enough to let me in.

CHAPTER 17

Brady

"Honestly, Mrs. Zeringue, I couldn't possible take any more cookies."

Harper's grandmother just laughs at me and shoves another box into my already full arms. "Don't you be testin' the Jesus in me now, son. You've been a mighty good friend to my darlin' Harper, so this is how I say thanks. I think it's swell he's gonna go stay for a little while with you boys in that big ol' house. That's what he needs. Not to be rattlin' around here with some fusspot like me."

Harper swoops down and kisses his grandma's cheek. "I'll *always* need you," he insists. "But this house isn't built for us both, and Brady's place has so many spare rooms."

"Uh-huh," June Zeringue says, like she knows full well he's not going to be sleeping in a spare room. Well, I guess technically he is. But he's going to have me there by his side.

We had a pack meeting last night, and all agreed that Harper seemed to be coming out of his shell as he was spending more time with us. It was Papa who pushed to ask him if he'd like to grab some more clothes from his grandma's and stay a little longer.

He's still working at the bar, so he's also socializing, but I think hanging out with my Daddies and me is doing him good. It feels like he's finally starting to face some of the things he went through with his awful ex. His grandma obviously loves him fiercely, but I understand if he doesn't want her knowing all his darkest secrets.

Papa reckons there was some kind of abuse going on. He's not sure what, but he thinks that it was so clever that Harper still might not even realize the extent of it. I think Papa sees it as his responsibility now to be there for Harper as he starts to pry open that can of worms. I know they had some sort of heart-to-heart the other day, but it warms me right down to my bones to see two people I care about bonding.

I know Daddy wants to fix whatever's wrong in Harper's life, but that's just his nature. He does that with everyone. What I'm hoping is if they can spend a little more time together, they'll start to connect like Harper and Papa have.

I don't know where this relationship is heading, but I know I want to keep dating Harper for as long as I can. If my Daddies want to date him too or try a scene again, well…that would mean so much to me. But we'll see.

First, we have to escape this house without a metric ton of baked goods. Apparently, June's love language is food.

"So these are raspberry and white chocolate," she's explaining as Harper and I try and head toward the door with his bag of stuff. "And these here are banana blueberry—don't knock 'em till you try 'em. And these are good ol' peanut butter chocolate. I hope you boys like 'em."

"They smell amazing," I say truthfully.

"Aren't you as cute as a button," she says sweetly. But as we reach the door, she points a finger in my face. "That being said, my boy is a goodun. He got wrapped up with a wrongun, but that's all over now. So I give this little vacation of his my blessing. But you better treat him right."

"Y-yes, ma'am," I promise, having no doubt she'd track me down and spank me with a slipper if I cause her boy harm. If she didn't do that to Harper's mysterious ex, I bet it was only because she couldn't find him. "I like your grandson very much."

That Southern belle smile comes back again. It doesn't matter about her age. It's not hard to understand how she won a lot of beauty pageants with that smile, because it's dazzling but also warm. "I can see that, son. I gotta tell you how it is anyhow. But I don't doubt you got nothin' but diamonds in your eyes for him. He's a very special boy."

Harper blushes, but I'm kind of glad to see that his low self-worth obviously doesn't come from this woman. She's strong like iron and speaks nothing but the truth.

"He is very special," I agree softly.

She pats my cheek. "Go on now. Get. And tell Harper which cookies you like the most so he can tell me. I'll whip you up another batch."

"I-I should really pay for—" I try and stammer, but Harper cuts me off.

"Stop right there if you want to leave with all your fingers intact," he says with a big laugh.

It's so wonderful to see him happy again like that. I was worried after the incident that he'd broken himself so badly. But I can see the pieces coming back together of the spunky young man who seized my interest the moment he walked into Creams.

"Bye, Grandma!" he calls out as he marches me down the garden path back toward my car. "I'll see you soon!"

"You message me every day, boy," she threatens with a cheery grin, waving us off with a handkerchief.

We pause for a second once we've both sitting in my car, catching our breath. "Did you get everything?" I ask.

Harper shrugs and slings his bag into the back seat. "If not, I can borrow stuff from you or come back, right? This is just for a little bit while I get my head screwed back on."

I reach over and squeeze his knee. "You're welcome to stay as long as you like, I promise. You don't need to pay for rent or groceries or anything, so you can just save your paychecks and take a moment to think about what you want to do next."

He nods and looks out of the window as I drive off. "Trey had some really interesting ideas about that. You know, what I might want to do next or at least something to work toward."

I glance over at him and beam. "That's fucking awesome," I say genuinely. Trey said they'd had a really productive talk but didn't elaborate on what. I didn't ask, either, wanting to respect Harper's privacy.

"I really like him, Brady," Harper says. I take my eyes off the road briefly to see him looking at me. "That's okay, right?"

I've still got my hand on his knee, so I rub his thigh reassuringly. "Sweetheart, that's wonderful. I really like him as well, in case that wasn't obvious."

He laughs, but then he's quiet for a while, nibbling on his thumbnail. The drive back to The Vineyard is about fifteen minutes, so we've got a little more time to talk just the two of us if he wants to discuss anything else.

Sure enough, after a minute or two, he sighs. "It's so incredibly nice of you guys to take me in like this," he says. "I could have stayed with my grandma, but well..."

"It's easier to have sex with this arrangement?" I supply. He laughs.

"Yeah, that."

We haven't actually been intimate since the incident in the barn when he safe-worded out. But I have a feeling we're getting back to that kind of place. We made out for quite a while with clothes on this morning. I don't want to rush him, but I hope the next time we start getting hot and heavy, it'll also involve an orgasm.

But my thoughts of sex are quelled with his next comment.

"I keep waiting for the other shoe to drop." I arch a questioning eyebrow over at him, and he squirms. "I keep waiting to find out what you expect in return for all this free housing, food, and therapy."

"Hey, no," I say firmly. I find his hand so I can intertwine our fingers. "It's not like that. We don't want anything from you. We'd like you to be happy, but that's not a condition. We like having you around, but don't feel you have to entertain us. You can just *exist*, all right? No strings attached."

He hums. "That seems a bit too good to be true, but thank you."

And this is why it was such a good idea for him to come stay with us. He needs it drilling into him that he doesn't owe anyone his existence but himself. I take his thanks and let the matter drop for now. These aren't conversations that we can rush through. Besides, we're coming up to the house, and I have other things on my mind.

I have a lot of friends from my time at school, college, on my old teams, and now at work. But there's something about having a *best* friend. That person who you share so many of your waking hours with or talking to. That's how I'm beginning to feel with Harper. Our energy is so different from what I have with my Daddies. It's like I have someone on my team who's just for me, if that makes sense.

There's a heightened sense of anticipation as Harper and I get out of my car and hurry into the house. Almost like we're in on a conspiracy together. I don't know why, but we start giggling as we scurry up to the spare room I've come to think of as 'our room.' That's where he's going to be staying.

And where I plan on spending a lot of time with him as well.

Without saying a word, we dash through the door and I close it behind us, then he launches at me, kissing me hard. I think we both appreciate that this is the start of something exciting for him, and we're feeling the hype.

I kiss him back with fervor, cupping either side of his face and walking him back toward the bed. "Come to the fundraiser," I mumble against his lips.

"Huh?"

"Daddy's big fundraiser at the house next week," I elaborate.

We've spoken about it a lot since he's been here, as it's all Daddy's really thinking about right now, but I know we've been skirting around whether or not Harper would like to come and indeed if it would be appropriate to have him there.

Fuck it. I want him there. I can invite friends if I want to. And he's so much more than a friend.

"The party in the garden?" he asks.

I nod and drag him down on the mattress with me. "I want you there. We all do. It'll be fun."

He opens his mouth as if to protest, but then he bites his lip and considers. "Okay," he says softly. "If you'll be there, I guess it will be fun, right?"

"Of course," I say with a grin.

"Will I have to dress up?"

I shake my head. "Don't worry about that now. We can sort something if you need help. I just want you there."

"Okay," he says again with more conviction. "Only because you asked nicely, Baby Wolf."

I groan and kiss his neck. "I want you, sweetheart."

"You can have me."

I don't waste any time in taking his T-shirt off, but I hesitate a second as I run my hands over his skin. "If you need to stop at any point—"

He presses a finger to my lips to shush me. "I know, Baby. I promise. I remember my colors. I want you."

I nod and yank my own shirt off. We kiss topless for a while, but I can feel our hard cocks rubbing together through our jeans, trying to find some friction. "I have an idea," I say between breaths.

He nips at my earlobe. "Yeah?"

I take hold of the back of his neck so we can properly stop for a second. "Do you want to try topping me?" I'm not sure why, but that's what I want right now, quite badly. No kink. No games. Just two people who care about each other making love.

He blinks, panting, but then gives me a little nod. "I don't normally do that. But yeah, actually. Yeah, that sounds really good."

I grin and capture his mouth for a hard kiss. "I know, right?"

We're both laughing as we scramble out of the rest of our clothes. I grab a pillow to shove under the back of my hips as well as a condom and some lube. Harper suits up while I force a couple of fingers inside myself. I'm well used to being stretched out and I don't want to waste too much time on prep. This isn't something I want to take hours. I just want to connect with my friend and share something deep with him.

I'm still working myself as he comes between my legs and hovers over me, kissing my lips. "Brady?"

"Yes, sweetheart?"

He brushes his nose against mine, apparently feeling a little shy. "I, um, went to the clinic before work a few days ago. I've only been with…you know…*him*…without protection, and only you after that with protection, but I want to be sure."

I withdraw my fingers and wipe as much of the mess off as I can on a tissue. Then I run my hands through his hair and kiss him reverently. "That's wonderful, little lamb," I say sincerely. "We get tested all the time. I'd love it if we could have nothing between us."

He looks relieved. "I should get the results soon."

We start making out again, eager and hungry. I absolutely trust him to be responsible, but I wouldn't put it past his ex to be stepping out on him, so I'm glad he went to go get tested of his own volition. I want to come deep inside him and claim him with my seed, with nothing getting in our way.

"I'm ready for you," I tell him, my cock already feeling like it wants to explode. He picks up the lube and adds some more to his own length as well as my hole. Then he angles himself and starts pushing his way inside.

I lift my hips and wrap my legs around his waist, crossing my ankles. It would be even better if I propped my heels up on his shoulders, but I want to make it easier to kiss him while we fuck. I want to look into his eyes and feel his breath on my lips.

Oh, god. I like him so much. It feels overwhelming in this moment as he sinks inside me. I seize his arms and pull him to me so our mouths can crash together. My little lamb. My good boy.

I'm scared to even think it, but I'm pretty sure I'm falling in love.

"Yes, Harper, yes," I hiss as he starts to rock his pelvis, hitting my prostate with the end of his pretty cock. He doesn't have the girth of either of my Daddies, but he still feels so good. If anything, the way he was able to slide into me easier than they do was quite exciting. Sometimes, it's nice not to have to spend ten minutes just trying to stretch out enough so nothing gets damaged.

"Brady," he mumbles between kisses and gasps for air. We slam together over and over, chasing our climaxes. His light blond hair is dripping sweat onto my chest, and the room stinks of us both, like we're marking it with our scent.

I reach over and take myself in hand, my cock already rock-hard, leaking, and ready to spit. It only takes a few strokes before I'm blowing my load all over my belly with a shout, gnashing my teeth. Harper grabs my hips and pistons like a machine until he drops his head back, and I can feel him throbbing as he comes in my hole.

Before we've even finished, I throw my arms around him and hug him against me, not caring about the mess smeared between our chests. It's raw and perfect, and I just have to hold him right now in this beautiful moment.

"Harper," I say with a happy sigh. "Thank you."

He chuckles. "For what?"

I kiss my way along his jaw and cheek until I find his mouth. "For being you," I tell him.

He shakes his head and laughs. "Such a himbo," he teases before kissing me some more.

That's okay. I really quite like being his baby himbo. I like being his everything. I don't know how long he's going to stay, but for now, this is good enough.

This is wonderful.

CHAPTER 18
Rick

WHEN I KNOCK ON THE SPARE BEDROOM DOOR, I'M GLAD IT'S
Brady who opens it. He's freshly showered and in the middle
of buttoning up his blue shirt. He beams at me like he always
does. Even after a couple of years, he still makes me feel like
he's delighted every time he sees me.

I know we're in a bit of a transitional period, and that's
fine, but I'd be lying if I said I didn't miss having my baby boy
around as much at the moment. Hopefully, though, that will
change soon.

"Hi, Daddy," he says a little breathlessly.

"Hello, little pup," I reply, leaning down for a sweet kiss.
"Are you almost ready for the party?"

"Getting there," he says as he works on a couple more
buttons. "You look sexy."

I grin and kiss him again. I know I look good, but it
doesn't really count if it's just me looking at my reflection. I
love hearing it from my little wolf more.

"Is Harper getting ready?" I ask, nodding toward the en
suite door where I can hear the shower running. I like that
Harper's made this his room, and I can see signs of him all

over it with his clothes and his art supplies. I want him to be comfortable, and I know that Brady's been doing all he can to help him settle in.

Now it's my turn.

"Yeah, he should be out in a minute," Brady says.

I wave my hand. "No rush. But don't let him put that on, all right?"

I jerk my chin toward the bed, where a pair of black pants are laid out with a light green shirt. Brady glances at Harper's clothes, then he lets out a little knowing 'ohh' sound.

"Put him in some sweats and send him down the hall to me, okay?"

Brady jiggles happily, then hugs me. "Will do, Daddy. Thank you."

"You're welcome, baby boy."

I wander back down to the master bedroom and into the walk-in closet. I take my time laying a few things out on the circular plush bench that's in between the full-length mirrors, occupying myself while I wait. Trey is already downstairs, mingling with the first few guests and talking with the caterers. I mentioned that I wanted to take a little time with our guest before the party and he was very supportive of the idea.

This is my house and my pack. While I wasn't expecting everything that's happened with Harper, I'm not opposed to it. However, it's about time that I made an effort to connect with our little lamb. Judging from the way the two men I love are falling for him, he's going to become an important part of our lives. I know he keeps saying that he doesn't know what he wants to do, but how can I help him figure that out if I don't make the time to get to know him one on one?

I suspect if he up and left tomorrow, that would break Brady's heart. I think it would bother me as well. So it's time to show this young man that when we say he's welcome, we mean it. We might fuck around a lot, but when this pack stakes a claim on someone, it's something to be taken seriously.

"Hello?" Harper's voice drifts through from the bedroom. I smile to myself and saunter back so I can stick my head out.

"In here."

He looks between me, the double king-sized bed, and the closet I've been working in. "Everything in here is huge," he says, and I chuckle.

"It's kind of necessary with three big-ass men sharing a space. Come on over. I've got a surprise for you."

He's dressed in sweats and a tee, so it looks like Brady relayed my message. He pads over the carpet barefoot, looking apprehensively at me.

"No need to be frightened, little lamb," I assure him.

But he folds his arms and nibbles his lower lip. "You didn't need to get me a gift. You're already letting me stay in your house and come to your party."

"Ah," I say, not surprised. I was expecting something like this. Brady warned me about their 'waiting for the other shoe to drop' conversation last week. "But you see, the thing is, while you're under my roof, that makes you one of my boys. And I take care of my boys. It's sort of my kink. I don't expect anything in return. Just seeing you happy will be enough, but only if you genuinely like your present."

I gently place my hand on his lower back and steer him to look at what I've laid out. His gaze roams over the burgundy silk suit with black lapels, the matching vest, white shirt, and black silk tie with a delicately embossed diamond pattern. He exhales and blinks. "This is for me?"

"Yes," I say. "If you like it. I estimated your size and took liberties picking the colors. If you're not keen on it, I have a few alternatives, but I honestly think you'll look stunning in this. Would you like to try it on?"

He stares at the suit a while longer, then flicks his gaze toward me. "I can say no, can't I? I don't have to wear it?"

Disappointment washes through me, but I make sure not to show it on my face. "Sweetheart, of course you don't have to. You don't *have* to do anything under this roof other than be honest with me."

He lets out a shaky breath and gives me a wobbly smile. "In that case, I absolutely love it," he says in a small voice.

"Oh," I say. Before I can stop myself, I step over to him, wrapping my arms around him. He hugs me back, fiercely.

"That's really nice of you, Rick," he mumbles into my chest.

I kiss the top of his head and rub his back. "It's my pleasure, I promise. Now, would you like to try it on?"

He nods against me, so I reluctantly let go of him, stepping out of the closet so he can get changed. Merlot, one of our fluffy cats, wanders in to keep me company, and I pet her to pass the time.

"Um…Rick?" Harper says after a few minutes, honestly sounding so cute I have to bite back a grin.

"Yes, darling?"

"I think the shirt is broken."

I can't help but laugh at that. I don't want him to think I'm laughing *at* him, though, so I quickly step back inside the closet to see him flapping his arms around.

"Oh, I'm sorry. That's my fault," I assure him. The poor little lamb must not have worn double cuffs before. "I should have explained. Come here."

I grab a small box from the side and sit on the bench, angling him so he's standing between my knees. He holds his arms out helplessly, and I can't stop myself from kissing the tender inside of his right wrist as I bring it closer.

His breath hitches. I like that. "Let Daddy do it," I say softly, fully aware of what I'm doing. Brady told me all about how Harper's ex was also his so-called Daddy, and I think we're long overdue healing some of that bullshit.

"Thank you," he whispers as I turn his hand around. Then I open the little box by my thigh and lift it up to show him the matching silver cufflinks inside. They're fat, fluffy sheep, and I know full well what a dorky gift it is. But our little lamb's eyes light up when he sees them.

"Brady has wolf heads," he says. My boy must have shown him before he came over to the closet. I nod and tug my jacket sleeve just enough so Harper can see that I too have silver wolves on my cuffs.

"Trey's are matching as well," I explain.

He bites his lip and looks at the box once more. "Are they really mine?"

"Yes, little lamb," I say. "To keep, just like the suit."

"That's very generous of you."

I shrug, taking the first sheep out so I can attach it to his cuff. "You're important to us, Harper. I wanted you to understand that. Just because we haven't known you long doesn't mean what we have isn't special."

He watches me silently as I secure both cufflinks, then he turns them this way and that, admiring them under the lights.

"Brady is important to me," he says. His words are firm. However, he's not looking me in the eye. "I tried to deny it, even to myself, but I knew it from the moment I laid eyes on him. He explained that first night how important you and Trey are to him as well, but that he was looking for something different with me and he had enough of a big heart to go around." He chews on his lip, his brow creasing. "But you three are all sort of a package deal, right? So...it's okay if you and Trey are starting to become special to me too, yeah? Like...that's allowed? I don't know how you feel about me, and it's okay if that's not—"

175

"You're already special to me and Trey," I say, cutting him off. "One of the most important things in open, polyam, non-monogamous relationships is good communication. Hell, that's important in *any* relationship. We like you very much, Harper. *I* like you very much. I want you to feel like you're a part of what we have for however long you want to stay."

Finally, his gaze reaches mine once more, his lip wobbling and his eyes glassy. "Yes, Daddy," he whispers.

My heart soars like an eagle. "Good boy," I rasp, rubbing up and down his arms before I stand. "Such a good boy." I take his hands to admire the cufflinks and caress the backs of his knuckles. Then I brush a lock of blond hair from his face and tilt my head. "May I kiss you, little lamb?"

He gulps, but after a second, he nods. "Yes, Daddy," he says softly.

We kissed previously on the porch before our ill-fated attempt at a hunt. I thought then he tasted of candy, and he does again now. But there's something entirely different about the way he opens up for me this time. Before, he was fighting me like he had something to prove. It was hot, I won't lie. But now he's sweet and compliant. I can feel his trust in me through the softness of his mouth. I wrap my arm around his back, holding his body against mine, trying to tell him without words that he is safe here. I have a feeling he knows.

His pale skin is rosy when I relinquish him. Twin tears have spilled from his hazel eyes, but they're now bright as he blinks up at me. I wipe the droplets from his chin with my thumb as we beam at each other.

"Good boy," I tell him once more.

He looks away and laughs like he doesn't believe me, but that's okay. We'll get there. He'll soon understand that I'm always right and I know what's best for him. Right now, I have the strong urge to show him off alongside my other gorgeous men in front of some of the wealthiest people I know. I'm collecting quite the harem, if I do say so myself.

"Would you like some help with your tie?" I ask, pleased when he nods gratefully.

"I'm never really good with them, although I don't have to wear them often. My grandma did her best for prom. She watched so many YouTube tutorials, bless her. My grandpa had passed away by then, you see, and my dad…well."

"Yeah," I say, getting the picture. I know I'm lucky. So are Trey and Brady. We all have strong relationships with our parents. Not everybody gets to be that fortunate.

I stand him in front of the mirror, then position myself behind him, explaining the Windsor knot as I tie it. Merlot joins us and hops up onto the bench, looking at the reflection, her tail thumping as I work. I love how Harper naturally leans his back against my chest, and I'm not afraid to press a kiss to his temple as I do my thing.

"There you go. That's how you make that top part so fat and sturdy."

"I look like a real man," Harper jokes.

I swat his ass. "None of that toxic masculinity bullshit here, thank you very much."

He bats his eyelashes at me. "But what if I want to get punished later, Daddy?" he asks, totally knocking me on my ass, figuratively speaking. I *knew* there was a naughty brat in there just dying to get free. We simply have to peel back all the layers of hurt and trauma to let that little shit out.

I kiss him through my grin. "Be a good boy, now. Then maybe later, you can show Daddy how bad you are."

"Oh, I can be bad," he says flirtily.

I restrain myself as I help him into the rest of his clothes. I've also bought him an aftershave that smells like the ocean. He has a naturally sweet and clean scent, but what can I say?

I am still basic in a lot of ways. I want to mark him with something I picked out for him myself.

"Gorgeous," I say as we both look at him in the mirror. Merlot gives a loud meow, which probably means she wants feeding, but I chose to interpret it my own way. "See? Our feline overlord agrees."

"Thank you, Rick," Harper says. "Daddy. I mean it. This is...everything. It's all everything."

I grin and kiss his cheek, loving how his clumsy words mean more than something perfectly articulated. "You're very welcome, little lamb. Now, do you feel like joining the party?"

He nods enthusiastically. "I promise to behave."

I scoff. "You'll do nothing of the sort. You'll promise to go have fun. I expect to hear that you and Brady have gotten yourself into shenanigans by the end of the night. Understood?"

He laughs and hugs me. I squeeze him tightly, not caring about either of our expensive suits. "Understood, Daddy," he says.

I love hearing that word from his mouth. I wonder if later I'll get the chance to make him moan it. But for now, I very much treasure this not-so-small moment we've shared together. He is a good boy. And I'm going to make him see that.

———

By the time we get downstairs, the party is in full swing. But that's absolutely fine by me. I like to make an entrance. I send Harper off with a kiss, loving the spring in his step as he ventures out into the garden to find Brady. Seeing those boys together makes my cold heart melt, I swear to god.

I snag a glass of red wine from one of the serving staff

I've hired for the night and head out onto the grounds myself. I've held this charity fundraiser ever since I inherited the company. It's an excellent way to get the majority of my business partners in one place at the same time, get them all drunk, then not-so-gently encourage them to spend all their cash on the auction. The proceeds go toward several of my favorite charities, and while everyone's feeling good, we all get the opportunity to make professional connections that might otherwise never be possible. Plus, it's a great way to bring the community of the little town together. It's not often the folks in Paddle Creek get to put their glad rags on. It's a win-win situation.

I find Treyvon mingling with his work colleagues from the garage. Despite being pretty rough around the edges, I have to say I genuinely like all of them. They're a solid bunch and Trey really enjoys working there.

"Hey, man!" his boss, Ruben Ward, cries out when I approach. He's a large guy with a heart of gold. He waves a meaty hand at me as I join their little throng. "Great party, as always."

I shake hands with everyone I know and say hello before Ruben proudly throws his arm around a sweet-looking young man. "I'd like you to meet my partner," he loudly proclaims.

"You must be Xander," I say warmly, and he blushes. "Ruben told me a lot about you."

"Oh no," the boy mumbles, and we all laugh.

"Don't worry, only good things," I assure him.

Trey and I gave Ruben some advice a couple of months ago about taking a leap and starting something with his best friend's younger brother. It looks like it's all worked out, and I don't mind taking a little credit for that. It makes me happy seeing two people together who seem so right for each other.

"And this here's Jackson Riggs," Ruben continues.

He slaps a dark-haired man on the back who I'd guess would be in his late twenties. He's wearing eyeliner and a pleated skirt that he's paired with combat boots and a polo shirt. I admire anyone with the guts to go against gender norms in a small town, especially when he's not your typical twink who you'd expect a more fem look from.

"It's a pleasure to meet you, Jackson," I tell him truthfully as we shake.

"Likewise," he agrees. "This is my partner, Benedict Knight," he says, indicating the slightly older man beside him.

"I rescued Jackson from the side of the road a couple of months back," Ruben announces proudly. "Escorted him to the airport so he could stop this idiot from getting on a plane."

Benedict laughs. "All right, all right," he says good-naturedly in an English accent. "Yes, I was almost the world's biggest idiot. Are we ever going to forget about that?"

Jackson grins, the love clear in his eyes. "Probably not," he says before kissing Benidict's cheek."

"Benedict's a professor at Brady's college," Trey informs me. "Bobbi Schultz is his department head. She invited him. It's a small world, huh?"

"It sure is in these parts," I admit. But that's the charm of a small town, isn't it? Ultimately, everyone knows everyone, and most of the time, they go out of their way to take care of one another.

That's my kind of people.

I wrap my arm around my own love, chatting with Trey and his friends for as long as I can get away with. Once my glass is empty, I use it as an excuse to slip away for a refill, knowing I have to go work now, pressing flesh and making my associates and clients all feel important. It gets easier the more I do it. I genuinely enjoy getting this time with people I

180

mostly only see on Zoom calls or for a couple of hours in boardrooms. This is far better.

Once the auction kicks off, I spy my two baby boys hanging out with some of the football kids. I think one of them might be Seth Eisen, who just got signed to the Spartans after his graduation. Brady told me a while back he's got himself two boyfriends as well, which is why I made sure to remember his name. It warms my heart seeing more polyamorous relationships out in the world.

"You must be the man himself," a deep voice drawls by my ear. I'm sure someone with less combat training than myself might have jumped, but as it is, I turn and give the speaker a smooth smile, offering out my hand.

"Rick Bryant," I say.

"Great party, Rick," the stranger says. "I'm Fernsby. Pleased to meet you."

He's built like a fucking fridge with ash-blond hair and a dazzling smile. I don't miss the watch on his wrist that I'd hazard a guess cost in the region of seventy-five grand. Obviously, this guy means business, but I'm kicking myself as I have no clue who he could be.

"Your first time joining us," I comment, knowing it to be true. He nods, not looking put out at all to my relief.

"A mutual friend put me on your radar," he says, tilting his whiskey glass my way. I know it makes me an ass, but I do silently judge people who come to my house and don't drink my wine. But hey, not everyone's a fan, and I know for a fact that the whiskey is also top notch. "I think I might have a proposition that could be of interest to you."

"Is that so," I say, never one to turn down an opportunity to grow my company. I can't say this guy has me warming to him yet, but you don't get to wear watches like that if you aren't a bit of an asshole. I'd know. No one would ever accuse me of being all sunshine and flowers.

That's why I have Brady and Trey. And maybe now Harper, although he perhaps adds more spice than sweetness, you could argue.

Fernsby slaps me on the back. "Let's not spoil a good night of drinking by bringing up work now," he says with a deep, rumbling laugh. "I can't stay much longer anyway. But I'll have my secretary call your secretary, and we can get into the nitty-gritty of it over dinner sometime, hmm?"

It's not escaped my notice that he's failed to mention the specifics of what he has on offer, but that's fine. I recognize a man who likes playing games and holding on to his power when I see one. It won't do me any harm to hear him out. Because at the end of the day, this is my little kingdom, and I don't have to answer to anyone but myself. I'll either be interested in his proposition or not. No harm, no foul.

"Sounds great," I say with a smile, shaking his hand once more. "You take care now."

He gives me a salute before slowly ambling off, looking around the grounds at my guests. I have no doubt he's got a net worth that far exceeds my own, but I also know without question that he's never seen a real day of combat in his life. I don't feel threatened by a man like that. I know who I am.

I'm blessed. I watch as the professional auctioneer closes yet another deal that means a hefty chunk of change will be going to help queer teens who've found themselves out on the streets. I see people here who have helped my business flourish. I know so many others personally from this town I'm glad to call home. I run a business and own a home that my parents worked their asses off to give me, and I know that I'm doing them both proud.

And I have my men. My boys. My wolf pack that I'm hopeful could now include a little lamb for longer than we might have initially anticipated.

Much, much longer.

Harper fits with us. He looks so perfect laughing with Brady, being hugged by Trey, joining in conversations with the people we call friends. He was lost when Brady found him.

Now I hope he realizes that he's been found. Because I say so, and I'm never wrong.

CHAPTER 19

Harper

I FEEL LIKE I'M IN A DREAM. LIKE I'M A PRINCE IN A FAIRY TALE or something. How did this even happen? I walked into that bar looking for a job, and I think what I found instead was my heart.

Who knew it could be so big?

I spend the party mostly by Brady's side, but we talk to so many cool people. He introduces me to his friends and colleagues. I meet Trey's coworkers too, including his boss's boyfriend, Xander, who, after a few glasses of rose wine, whispers to me that Ruben is actually his Daddy, and he has the bestest dinosaur-themed playroom back at their house.

I feel connected. Part of the community. Even the damn cats—who I still can't tell apart—seem to be warming up to me. One of them winds her way around my legs as I brush my teeth, thinking over what a lovely night I've had.

Nobody told me off or tried to control me. I didn't feel like I was getting in the way or embarrassing anyone. Hell, Lowell just flat out stopped inviting me to big events like that because he said I didn't know how to behave. But Rick pointedly *told* me to go get into mischief.

FOUR PLAY

Right after he kissed me.

I called him Daddy.

I know he's technically Brady's Daddy, but even if I only get to borrow him, he's already a million times better than Lowell ever was. Yeah, he's still a bit scary, but it's because he cares. Just like Brady. Just like Trey.

"Psst," I say as I come back into my bedroom. Brady's already brushed his teeth and changed into pajama bottoms. He's lying on the bed, scrolling on his phone while he waited for me.

He raises his eyebrows as he looks at me and grins. "What?" he says at a normal volume. But I'm a bit drunk, and I think it's funnier to whisper.

I beckon to him with my finger. "Come here."

He shakes his head, but he still laughs and gets off the bed to come stand by me. "What is it, sweetheart?"

I intertwine our fingers and swing our hands between us. "Do you think we could go say hi to your Daddies?"

His eyes light up, and his brows shoot into his hair. "You want to go see them?" he says, clearly excited.

I've had enough wine that I'm feeling brave, but I'm definitely in control of what I'm doing. I nod earnestly at him. "I thought maybe they'd like to snuggle with us. Could you ask them?"

He surges forward, crashing his mouth onto mine. There's my big himbo. Such a puppy. "I'd love to ask them," he mumbles against my lips. "Now? Shall we go now?"

I giggle. "That's the plan, yeah."

We all just said goodnight as the party was winding down. Rick's so fancy he has security to make sure people leave the grounds and a professional cleaning crew who will work through the night so we'll wake up tomorrow like nothing happened. Brady confessed to me in a clear moment of pride that Rick always pays his crews two or three times

185

what they'd normally earn, so I don't feel like a douche about it.

That's a rambling way of my tipsy brain reminding me that Rick and Trey only just went to bed, so we shouldn't be in danger of them already having fallen asleep. They *might* be getting frisky, but hey—I don't have a problem interrupting that.

I feel safe. So completely different from that night in the barn where I was convinced I had something to prove. Tonight, I feel secure enough to ask if I can share a little of what these three remarkable men have together.

Lowell is still lurking in my mind, of course. I haven't had another message like the one that freaked me out so badly before, but I keep getting the same three emojis on my posts from different unknown accounts. Lowell used to call me his monkey, and the messages I'm seeing lately are the 'see no evil, hear no evil, speak no evil' symbols all in a row. I know it's him. But if that's all he's got in his arsenal, I have to say I'm feeling pretty confident.

So much so I posted a selfie of Brady and me tonight with me kissing his cheek while he was laughing. I only captioned it "This one" with a few cute emojis, but it feels kind of significant to me. It proves that I'm moving on. That I'm not a prisoner anymore.

Besides, Lowell's easier to forget about after several hours of good food and wine and even better company. I'm so fucking lucky that this is my life right now. I don't know what tomorrow's going to bring. This feels far too good to be true for much longer. But in this moment, I want to enjoy myself.

And if that happens to include some alone time with three smoking hot dudes, I'm so down with that.

Brady's squeezing my hand so tightly I'm worried about bruising. But I also love his excitement so much that I don't complain as he drags me down the hall toward the master bedroom.

I think back to when I was in there earlier this evening for that remarkable exchange with Rick. So much shifted for me in such a short period of time. Not only did he make me feel incredibly special, but I think I finally trusted that it's okay for me to be interested in all of these men at once. That's actually kind of their *thing.* Lowell accused me of cheating and having wandering eyes all the time, so it doesn't come naturally to me. Yes, getting into something with three other men is unusual.

But nothing about Rick, Trey, or Brady is usual.

I think of Brady's mom, who's so supportive of him being in an unconventional relationship because of the prejudice she's faced in her own life. I think of my own grandma waving me off last week and all her encouraging messages since. The only person's opinion who really matters on this is mine. But I'm still a little shaky trusting myself. So knowing that actually I'm not alone and people I value do approve of me choosing happiness—even in an extraordinary way— gives me confidence.

Brady stops at the threshold of the open bedroom door, pulling me against his side. Rick and Trey are in bed with a lamp still on beside Rick. Trey has his eyes closed as he rests against Rick, but Rick is scrolling on his phone before he glances up at us.

"You're hovering, baby boy," he says with a grin.

Brady giggles, and I wonder if there's a joke here that I'm missing. Rick's smile and his tone of voice are warm, however, so I don't worry about it for too long.

"Hey there, little ones," Trey says. He was clearly not asleep, and his eyes blink open at us, his expression one of curiosity. "What are you up to?"

Brady bounces on his heels and glances over at me before

looking back at them. "Harper was wondering if we could come snuggle."

Trey's eyes go wide, but Rick's darken, and he suddenly looks hungry. "Oh we'd *love* some snuggling, wouldn't we, Papa?"

Trey sits up in bed, moving over to the side so there's quite a gap between him and Rick. I'm not sure if it was like that before or if I just didn't notice, but there are definitely four sets of pillows on that massive bed now.

I try not to read too much into what that might mean.

"Come snuggle, babies," Trey says, his voice warm like honey.

Brady lets out an excitable little squeak, pecks a kiss on my cheek, then bounds over to the bed where he settles between his Daddies. I try my best to hold on to my courage from before as I approach the edge, reminding myself that there's nothing to be afraid of. I like these men very much. I only want to spend time with them. And if anything makes me uncomfortable, I just have to use my safe word and I know without a shadow or a doubt that they'll stop.

I take a breath before crawling up onto the bed and over the mattress toward the pillows. Brady has flopped against Trey, who's pulled back the covers so they're not getting in the way. That leaves me to go between Brady and Rick. It doesn't escape my attention that it's the same configuration as the other night after my meltdown—the only previous time we fell asleep together.

Those were very different and much less pleasant circumstances. Still, I can't help but feel a little nervous as I flop down with my head on the pillow. It feels natural for me to face Brady, but I can't help but gasp when the lamp goes out and Rick presses himself up against me without hesitation. He and Trey are only wearing boxers, and I can feel his length against my thigh through my pajama bottoms, even though he's not hard.

Yet. I feel like the 'yet' is implied.

I blink in the darkness, realizing that there is a little light from the moon outside and a lamp that's still on in the hallway. But the gloom helps bring some of my confidence back. It's easier for me to be brave when I feel like I'm not being watched and scrutinized. In fact, I feel my old self creeping back in.

"Fancy seeing you guys here," I say in a clearly flirtatious tone. Trey snorts. Brady grins at me and links our hands together.

And Rick? He starts kissing my neck and running his hand over my tummy.

"Was this the kind of snuggling you had in mind, little lamb?" he growls into my ear.

I'm already breathless. I nod, but then I find my voice. "Y-yes."

"Yes, what?" he asks, tracing his fingers in circles below my belly button. My pants are silky, so it feels so nice and sends shivers all over my body.

I have to think what he means for a second, but then my heart glows with pride. "Yes, *Daddy*," I say purposefully.

"Oh," Brady squeaks. He pulls our hands to hold them to his chest. "Daddy?"

"That's right, little pup," Rick tells him. He's nuzzling his nose against my cheek, so his words vibrate off my skin. "Daddy and little lamb had a nice chat earlier. It's about time we updated this relationship status."

I giggle nervously, but not because I'm anxious about what he's got in mind. I'm a little nervous about making any kind of commitment so soon after escaping Lowell, but not enough that I'd argue with Rick—with *Daddy*—right now.

He's the good kind of scary. I like just letting him take charge. A lot.

"What do you want, little lamb?" Trey asks. I look into his eyes and allow myself to think of him as Papa. I'm pretty sure that's allowed now. "Just snuggling?"

My breath is ragged, and my heart is hammering in my chest. I'm not ready for some big scene. But it's pretty obvious how hard I am in my pants, even in the dark, and I think if I don't have an orgasm soon, I might find it quite painful.

"Maybe some *sexy* snuggling?" I suggest.

That gets a laugh out of everyone. Well, Brady is laughing until Trey kisses the side of his neck and drops his hand to caress Brady's cock. Then Brady lets out the prettiest, filthiest moan, his eyes fluttering closed. I watch on, transfixed. Brady said he loves his Daddies watching him as he gets fucked by strangers. I couldn't really picture it before now, as it's only ever been the two of us.

But he looks glorious in this moment. I kind of wish we'd left the lamp on.

Maybe next time.

"Do you like that, little lamb?" Rick whispers in my ear. I nod. "Is our little pup hot?"

He's still caressing my stomach, but he hasn't moved farther south yet. My cock is jumping in my pajama bottoms, though.

"S-so hot, Daddy."

"Tell him," Rick urges me.

Brady's still holding me, so I keep our fingers intertwined and pull his hand to my lips so I can kiss his knuckles. "You look so hot, Baby Wolf, with Papa Wolf touching you like that."

Brady groans, twisting against Trey's body. "Do you want

to watch me come, little lamb?" I nod eagerly. That sounds awesome.

Rick laughs in my ear. "Such sweet, pretty boys we have here, Papa. Shall we make them watch each other as we make them come?"

"I think that's a wonderful plan, Daddy," he says playfully.

Even though it was what I desperately wanted, I'm still surprised when Rick suddenly slips his hand down my pants and finds my hardening cock. Within seconds both mine and Brady's pajama bottoms are thrust down to our thighs, Daddy's and Papa's hands wrapped around our lengths respectively, and we're looking into each other's eyes as they both start leisurely jerking us off. My breath hitches, and Brady bites his lip. Our entwined hands are clutched between our chests. I can feel Daddy's cock pressed against my ass cheek, and I watch as Papa grinds his hips against Brady's backside.

I'm radiating heat and gasping for air as Daddy lets me go for a second. I wonder where he could be going as he reaches back, but then he returns, his slippery hand gliding over my dick before sharing the lube with Brady and Trey as well.

"Do you like this?" Daddy asks me as he starts working my cock again. It feels ten times better now that it's flying over the sensitive skin so fast. I moan and nod. "What was that?" he asks with a chuckle.

"I love it, Daddy," I yell, arching back into him. He laughs and nips at my earlobe.

"Settle down, little lamb," he warns. Not in a way that makes me feel like I've done something wrong. In a way that sets boundaries and it warms my heart. "Do you like it, little wolf?" Daddy asks Brady. "Watching Daddy touch our little lamb while Papa touches you?"

Brady squirms. "Yes, Daddy," he pants. "Harper looks so hot. I want to see him come all over me."

It's pretty mild dirty talk, but it still gets me off. I knew he was an exhibitionist when I jerked him off under that table at Creams. I'd never really thought about us doing it together, though, or us watching each other.

I have to admit I am having a very, very fun time right now.

Rick's arm around me is like a vise, keeping me in place. I swore I'd never let myself feel trapped again, but this is the good sort of trapped. The best, actually.

This—*this* is what I love about submission. I don't have to decide what's right or wrong. Daddy knows best. He's going to hold me down and make me come, looking into the eyes of the guy I've started to realize is my best friend. I love being with Brady. I love experiencing this brand-new kinky stuff with him.

It might be the impending orgasm talking, but I think I might love Brady. Who knows? I thought I loved Lowell back in the beginning, but it never felt like this. Like I had a hole in my heart that I didn't even realize was there until my baby himbo came along and filled it.

"Kiss," Rick commands into my ear, and I surge forward to capture Brady's mouth like a starving man. I moan against his lips as our Daddies make us fuck into their hands. Brady's grip on me feels like it could shatter the bones in my fingers, but I don't care. I feel so connected to something incredibly big and important.

I matter. I'm special. And I'm sharing it all with Brady.

"Stop kissing," Rick instructs.

Brady pulls away immediately. I was ready to let my brat take over and defy Daddy to see where that got me, but instead, I writhe against Rick as he jerks me off even faster. He's looking at Brady when he talks, though.

"What are you, little pup?"

Brady's a mess as he undulates against Trey, clearly

desperate to come. I'm not far off myself. "A good boy," he rasps, tears in his eyes. "Yours. Your good boy."

"That's right," Rick says proudly. "So good for your Daddies. So pretty while we watch you come. You love your Daddies, don't you?"

"Yes, yes!" he cries out.

Rick bites my earlobe, making me gasp at the jolt of pain. It certainly gets my attention, though. "How about you, little lamb? What are you?"

I scoff, thrusting my pelvis up to meet Rick's hand as he works my cock. I'm so close to spilling. I keep my eyes locked with Brady's. "A naughty little slut," I say with a snicker.

Rick squeezes my cock like it's suddenly caught in a cage. I wail and try and thrash against him, but he's too strong.

"Bad boy," he growls, and he genuinely sounds cross.

Brady pulls our hands against his chest. Trey's slowed down his hand on his cock as well. Brady looks upset. "No, Harper," he says. "You're a good, sweet boy. You're *good* for our Daddies."

I'm trembling and scowling. My eyes feel hot. Why are they spoiling this? I'm basically in an orgy. I'm bad. I want to be *bad!*

"No, I'm a slut," I spit out. "Brady's good, and I'm bad!"

"Little lamb," says Rick in his warning voice again. "Do you need to use your safe word?"

"No, no," I say, feeling so confused. I'm still horny and feel like I'm about to tip off the edge of a cliff. But he's got it wrong. I'm not the good one. Brady is!

My friend leans forward and kisses my mouth. "You can do this, Harper. Look at me. Look me in the eye and say that you're good and special and that you deserve this. You deserve to be loved. I want you here with me. I want to come with you."

Fuck. I had no idea I had this hangup lurking within me.

How did Rick know? Now he's holding my climax hostage until I say...I say...

I don't know if I can. Am I good? I'm *lucky*, I know that. Otherwise, I wouldn't have met these amazing guys. I would be here. I'm grateful. I'm happy.

But do I truly believe that I'm good? That I deserve this?

Rick is slowly stroking my cock, teasing me. Brady is holding on to me for dear life, and Trey's eyes are locked on mine.

"You're a good boy, Harper," he says. "Remember what I told you? You can be anything you want to be. It's up to you. You're a good, sweet person, and we all care about you very much."

He made me feel invincible when we sat on that garage floor. I truly believed him when he said my art wasn't stupid. That it mattered. That *I* mattered.

I screw my eyes shut, feeling the tears fall down my face. "I'm a good boy," I manage to utter.

"Yes, yes, you are," Brady cries.

"Say it again, little lamb," Rick says, his hand flying over my cock once more. "Open your eyes and say it louder. We want to hear you."

I gulp, but I do blink my eyes back open, staring at Brady, who's smiling at me. He's closer so it's easier for him to lean over and kiss me. "You're a good boy, Harper. You belong here. You deserve this."

My chest is heaving, and I'm practically sobbing, but I do my best to keep my eyes on him this time instead of hiding away by closing them. "I'm a good boy," I say in a slightly louder voice. The words still come out all trembly, so I grit my teeth and try again. "I'm a good boy who deserves good things!"

"Good boy," Rick repeats firmly, pushing me over the

edge. Brady is jerking and gasping too. "Come, boys. Come for Daddy right now and kiss."

"That's it, sweet ones," Trey adds as I crash my mouth against Brady's. Our screams mingle together as we both start spilling over our Daddies' hands as well as our bellies and the bed sheets. It feels like I come my brains out. It just keeps going and going. I cling to Brady as Daddy wrings every last drop of pleasure from me.

I'm not sure when I stop spurting and start crying or if it was all happening at once all along. Eventually, I'm spent as far as my poor cock is concerned, and I'm left with my forehead pressed against Brady's and my fingers digging into his hand. But then I'm vaguely aware of hands moving between us. Oh, god. Rick and Trey are cleaning up our mess with tissues. I feel embarrassed but not enough to stop them, so it seems. In fact, I do nothing as my pajama bottoms are carefully eased up again, as are Brady's, and I find myself in the middle of a cuddle pile between three pretty large men.

"Good boys," Rick and Trey murmur over and over as they stroke and kiss Brady and me. "Such good boys."

"You need to come," I mumble. I doubt that I have much energy to help them out with that, but I don't want to be selfish.

Daddy chuckles in my ear, gently caressing my arm and pressing a sweet kiss to my neck. "We're fine, little lamb. Watching you both was pleasure enough."

I grumble sleepily, already planning on seeing if Brady wants to wake them both up with blow jobs in the morning. That seems like the sort of thing they'd all enjoy. That way, I can still be a bit naughty. But not *bad*.

Apparently, I'm a good boy now.

When I suggested that Brady and I come find his Daddies earlier, I was expecting some fumbling and kissing at most. I just wanted to feel like I belonged.

Of course Daddy knew what I *really* needed. I'm fucking exhausted as my eyes soon droop closed, and I feel raw. But I also feel content. Safe.

I think maybe *that* was the best sex of my life? Because it wasn't just my cock that exploded.

It was my heart, too.

CHAPTER 20

Brady

It's always strange being on campus during the long vacation. Of course there are people still around taking summer classes to make up credits, and I train the boys on the team a couple of times a week so they can keep up their fitness. But it's so much quieter without the majority of the students around. Even Clayton—the thieving raccoon who's audaciously made the college his stomping ground—leisurely strolls in front of me as I walk along the path, carrying an entire bag of burgers and fries from the Dino-Mite fast food place in town. He's even got a slice of pizza hanging from his mouth, and all he does when he sees me is shimmy his bushy tail. I swear he even grins.

I chuckle to myself and shake my head. It's good that the pace slows down for a few months. It would be hard to keep everything going full on all year round. I inhale the warm air into my lungs and appreciate the lull. Soon enough, the days will cool, we'll have a new batch of freshmen, and the chaos will all begin again.

I have some time before I need to get down to the field. The boys know what they're doing anyway. Mostly running laps, throwing balls, and working on their strength. Nothing groundbreaking. So I seize the chance to take a little detour and catch up with my friend first.

I've always found libraries a little intimidating. Even the small one back at Paddle Creek High. The college library is full of cracked and dusty old books that seem to judge me the moment I step through the door. The silence is deafening, especially without any students around tapping on keyboards or scribbling notes down on paper. I'm sure it's not all that big, but I always get the feeling I could easily get lost in here if I venture too far from the central aisles.

There's no one at the desk, though, so I lean over to look in the back office. Nothing. I drum my fingers on the counter, careful to avoid the pentagram carved into the wood by the bell, then start wandering toward some of the empty tables where I spent so much of my own time studying for finals. I'm really glad those days are done. I hated exams.

"Hello?" I call out.

"Your third eye is being lazy," a soft voice drawls right by my ear, making me jump three feet in the air. I spin around and clutch my chest, but Ms. Maude just watches me calmly. "I saw you coming at least ten minutes ago."

"Right," I say with a gulp.

The librarian peers over her glittering black horn-rimmed glasses. It might be summer outside, but the A/C is cranked up in here, so it's not surprising that she's wearing a black polo-neck sweater along with a floor-length skirt, her pointy boots just peeking out the bottom. Around her feet twirls a cat as black as the rest of her ensemble. Even after all these years, I've still never learned the creature's name.

"Uh, hi!" I say brightly with a wave. Now that my heart is slowing down again, I'm remembering that I actually chose to come in here of my own volition and that Ms. Maude is my friend and not someone to be afraid of.

Probably.

"You were right," I blurt out.

"Of course I was," she says, swishing her way back to her desk. "About what in particular?"

I follow her, shoving my hands into my jeans pockets and grinning. "Last spring at the faculty meeting. You told me to put the beer down and go talk to my soul about what I really wanted." I don't mention that it took me another couple of months to drum up the courage to do it. She still gave me the push I needed, even if I dawdled acting on it.

I've never mentioned my Daddies to her or even the fact that I have two partners, but I worked out that was what she meant by 'soul.' She still gave me a three-fingered salute when she threatened—I mean, *suggested*—that to me a few months ago. I'd thought it odd at the time and assumed maybe it was a reference to my Daddies' military background.

Now I think the three digits were more significant than I realized. Ms. Maude's like that. Always telling you to do stuff in a tone that suggests you dare not ignore her, then acting like she has no idea what you're on about.

Sure enough, she arches a dark eyebrow at me as she swoops around the other side of her desk. "If you say so, child." She calls everyone that. It's fine, except I literally can't work out if she's like twenty years old or fifty.

When I was a student here, she scared me and my friends so much we'd honestly draw straws as to who was going to come inside and get the books we needed so we could go study out on the bleachers. When it was my turn, I would sprint inside, hold my breath, and practically pass out by the time I launched myself back outside with what I hoped was the required reading material.

But when I made the scary jump to assistant coach and switched from student to staff, Maude was the first to approach me, pressing a bracelet made of jade beads into my palm, telling me it was for good luck. I'm not sure I believed her, but I thought it was really nice of her to make me feel welcome. Plus, the Panthers won the first three games we played that season until the bracelet mysteriously broke right off my wrist, the green beads bouncing in every possible direction. I swear Clayton has several tucked away in his nest, from things I've heard people say.

So, yeah. I'm not sure if Maude is necessarily a friend in the same sense as any of my other buddies, but I like her. I trust her. And she gives good advice.

"Well, yeah," I continue to say. "I followed my heart, and I made a new friend. He's really special."

She pauses, looking up from the notebook she's writing in with handwriting so ridiculously swirly I think I'd need to run it through Google Translate to understand it, even though I'm pretty sure it's in English.

"You have a hesitation," she says. It's not a question.

I shrug. "This guy's just come out of a bad situation, and he's not really sure what he wants. I know I want him, but I also have to be respectful and give him space."

She rolls her eyes. "Men," she says with a sigh. "They come, they go, the faces all different, the words all the same." She jabs her fingers at me. I realize she wasn't writing with a pen but an honest-to-god quill that she's dipping in an inkwell. "Tell him how you feel. Use small words. Perhaps draw a picture."

"Ha!" I cry. "He does actually draw. He's an artist, and he's really good at it."

She gives me a withering look and I can't decide if it's because that information is totally irrelevant or that she knew it all along.

She goes back to writing. The black cat hops up onto the counter, delicately winding their way around the interminable amount of knickknacks Maude has sitting around. However, among all the colorful crystals, bundles of twigs, locks of hair, and dried-up animal parts, I spot something that definitely wasn't there before.

A couple of snow globes. One looks to have a cartoonesque haunted house and the other a cheerful graveyard complete with a little ghost crying "BOO!" in a small speech bubble.

"What are those?" I ask with a grin, pointing rather than trying to touch them, even though I *really* want to give them a shake. I know better than to cross the line over to Ms. Maude's desk, though.

She glances at the snow globes, and a slightly maniacal grin spreads over her face. "They are from a *girl*," she growls. I can't tell if she thinks this girl is pretty or if she's planning to sacrifice her at the next full moon.

Maybe both.

The smile vanishes as quickly as it appeared. She snatches her hand forward to grab something out of my line of sight under the counter, then she thrusts her closed fist toward me. "Do not be afraid of the boy. He needs you. Do not be a jackass."

I blink and hold out my hand. "No, ma'am. I don't intend to be."

Wordlessly, she drops something black and cold into my opened palm. It's a clear, dark stone that's been beautifully carved into a pair of feathery wings.

"Oh, wow," I say, turning the trinket over in my hand. "That's gorgeous. Can I...is it for me?"

She scowls at me as if I just asked her why the sky was blue, then goes back to whatever she's writing with her quill.

"Well, uh, thank you so much," I say sincerely. I might not

understand the gift, but it's pretty, and it feels good as I slip it into my pocket. "That's really nice of—"

"Water," she says, snapping her head up.

"Huh?"

She frowns and stares off toward the door. "Check the plumbing."

I'm not really sure what that means, but I take it as my cue to leave. I rub my thumb against the black wings as I walk across campus to the Panthers' stadium, thinking over what she said about Harper. She is right about that. I'm scared of pushing him too much, but I know how I'll feel if he goes through with his plan of upping and leaving for Chicago at a moment's notice.

I need to give him a reason to stay.

Because I'm pretty certain that I'm falling in love with him.

However, I forget all about that the second I enter the building, as it appears we've had a leak in the women's changing rooms. It takes me at least an hour and a change of clothes later to remember what Maude said about the plumbing. I look at the black wings once more.

What else does she know?

CHAPTER 21

Harper

THIS IS MY LIFE. IT'S ACTUALLY MY LIFE.

"What are you grinning about?" Skylar asks.

"No-thing," I say in a sing-song voice, shaking my ass in time to the music as I spin around, pouring tequila into shot glasses.

It's funny, but I've enjoyed work a lot more these past few shifts ever since I figured out that this isn't someplace where I'm stuck. It's a fun summer job. And soon enough, I'll be moving on to something more challenging.

Trey made me understand that. Brady makes me believe it. And when the time comes, I have no doubt Rick will tell me what I have to do because he knows best.

Three amazing men and they all care about me. They're invested in me. When I enter their house, they ask how my day has been and how my grandma is.

Yesterday, they gave me my own key.

This is my life.

A couple of months ago, I was still trapped in that soulless penthouse of Lowell's, practically a prisoner, too afraid to leave and go live my life the way I wanted to. But the real me was always lurking just beneath the surface, fighting to get out.

I was never that scared little boy who Lowell tried to convince me I was. I'm a firecracker, just like Grandma always said. I simply had to get away from him to realize that, not to mention keep much better company.

Between serving customers, I glance over at the table where Brady and I shared our first scintillating encounter right before I ran out the door to see if he was being serious when he said he wanted to hunt me.

I had no idea what I was letting myself in for, but oh boy, am I glad I let my bratty impulses take over that night. *That's* who I am.

I just needed to meet Brady to remember it.

It's a Saturday afternoon, so there's a fair-sized crowd, but it'll get much crazier in a couple of hours. As usual for a Saturday, we've got our resident drag queen, Kimmi Sugar, performing later, so I make the most of the slower demand for service while it lasts. Usually, I wouldn't be able to hear myself think until we kick everyone out in the small hours of the morning, but today, I'm getting off at seven.

My wolf pack is taking me on a date. A real date. It's just dinner and drinks, but I'm ridiculously excited about it. That says to me that they're proud to be seen with me. That this is becoming something…real.

When I'm not totally preoccupied with the incredible sex I've been having and daydreaming about the next time all three of my men want to play with me, I can't stop thinking about what Trey said. The trouble with my life being confined to one luxurious but still very limited penthouse is that I couldn't see what opportunities were even out there waiting for me. That's all changed now.

I can't remember a time when I didn't draw, doodle, paint, or make silly but pretty things out of trash. Grandma's fridge used to be covered in my creations, and I got top marks at school in all my art classes. My teachers tried so badly to get me to keep studying at college. But my dad would never have paid for that. He didn't say it, but I knew the expectation was if I took him up on his offer, that I would have to study something 'useful to society.' If I couldn't follow my passion, then what was the point in going?

He still won't be interested in supporting his 'sissy' son like that, but I wouldn't want to ask him anyway. However, I have been looking into different loan options, as well as scholarships and community college opportunities. It turns out that right here in Paddle Creek, they have an okay-ish art department as well as a pretty decent psychology program.

I love art, but there's always been something nagging inside me that I didn't honestly think it had a point. Art for art's sake, as the saying goes. That didn't seem like a good way to earn a living or contribute to society. But art therapy? Phew. It's like Trey has lit a fire under my ass. The idea that I could help people process their trauma by bringing beautiful, cathartic things into the world has me so excited. Having not drawn anything in my diary for years, now I'm adding a new page almost every day.

This is my life. And I've never felt so alive.

I hum to myself as I finish unloading the dishwasher out back, grabbing the next lot of used glasses that are already stacking up to be washed. I knew working at a bar wouldn't be as fun as partying and drinking in one, but I am genuinely enjoying my time being surrounded by queer people.

I've never felt part of a community like this in my life. School was certainly a lonely time for me. It surprised me to learn that in the time I'd been away from Paddle Creek it had become so much more queer. But I guess it makes sense what with the Panthers coach being openly gay. It's meant so many queer players have joined the team, and this town has always lived for football. That kind of representation matters.

It makes me wonder if *I* could ever inspire someone like that. I appreciate that on TV and other media, LGBT representation has improved so much since I was a kid. Drag queens are so commonplace now, and your average Joe has heard words like 'trans' and 'nonbinary.' There's an abundance of resources these days for people questioning themselves so they don't have to feel alone.

But there's something to be said for in-person inspiration as well. I'm sure if I'd known an older gay man as a teenager who could have been a role model for me, I would have been less likely to fall prey to the likes of Lowell. He was the first 'father figure' I ever had a conversation with, and I think he bewitched me because I didn't know any better.

What if some young gay boy met me and thought 'I could make something of my life, just like this guy has.' I know I should want to achieve things for my own pride and happiness, but I can't deny that imagining a scenario like that is also making me braver.

I never dreamed that I'd get to go to college or make anything of myself. Thanks to the efforts of a certain wolf pack, I'm starting to believe that anything's possible.

I grab a tray of still-hot tumbler glasses and use my ass to push my way through the swing door back out behind the bar. It's gotten a little busier since I went out, so I hastily shove the crate under the counter where it lives, wipe my hands, then make sure I'm smiling when I look up to see who's waiting to be served.

It's Lowell.

"Hello, monkey," he says warmly.

I'm quite impressed that I don't stagger back into the glasses I just put down and knock them all to the floor. As it is, I grab the edge of the prep counter and let out an involuntary whimper. The dream I was walking around in has turned into a nightmare in the blink of an eye.

"What are you doing here?" I utter. It's so wrong for him to be in this place—The Ice Cream Parlor, Paddle Creek, both—that my brain is having trouble processing it. It's as if everything's gone into slow motion. I'd genuinely started to believe that I'd never see him again.

I should have known it wouldn't be that easy.

"I missed you," Lowell says, his face dropping like he's really concerned. I don't fall for it. It's all an act.

"Well, I left you," I spit out. "I thought the letter I wrote you made that very clear. I also said not to try and contact me or to find me."

Lowell shakes his head. I forgot just how *big* he is. I used to think it was attractive. That I liked being pinned down by such a beast.

It turns out it takes more than just size to earn the right to dominate me.

"I gave you some space," Lowell says sadly. "But you can't just leave me, monkey. We need to talk this through."

"Sorry, there's nothing to say," I tell him, crossing my arms. I can feel my coworkers glancing my way, but we're not so busy that they're drowning without me. I won't be talking to this asshole any longer than I have to, though, I promise. I do move farther down the bar, however, so I can try and maintain some privacy.

Lowell laughs like I'm adorable and follows me along the counter. "Of course there's something to say. We were together for five years. You can't just sneak off without a word. That's cruel."

My temper flares. I can't think of a time when I ever got angry with him, but I sure am now.

"What's *cruel* is the way you tried to crush my spirit," I snarl, leaning forward and jabbing my finger at his face.

"Crush your…Harper, what are you talking about?"

"You controlled me," I snap.

"I cared for you," he says, sounding genuinely confused. "I set boundaries. That's what good Daddies are supposed to do."

Guilt flashes through me, and I'm immediately questioning if I'm wrong and he's right—like I always used to do. But then I dig my fingernails into my palms and angrily shake my head. "No—nope. You're not turning this around on me. I wasn't happy. I was pretty much a prisoner in that place. I could never do anything right, and you basically…"

I feel my face getting hot and tears pricking in my eyes. But I lean forward and make myself say it, even if it's painful.

"You *forced* yourself on me."

His frown is looking less upset and more cross now. Good. I can deal with that easier. "I was your Dom, Harper," he says, a hint of a warning creeping into his words. "I took charge of those situations. That's what you consented to."

"Well…maybe I didn't understand what I was consenting to," I fire back, aware that I sound petulant, but I don't really care. "I certainly didn't understand that I could safe-word out if I wasn't enjoying it. I just thought I had to suffer through it."

"That's not my fault—" he starts to scoff, but I cut him off.

"You were the Dom," I snarl, my heart beating like a jack-hammer. I never thought I'd get to say all these things to him. I didn't really want to ever see him again, but now that I am, I'm getting some things off my chest. "It was your job to take care of me and make sure I knew those things. It was your *job* to give me *aftercare.* Daddies are supposed to help their boys flourish, not break them down into tiny bits."

Lowell shakes his head, pretty much openly scowling now. "You know I hate when you act like this, boy," he says, his voice low. "Being a brat isn't cute."

"It's fucking adorable, actually," I say smugly, putting my hands on my hips. I have *three* partners now who say so, vastly outnumbering Lowell.

He grits his teeth before shooting a fierce glare my way. "This is unacceptable behavior, boy."

I shrug. "Tough. I'm not your boy anymore. You don't get to manipulate me like that. In fact, you should just leave. I don't ever want to see you again."

"No, no," he says, that sadness reappearing. "We need to talk, monkey. I'm sorry if you were confused, but I can fix it. You just have to come home."

Those words send ice through my veins. "I'm not going anywhere with you," I say, taking a step backward, like he might reach over the bar and grab my shirt. "That place isn't my home—it never was. I don't need to talk to you ever again. Leave."

He drops his head and rests his hands on the bar. Then he looks up at me with puppy-dog eyes. "I didn't want to believe it's true, but it is, isn't it?"

"What is?" I demand. I'm so not in the mood for his games.

He sighs. "You're *cheating* on me, aren't you?"

I splutter out a laugh. It's not like I want to aggravate him, but that's such a ridiculous thing to say I can't help it. "I *left* you," I remind him. "I can do whatever or *whoever* I want, and you get absolutely no say in it. Now seriously, fuck off before I call the police."

He licks his lip and nods thoughtfully. "Yes, the police," he says. "I was considering whether or not I needed to give them a call myself. In the name of public interest, of course."

"What the fuck are you talking about?" I snap.

He gives a lazy shrug. "What's that assistant coach's name? Brady Ritter?" Coldness washes over me again as I don't dare breathe. I just stand there, frozen, watching him stroke his chin like a goddamned silent movie villain. "I heard some very unsavory things about that young man. Accusations of gambling on his own team, throwing games, that sort of thing. Totally illegal, of course. I feel like it's my duty to notify the police so they can intervene at the college. He shouldn't be in a position of power over students, should he?"

"You wouldn't," I whisper, feeling faint. I have absolutely no doubt he's making up every word he's saying, but an allegation like that could destroy Brady's career in an instant. He *loves* coaching those kids. Lowell can't do that to him!

Except he can. Easily. I shouldn't have gotten ahead of myself, thinking that he can't manipulate me anymore.

He inspects his nails and sighs. "You should really get to know someone before you jump into bed with them, Harper. That's what whores do. This man isn't what he seems."

I can feel myself getting hot and tearful again, but I'm not backing down. "You're a *liar*," I spit out. "Brady is one of the nicest and best people I've ever met in my life! You're just jealous of him."

He laughs. It's a cold sound. "Speaking of cheaters and whores, you do know that he's already seeing a married couple?"

It's my turn to laugh scathingly. "Perfectly well aware, thank you very much. And you can call us whores all you want. I don't care. I *am* fucking all *three* of them and every single one of them is a better man than you ever were."

I know I should be more freaked out over the fact that he's clearly been stalking me way more than I suspected. He's delved into Brady's life as well, and that does scare the shit out of me. But the funny thing about being cared for by Brady and Trey and Rick is that I know what good people they are, and their affection makes me feel invincible.

"I'm so disappointed in you, Harper," he says.

For the briefest second, I feel ashamed. But then I realize *I don't care* what he thinks of me anymore. I shrug and cross my arms. "So? I don't know how many times I can say it, but I *left* you. It's over. You're just going to have to deal with that."

"Like Mr. Ritter will have to deal with those very serious allegations?" Lowell asks with a crooked eyebrow. "How about Mr. Bryant, who owns the wine company? Word on the grapevine is that he's involved with insider trading."

He tuts as if he's talking about a naughty schoolboy, but my heart has dropped down to my toes. He can't be serious, can he? He wouldn't go after both of them?

I should know better by now.

"I also heard there's a problem with Mr. Caldwell's disability benefits, maybe? Apparently, he's claiming more than he should be. That could affect his pension. Wouldn't that be a shame if he lost that vital support? And the street where your grandmother lives—"

"What about it?" I cry. I know I shouldn't be rising to his bait, but I can't stop the panic that's flooding my chest.

He can't trick me like he used to, so he's going after the people I love. I wish I could say that I'm sure he's just bluffing...but after five years, I think I sadly know exactly what this douchebag is capable of.

"The street?" I prompt him as he just stands there grinning at me. He knows he's got me by the shorthairs.

"Oh," he says with a shrug. "I heard it had been bought out. I think whatever company owns it now intends to raze the properties to the ground and build a strip mall in their place."

I clench my jaw, feeling murderous as I glower at him. No prizes for guessing which construction company he's talking about. That's how he got filthy rich—by buying up homes people couldn't afford anymore, demolishing them, and putting up cheap crap. He really is a crook, and I'm ashamed I ever warmed his bed. Everything he ever bought me was paid for with dirty money.

But I don't believe for one second that he's bluffing.

I swallow and look around. My colleagues are all busy working. There's no one here to help me. I have to stand up for myself. Except I close my eyes for a second and imagine that my wolf pack is standing right there behind me.

I'm not alone. I can do this.

"Please, Lowell," I say. I'm not above begging in this moment for the people I care about. "You don't have to sink this low. It's over. I don't love you. I never did, and if we're honest, I don't think you ever loved me. You just liked having someone to control. I can't live like that again. I don't want to be with you. Have some dignity and find someone who does want you."

His laugh is chilling as his eyes narrow at me. "You don't get to tell me what I can and can't do, boy. What I want and what I don't. *I'm* in charge, a fact that you've clearly forgotten and need to be reminded of. That's it. I'm done fucking around. We're leaving."

"I'm at work," I say pathetically. I should tell him to fuck off. That I'm not going because I don't *want* to. It feels easier to come up with an excuse. But I should have known that wouldn't be enough to even make him pause.

"Ah, yes," he says with a sneer, rolling his eyes. "This charming establishment is clearly going to fall apart without you. You don't need a job anyway. What are you playing at? Come with me this instant. We're going home."

I take a couple of breaths, my fists clenched and my heart racing. "No," I manage to utter.

He shrugs as if what I say is inconsequential. Then he pulls his phone out of his suit pocket, quickly dialing a number before holding the cell up to his ear. "Yes, hello?" he says after a couple of seconds. "Police? Yes, I have some information regarding an employee at Paddle Creek College."

"STOP!" I yell, not caring how many people's heads snap in my direction.

He raises his eyebrows at me. "You have something to say, Harper?"

I think I'm going to be sick. I knew he wasn't bluffing, but I didn't think he'd call the cops right in front of me. "I...I... hang up. I'll do it. Come with you. Just leave Brady alone. Leave them all alone."

He chuckles darkly and closes the call, probably confusing the operator at the other end of the line. I can't worry about them, though. I have my own people to protect right now.

My insides are boiling with fury and I don't know what to do. I just have to stop him from making that malicious call until I can work out what to do.

Until I can talk to Rick. He'll know how to fix this, I have no doubt.

"I finish work at seven," I say. My insides plummet.

I was supposed to be going on a date. Oh, *god.* I could cry, but I won't. I won't give him the satisfaction.

Lowell shakes his head and grins. "I don't think we need to wait that long, do we?" he says slyly. "You're quitting, after all. Just walk out right now." He narrows his eyes. "Do as you're told, boy, or you won't enjoy the consequences."

I gulp. I'm trapped. This is the old kind of awful trapped. The real kind. I feel powerless. He's in control. He's holding all the cards.

For now.

"Fine," I snarl.

I'll play his game. Anything to stop him from picking up

his cell again and making that call. At least until I can speak to Rick.

He's smarter than me, though. He holds out his hand and arches an eyebrow. "Give me your phone."

"What?"

"You can have it back when I trust you." That'll be never, then. "Come on. We need to get on the road. Otherwise, we'll get stuck in traffic. Stop wasting time."

Oh, *fuck.* He's really taking me back to Indianapolis, isn't he? And if I hand over my phone, I have no way of letting Brady know. Lowell's got his hand stuck out, looking hulking and terrifying. I don't know what else to do for now, but I can't see any option but to do what he says.

I hand it over.

"Uh, Skylar," I say, catching my colleague in the middle of him pouring glasses of pink wine. "I have to go. It's an emergency."

Skylar's eyebrows shoot up, and he glances at Lowell. "Everything okay, buddy?"

"Yeah, I—"

"Harper, *now,*" Lowell barks.

I wince. Of course he doesn't want me to say anything. I don't want to drag my colleagues into this either, so I just shrug at Skylar. "See you," I say.

I feel like I'm folding in on myself as I walk around the bar and trudge toward the door with Lowell. *This isn't the end,* I promise myself. I don't care how long it takes. I'll play along and let Lowell think he's won. But sooner or later, I will be able to call, email, send fucking smoke signals, and I'll make it back to my wolves.

Right now, I just have to survive.

So I push down my revulsion and slip my hand into his as we walk out of the door. I see Dijon, the host, raise their eyebrows at me, but I have to ignore them. "I'm sorry,

Daddy," I say to Lowell in a small voice. "I never should have left."

For someone so smart I do think that Lowell's arrogance makes him remarkably stupid sometimes. He sighs and looks down at me, visibly mollified. "Good boy," he says. "Don't worry. Daddy will fix this silly mess."

I give him a simpering smile, but inside me, a storm is raging.

I *am* a good boy. And I'm going to do everything I can to fight my way back to Brady, Trey, and Rick.

They made me believe in myself, and I'll be damned if I'm giving up now.

CHAPTER 22

Trey

"Sorry I'm late."

I rise to greet Rick with a kiss, shaking my head. "You're fine. We're still waiting on Harper. How was golf?"

Rick scoffs as he takes a seat in the booth Brady and I have occupied for the past hour. As we're all coming from three different locations, we agreed that we'd meet at O'Toole's pub first, then head out for dinner. I'm driving, so I've been nursing a small glass of red, but Brady's had a large one, and his cheeks are adorably rosy.

"Hey, Daddy," he says warmly as Rick leans over and hugs him.

"Hello, gorgeous." Rick shakes his head. "Golf was golf. It's a stupid way to do business, but whatever. Business was accomplished, and now my day is looking much brighter." He checks his watch and frowns. "Shouldn't Harper be here by now?"

I look down at my phone. "Yeah, but maybe he got chatting to someone after his shift."

"He hasn't texted me," Brady says, also checking his phone. But then he shrugs. "I'll message him now. I bet he's walking over here as we speak. Do you want a drink, Daddy?"

He holds up the bottle, and even after all this time I feel a rush of warmth toward our baby boy. He's got such a big heart, looking after us as much as we look after him.

We don't often make time for dates out anymore. It's nice to cook at home, and certainly easier to go from flirting across the table to naked fun times in under thirty seconds. But Brady wanted Harper to feel special. Things like this help assure him that all our feelings are real and quite strong for him. As it transpires, Rick and I are planning to officially ask him to be our boyfriend this evening. He's basically living with us already, but we thought the pomp and ceremony might be nice.

It's been a long time since Harper brought up moving back to Chicago or anything like that. In fact, Brady said he's been not too subtly asking about courses at Paddle Creek College.

I want Harper to be happy and choose what's best for him. But I feel strongly that would be to stay here with us, explore where this relationship is going, and have a support network to be there for him while he investigates what he wants to do next with his life.

Again, I don't want to pressure him into making any big decisions, but Rick has already made a dismissive offhand comment about how he'd naturally pay Harper's tuition fees if he wanted to go back into education. I made Rick swear he'd keep that opinion to himself, even though I'm pretty sure he thinks I'm crazy. As far as he sees it, it's too late.

Harper is already his. So why wouldn't he take care of him?

But I'm keenly aware that Harper is still very raw from his relationship breakup with his ex. We haven't even tried another primal play scene yet. We've been sharing the main bed more and more, though, and things have gotten deliciously handsy. But we need to still go slow with our little lamb. He's not like Brady, ready to jump in with both feet right away. What we need is baby steps so as not to spook him. We haven't even tried anything more than hand jobs between us. There's still a great deal left for us to explore intimately as well as emotionally.

"Let's give him a few more minutes before we go to red alert," Rick says with a grin. He unbuttons his jacket as he sits and picks up the spare glass we already procured up for him. He holds it so that Brady can pour him some wine. "How were your days? Get up to anything exciting?"

"I went to the gym and then played video games," Brady says proudly. "It was ridiculously relaxing."

I snort. "Well, Papa here got stuck chasing our cats around the house to give them their flea treatment. You'd think I was trying to murder them, honestly." We all laugh, knowing how true that is. Merlot, in particular, will be giving me the cold shoulder for days. "But then I did some more work on Ariana, and she's actually road-worthy again."

"Shut up," Rick says, a twinkle in his eye.

"It's true, I swear!" I protest.

Brady smirks. "For now, at least."

Rick shakes his head but holds up his glass. "To Ariana and Papa's exciting road trips." He winks. "Until he pulls her apart again."

I roll my eyes but toast with him and Brady anyway. Brady's phone starts ringing, making him jump, so he hastily places his drink back down.

"That's probably Harper," he says excitedly, but then his expression drops. "No...it's June. His grandma." Clearly confused, he accepts the call and presses the phone to his ear. "Hello? Yes, this is Brady." He frowns for a moment. "One second, Mrs. Zeringue. I'm here with Rick and Trey. I'm going to put you on speakerphone." He changes the setting, then holds out his cell in the middle of us over the table. "Say that again."

"Hello, boys," says a woman in a strong Southern accent. I've heard about Harper's grandma, but this is my first inter-action with her.

"Good evening, ma'am," Rick says. "Is everything okay?"

"Well, I don't reckon it is, sweetheart. Harper's manager called me from the bar. He said that Harper up and left right in the middle of his shift with an older gentleman in a suit. Said they exchanged harsh words. Harper hasn't come home, so I was just hopin' that perhaps one of you boys had seen him or if you were the fella who took him away from the bar?"

My stomach drops. "No, ma'am," I tell her. "None of us have heard from him, and he's certainly not with us now."

"In fact, he's running late," Brady adds in a worried voice.

Rick looks positively murderous, with a vein pulsing in his temple. He grinds his teeth for a second before responding calmly. "Mrs. Zeringue, do you have any idea who your grandson could have left with?"

The lady scoffs down the end of the line. "Oh, I sure do, son. I'll bet my bottom dollar it was that no-good Lowell Fernsby come sniffin' around. I knew he wouldn't let Harper be after he left. He's a bully, and he always gets his own way, one way or another."

"Wait, did you say Fernsby?" Rick cries, his eyes going wide with horror. "Big guy, like a linebacker? Ash-blond hair? Rich?"

June sighs. "Well, I never did meet the fella myself, but that sounds about right from the photos Harper sent me. And he's rich, for sure. Oil man rich. The kind that thinks he can buy people."

"Or steal them," Rick says darkly.

I slip my hand over his. My heart is pounding in my chest, that familiar adrenaline sending a million instructions around my body. I'm ready to jump into action, but right now, we don't have a direction in which to point our efforts.

It's probably fruitless, but I grab my phone and try to dial Harper's number. "Straight to voice mail," I tell the others. That doesn't exactly give us answers, but it goes some way to confirming that something nefarious is going on.

"Mrs. Zeringue?" Rick says. "Do you have any idea where Fernsby might have taken Harper? And what time did The Ice Cream Parlor call you?"

"Well, they called me about twenty minutes before I called you," she says. "I'm so sorry, son. I thought I should just wait and see if Harper came on home. The second it occurred to me that you might have some information, I picked up my phone. They said he'd left about an hour before that. The boys on shift weren't sure what to do, but when their manager came on-site, he had me down as Harper's emergency contact on his file, so he rang me lickity-split."

"It's okay, Mrs. Zeringue," Rick says, shaking his head. "That's understandable. But do you think they'd be staying in town?"

June scoffs in a very unladylike manner. "No sir-ee. As sure as eggs is eggs he'll have taken Harper back to Indianapolis. He thinks that place is his damned castle in the sky. He'll want to keep Harper like a princess in a tower again. Mr. Bryant—my boy ain't no dummy. If he did really go, it's because that ogre made him somehow. Do you reckon we should call the cops?"

Rick chews his lip and looks at Brady and me. "The police might not be able to do anything if Harper supposedly left of his own free will. Do you know the address?"

"I sure do, sweetheart. I picked him up myself so he could escape the first time."

Rick nods at me, silently asking for my permission. It's cute that we both pretend he needs it, but I know there would be no stopping him now, not if the entire Marine Corps themselves stood in our way.

"Do you think you could send that address to Brady's phone, ma'am? We're going to head down there now and straighten this all out."

June gasps down the other end of the line. "Oh, you are good boys, I knew it. Of course I'll send that to you this instant. You go with God now, you hear me? Harper belongs with you fellas. You make him happy. That Lowell is a brute and deserves everything comin' to him."

"You have our word, ma'am," Rick says grimly. "We won't come home without Harper."

He closes the call and hands Brady's phone back to him. Our little pup clings to my arm and looks fretfully between me and Rick. "Is Harper in danger?" he squeaks.

Rick clenches his jaw for a second before answering. "This guy, Fernsby? He approached me at the fundraiser. He was in our *goddamned* house doing recon on Harper. Now he's dragged him out of work under who knows what pretenses. So I don't want to scare you, baby boy, but this feels like a kidnapping to me. And we all know that this prick didn't treat Harper right before."

Brady's phone pings, and he turns the screen toward us to show us that he's got the address. "But we're going to go help him, right?"

"You're fucking right we are," Rick growls, and my love for him grows yet again, if that's even possible. "But it could be dangerous. You can stay here if you—"

"I'm going!" Brady cries, his eyes blazing. "I'm not abandoning him. He's mine. He's ours."

"Damn right he is," I agree.

"Is everything okay over here, gentlemen?" Donna, the

manager of O'Toole's, asks in concern as she comes over with her hands on her hips. "Only you're looking all agitated and throwing around words like 'dangerous' and 'kidnapping.'"

"You were listening?" Rick asks coldly with a raised eyebrow.

Donna scoffs and crosses her arms over her chest. As a proud self-proclaimed leather dyke, there isn't much that rattles her. "You fellas were practically yelling toward the end of that exchange, and folks can't help but pay attention."

Oh, wow. She's right. There's a Rolling Stones track playing quietly over the sound system, but no one's talking, and everyone's looking our way.

"Your friend's been kidnapped?" a large ginger bear asks in concern.

I swallow around the lump of fear in my throat for Harper and glance at the rainbow flag above the door to the pub. Everyone in here is queer, and sometimes I forget how protective people like this can be of complete strangers.

"We think our friend..." I glance at Brady's stricken face and decide to fuck pretenses. "We think our *boyfriend* might have been taken against his will by his ex."

"I don't care how rich and powerful this fucker thinks he is," Rick snarls as he gets to his feet and buttons up his suit jacket. "Harper is *ours*, and we're going to get him back. So if you'll excuse us, Donna, we need to get to Indianapolis right now."

"Whoa, whoa," she cries, throwing up her hands. "You've called the police, right?"

Rick shrugs. "We think Harper might have been coerced. Otherwise, why would he walk away with this guy like that? So the police might not be able to do anything if they can't prove he's really in danger."

"Besides," I add darkly. "If this Fernsby is as big a shot as he seems, he might have the police in his pocket. Men like that don't get filthy rich and powerful enough to run around kidnapping people without paying certain authorities to look the other way."

"Exactly," Rick agrees. "So at least for now, we need to handle this ourselves. They've got a head start, so we need to drive down there immediately."

Donna shakes her head. "Just you three against him and potentially the actual police department, worst-case scenario? Nah."

"Harper needs us!" Brady says desperately. "We won't abandon him."

"We don't have a choice," Rick growls. "We're going."

Donna smirks and looks around the bar. "I didn't say anything about not going, did I? But maybe you have a choice about how *many* of you go, hmm?"

I look between her and Rick, whose face slowly lights up. I'm not sure what she's talking about, but I think Rick does. Then Brady fishes something out of his pocket, a look of wonder on his face. It's a little pair of black stone wings. He looks over at the ginger guy—specifically at the Harley-Davidson patch on his leather jacket.

The one with a pair of black wings around the logo, just like the poster I've got on the wall in our garage.

Realization starts to dawn on me.

"Hey, baby," Rick says to me, his voice low and dangerous, and his eyes sparkling. "You fancy going for a ride?"

"Ariana's outside and waiting," I assure him.

He nods. "Let's go get our little lamb back, then."

CHAPTER 23

Harper

I'm starting to get really scared.

Stepping back into this damned penthouse was almost enough to make me blackout. I can't quite believe this is where I lived for five years and that I only escaped from here a couple of months ago. It feels like something that happened to somebody else. Everything is horribly familiar, and yet at the same time, it all seems so alien.

Lowell took me right from Creams with nothing but the contents of my pockets—and that's with him still holding on to my phone. I left everything else either at The Vineyard or at my grandma's. He insisted that I'd have everything I could possibly need here in the apartment.

He's left me standing in the bedroom we used to share. He's laid out an outfit for me. It's all brand new and designer labels. Ralph Lauren jeans, Alexander McQueen T-shirt, Calvin Klein button down, and a pair of Nike sneakers. Even the underwear and socks are from Tom Ford, and there's an Omega watch box that I haven't dared open. The most terrifying part is that I know that for him, this is nothing. An outfit to wear around the fucking house. He's dropped hundreds of dollars on this when I know he could easily splurge thousands—*tens* of thousands.

It's strange how completely different I feel looking at this compared to the burgundy suit that Rick surprised me with. It's so clear to me now that he did that because he wanted to do something nice for me. He specifically said I had no obligation to wear it if I didn't want to.

I know without a doubt that if I resist putting this on, there will be unpleasant consequences from Lowell.

I feel sick just looking at it all. He's buying me again. Before, I would have been grateful that he was spoiling me. I would have just said 'thank you' and put it on, letting him dress me like a doll that he could control every movement of. But the idea of wearing that stuff now leaves me cold. I'd rather put on a prison jumpsuit.

Which would be appropriate because I really am trapped. The front door now has a key panel on it, and I have no idea what the code could be. I'm locked inside. Lowell has taken himself off to have a shower, graciously giving me space to 'calm down and put on something nice for dinner.' Instead, I rushed straight to the landline, desperate to call my grandma as that's the only number I know by heart. But it just connected down to the front desk. They very nicely asked what they could do for me, but I just panicked and said I was fine before hanging up.

I dread to think what will happen to me if he asks at the desk if I tried to call out. Actually, I dread to think what's going to happen to me, period.

Lowell announced that we were going out to 'celebrate.' I think the safest thing is to go along with his plans, but I'm absolutely petrified that he's going to want to have sex later, and I can't do that. I just can't. During the last couple of years that we were together, I definitely lost my enthusiasm for being intimate with him, but I made myself rally. I told myself it was what I wanted and went along with it. Often I'd just switch off and do whatever he asked me to or simply lie back and take it.

The mere thought of doing that now makes me want to vomit. I won't let him abuse me again. But…he is *so* much bigger than me.

I'm not sure if he'll give me the choice.

I don't know how long I've been standing there staring at the new clothes laid out on the bed, trembling. But when the en suite door opens and Lowell steps out, I jump a mile, clutching my hands to my chest.

Lowell laughs at me as he emerges in a steamy cloud, a towel wrapped around his waist. He really is built like a wrestler, something I used to find hot. But now I feel myself shrinking away from him.

"You're not dressed," he comments as he uses another towel to dry off his hair.

"Um, yeah, sorry," I mumble. "I just…I guess I'm tired. I'm not sure I feel like dinner…"

I realize my mistake as soon as I've said the words. If we go out, that's more chances for me to slip away or to ask someone for help. I don't care what he thinks is happening here. I know I've been kidnapped and am in very great danger of being assaulted.

I shake myself. "I'm being silly, Daddy. I'm tired, but the outfit is such a lovely present. I'll be fine once we get some food. I'm starving!"

He grins as I slip back into that little boy persona he preferred. It took escaping from him to realize that's not my style at all. If he wanted someone who enjoys age play, that's who he should be dating. But he'd rather bully someone into doing what he wants instead. I repress a shiver.

"Good boy," Lowell says warmly. It sounds nice enough, and I almost believe him. Almost. "I've made a reservation at your favorite place—the sushi bar with the huge tropical fish tanks."

He beams at me, and I smile back, pressing my hands to my chest like I really am thrilled.

"Yay! Yummy. Okay, I'll get changed right now, and—"

The landline rings, and my stomach drops right down to my toes. *Oh fuck!* Are they ratting me out for trying to make a call?

Lowell looks amused, going out into the main living space to answer it. "Fernsby speaking." He continues to look amused for about five seconds before his face drops. "I'm sorry, what? They...? Have you called the police?" There's a pause. "No, no. We don't want that. This is just a misunderstanding. I'll come down and fix it. I'm mortified for any disruption this might be causing the staff or other tenants. I sincerely apologize and will be donating a substantial amount to your Christmas party fund, I promise. Right, yes. Okay, I'll be there shortly."

He slams the phone down, screwing his eyes shut and taking a deep, angry breath in. I clutch my hands to my chest and take a step away from him. I want to know what's happening, but I don't want to piss him off any more than he already is.

The seconds tick by, and my nerves keep getting bigger and bigger. But finally, he speaks.

"There are some people downstairs refusing to leave because they are concerned for your safety, Harper. We are going to take the elevator down, and you are going to assure them that everything is fine. That you are home where you belong. If you do not do this, you will leave me no choice but to report all the illegal activity that's been brought to my attention. That is your decision. I am doing you a favor by not making those reports. So you are going to tell them the truth—that you are happy here and you want to be with me. That you never should have left. Do I make myself clear?"

I swallow, trying to hide the hope that's exploded inside me. Someone is here? Maybe Rick or my grandma? Either would be unafraid to stand up to Lowell.

But he's right. He still has all those bullshit lies that he's no doubt ready to spread at the drop of a hat with devastating consequences. I need to play this very, very carefully.

"Of course, Daddy," I say contritely. "I'm so sorry I've caused you trouble. But I'm home now. Everything will be better."

He sighs fondly and reaches out to cup my face. I dig my fingernails into my palms to stop myself from flinching away. "That's my boy. Right. Let's get this over with."

He had a fancier suit hanging from the wardrobe door that I assumed he was going to change into for going to dinner. But he throws on what he wore to Paddle Creek instead, obviously not wanting to waste his exquisite Saville Row tailoring on the plebeians.

I'm trembling as we head out the door. He shields the passcode from me, but hopefully, I can work it out soon. If I can get a message through to whoever's downstairs that I don't actually want to be here, I might not need to escape by myself. But I'm going to try everything possible to get out of here.

The ride down feels like it takes an eternity, but I forcibly focus on my breathing. *It's going to be okay*, I tell myself over and over again. *Someone came for you! Someone cares. You DO matter!*

I cling to that thought as we enter into the lobby. It's past nine o'clock, and it's dark outside. As we're right on Monument Circle, it's usual for it to be brightly lit. But as we approach the glass doors at the front, something seems off that I can't put my finger on.

"I'm so sorry, sir," Gerry, the head security officer says as Lowell marches past the desk. "I didn't know what to do."

Lowell waves his hand. "Not at all. You were right not to involve the authorities. I can handle this quietly."

Gerry doesn't look so sure about that, but I don't have time to analyze his face any longer as I hastily scuttle by, following in Lowell's wake. He storms through the front doors into the night...and stops. I slow down behind him, coming outside more cautiously.

I see why he froze. I do, too.

There have got to be at least fifty motorcycles all parked up on the wide sidewalk, all with their lights pointing toward Lowell's building, and each with a driver either straddling the seat or standing beside the bike. There is so much leather, scowling, body piercings, and tattoos between them, and they all appear to be fucking pissed.

Not to mention that they're all looking right at Lowell.

"What's the meaning of this?" he bellows. To his credit, he sounds furious when if I were him, I'd be quaking in my boots. "Which one of you little punks called me out here? You're trespassing. This is harassment, and I will be calling the police!"

"Then why haven't you already?" a gut-wrenchingly familiar voice calls out. I snap my head to see Rick emerging from the throng. In fact, I can see his red Jaguar among the sea of bikes. Brady is also walking from the car, but Trey comes from next to it where Ariana is parked.

My wolves are here. They're all really here. Hope explodes in my chest.

"You're wasting your time," Lowell says to Rick, but then he looks around at the rest of the crowd who is just brimming with hostility. "Harper came with me of his own free will. He made a mistake in leaving, and now he's chosen to come back. So you can all just turn around and head back to that sad little rundown town where I rescued him from."

"Oh, honey," a muscular blonde woman says with a laugh. "These fine folk here are from all along route 31. When I put the call out that one of our own had been kidnapped by some rich sleazebag, all kinds of chapters wanted to saddle up."

"Some of us don't even have bikes," a man pipes up. I squint through the headlights, and my heart skips a beat when I see it's Trey's boss from the garage, Ruben. By his side is his boy, Xander, who gives me a shy little wave. There are Leandra and Lewis as well—all the people from Horowitz's garage.

I could cry. What are they doing here? What are *any* of them doing here?

"Like I give a shit what rocks you crawled out from under," Lowell sneers. He straightens his lapels and sniffs in contempt. "I've done you a courtesy by not informing the authorities. This is just a misunderstanding. If you all leave now, I see no need to press any charges."

"Agreed," says Rick with a shit-eating grin that I've come to love dearly. "Let Harper come with us, and we'll forget all of this ever happened."

Brady pushes forward, his face stricken. "Harper!" he yells at me. "Are you okay? Did he hurt you?"

"Why would I hurt him?" Lowell asks with a booming laugh. "He's my boyfriend. I love him."

Trey visibly flinches at that, stepping forward like he's going to start something. Rick holds out an arm, silently urging him to stay where he is.

"Tell them, Harper," Lowell barks.

I lick my lips, thinking about all the horrendous things he's threatened to do if I don't comply. "He hasn't hurt me," I say truthfully.

Brady's clutching his hands to his chest tearfully. "I don't care what he's said to you," he cries out. "What twisted lies he's tried to make you believe. You're a good person. You don't belong to *him*. You belong with *us*. I've known it since the moment I met you. You're special, Harper! He made you believe you were nothing! Don't fall for his manipulation, please!"

I don't know what to say. I don't know how to tell him that what he thinks has happened didn't at all. That I was strong enough to fend off his gaslighting. I'm only here because I had to protect him, our Daddies, and my grandma.

"I—"

"You don't know me, boy," Lowell sneers at Brady. "You or any of the misfits you hang around with. Harper doesn't belong with you. He's better than that. He belongs with me in my world where I can give him the best of everything."

"Except love," Rick says loudly and clearly. "You don't love him. He's just a plaything for you to control."

Lowell laughs cruelly. I wince, hating that he's being so disrespectful to some of the best people I've ever met in my life. "Oh, and you freaks love him? You're like a pack of wild animals, fucking in the dirt. No morals or standards. I can offer Harper structure, not to mention the finer things in life. No wonder he came to his senses and chose to return back home with me."

I'm so torn between telling him he's full of shit and protecting my pack. How funny that's the very word he used, thinking it would be an insult. I open my mouth, but I'm not sure what I can say.

Then another pair of headlights swing through the crowd, and a horn blares. I jump as several of the bikers look around in interest. There's the sound of a car door slamming, and through the throng of grisly leather-clad ruffians emerges a small woman in her finest Sunday best— complete with three-inch heels and a lacy fascinator in her hair—brandishing a skillet like she's about to take on an army.

"Grandma?" I splutter.

"Harper John Kendall! You stop this nonsense right now, and you get your behind in this here car, you hear me? That man is the devil! I don't care what pretty lies he's told you, he's an agent of Satan and I won't let him take you again!"

"No, no," I throw my hands up, looking desperately between her and Lowell. He threatened to evict her and tear down her house. I can't do that to her! But I can't have her thinking that I chose to come back to him after everything she knows I've been through. "I…uh…"

"Harper," Lowell growls in a warning tone.

But then Brady comes forward so he's only a few feet away from me. He's holding something in his hands that he's trying to show me. "See?" he says, tears flowing freely down his face. "I mean it. I knew you were special from that very first night. I…I love you, Harper. I really do. I want you to stay with me."

I have to blink away my own tears because I realize that what he's got is a crappy plastic doubloon. A gold coin that he must have taken from that cheesy motel where he hunted me down and claimed me for his own for the first time.

And somewhere inside me, I've known that I've been his ever since.

"I love you, too, Harper," Trey speaks up. "You're kind and bright and a sassy little shit. Please don't throw your life away because this man convinced you that you were worth so much less."

"I love you, Harper," Rick says calmly. "You're mine. You're a part of my pack, and you know it. Not because I made you. Because you want to be. It's where you belong. Where you'll be free. Don't make this mistake."

I look into his eyes. He really thinks I chose this?

That's what breaks me.

"Daddy, no," I cry pitifully.

"*I'm* your Daddy," Lowell snarls, reaching over to grab my wrist.

I stumble backward out of his reach. "NO!" I scream at him, clutching my hands to my chest. "Enough! I *hate* you! I'm only here because you threatened to ruin the lives of everyone I *do* love!" I turn once more to my pack, desperately shaking my head. "He said he'd tell Brady's college that he was making illegal bets and getting players to throw games. That Trey was cheating on his disability payments and that Rick was guilty of insider trading. He wasn't just going to take all your jobs and money away from you, but ruin your reputations, too! And Grandma—" I whirl around to face her. "He was going to demolish your house and throw you out onto the streets!"

She thwacks her skillet against her open palm. "Well, bless his heart. I'd sure like to see him try."

The crowd is getting vocally agitated now. "You were going after a disabled veteran?" somebody shouts, sounding utterly incensed.

Lowell is waving his hands, trying to calm the increasingly rowdy group down. "I have several reliable sources that brought me information that I was considering sharing with the police. It was for Harper's own good! He needed to know what kind of people he was really getting involved with!"

"And that includes destroying an elderly lady's home?" Donna pipes up.

Grandma straightens up her pencil dress. "Less of the 'elderly,' thank you."

Donna smirks at her and gives her a salute.

"I was looking into some perfectly legal property development—" Lowell begins, but Rick isn't having any of it.

"Save the bullshit for a judge," he snaps. "If Harper says

you threatened him to make him go with you, that makes perfect sense to me. He hates you and never wants to see you again. He's told us that countless times."

"Countless," Brady agrees earnestly. "I knew there had to be a reason like that."

"I knew that Harper wouldn't throw his life away," Trey says, nodding at me in a way that melts my heart into a puddle. "He knows he's got a bright future ahead of him, and we're here to support him in it if that's what he wants."

"It is what I want!" I cry, tears openly flowing down my face now. "I…I love you all. So much. I want to be with you. I want to start a new life with you. All of you!"

"Harper," Lowell barks, but I turn on him, shaking my finger in his face.

"No! You're a bully, and I don't care what you say. You have nothing on these people. You made it all up. It's so obvious you did. They're my family, and they're honest and good. You can try and lie about them, but we're stronger than you. We won't back down!"

He's still not giving up, though. His grin is like a shark that smells blood in the water. "You? The four of you. Against my fleet of lawyers. Good luck. It's your word against mine."

"And the court of public opinion," a calm voice says.

I don't recognize it, so I look around. I see a man stepping forward with his phone held up, the light on to indicate that he's recording. He's like most of the other bikers here—big, leather, lots of tattoos. His hair is closely shaved, he's got stubble on his face and a mean look in his eyes.

But he's also got a black cat wrapped around his shoulders.

"What?" Lowell demands.

"The court of public opinion," the guy says again. I have a feeling he might be the owner of that cat café Brady took me to on our first proper date. It would explain the creature currently wrapped around his neck, swishing their tail like they're ready to pounce.

Donna hops across to the guy and checks out his screen. "Oh, boy," she chortles, smacking his arm in delight. "Nim here's gone live on Instagram. How many followers do you have now, buddy?"

Nim creases his eyebrows. "Don't know. Maybe fifty?"

"Fifty followers?" Lowell crows.

"Fifty thousand," Donna corrects him smoothly. "People just love rescue kitties. Like the ones Rick and Trey over there adopted. British shorthairs. Cute as buttons. Yep, Nim did good when he let his coworker start up this channel. People tune in every single day. And let me tell you something, they do *not* like you right now."

"Say 'hello,'" Nim grunts, pointing his camera directly at Lowell.

"I'm live, too," another woman says, holding up her phone. She shrugs. "I've only got like a hundred people watching, but they *all* think you're a massive tool, dude."

Donna crosses her arms. "If the press runs with this story, Lowell Fernsby of Fernsby Incorporated, I wonder what that would do to your shares and stocks, huh?"

More and more people come forward with their phones raised high. I consider how long they might have been recording. I sort of hate the idea of my private business being made public like this, but if it makes Lowell back down and means he can't follow through with his awful threats...

Well...I'll do a song and dance for the cameras if they'd like.

Lowell's waving his hands again, but he doesn't look cocky like before.

He looks worried.

"Now, now, there's no need for any of this," he says, plastering a smile on his face that doesn't reach his eyes.

"You're right," Rick agrees. "No need for any of it so long as you let Harper walk away right now. If you follow through on any of those bogus threats, I bet it would be really easy to convince a jury of who was behind them with all this evidence, wouldn't you say?"

Lowell opens and closes his mouth like a fish. He flashes his eyes at me, clearly enraged. But then he spits on the ground.

"Fuck you, then, you useless piece of shit. I could have given you everything. If you'd rather waste your life with these freaks, fine."

I want to make a run for it immediately, but luckily, I remember something just in time. I hold out my hand to him defiantly. "Give me back my phone," I say. "I know you've still got it in your pocket. Give it back right now and never, *ever* contact me again."

"We'll be filing a restraining order as soon as offices open on Monday," Rick adds cheerfully.

Lowell scowls, probably wanting to have this one last bit of power over me. But he's grossly outnumbered, and all the camera phones are still pointed his way.

"You ungrateful prick," he growls, snatching my cell out of his pocket and thrusting it into my hands.

I don't waste a second more of my time on him. I break into a sprint, throwing myself into Brady's arms as we both cry. "I never wanted to leave," I tell him urgently.

"I never doubted you for a second," he assures me.

He presses the plastic gold coin into my hand as Trey also wraps us up in his arms. There's a cheer from the crowd, and I peek out to see Lowell skulking back into his shiny glass tower where he belongs. My grandma is waving her skillet around like she's just won a sporting trophy. A couple of the big, scary bikers pick her up and put her on their shoulders.

She sits there perfectly happy like the retired cheerleader she is.

Then Rick throws himself on me, Brady, and Trey, and I allow myself to be consumed by the hug. "Let's go *home*," he says firmly.

I sniff and laugh wetly. "Home," I repeat. "It's where the heart is."

"And where my fucking two-million-dollar mansion stands," Rick grumbles, making me laugh. I can't stop laughing. I think it's relief and happiness and hope all spilling out of me.

We're going home. Me and my wolf pack.

It's where I belong.

CHAPTER 24

Harper

I SPEND THE DRIVE BACK TO PADDLE CREEK curled up in the back seat of Rick's Jaguar with Brady clinging to me. I think I'm in a state of mild shock. Rick wrapped us up in a blanket before we started driving home, and I'm pressed against Brady's always hot body, but I'm still shivering. My attention keeps wandering in and out of focus, but all I really need to know is that I'm safe.

It's over. Really over.

Grandma's purple VW bug is apparently behind us, and we get a motorcycle chaperone the whole drive back. Rick says something about various chapters peeling off as we pass their towns, so there are only maybe half a dozen bikers still with us by the time we cross back into Paddle Creek, but by that point, I feel so safe it doesn't matter.

Lowell can't hurt me now. I doubt he'll ever try and hurt me ever again.

I think I finally feel like Paddle Creek is my home. When I moved in with my grandma when I was a teenager, it always felt temporary, even though I was here for years. And again when she rescued me a couple of months ago, I assumed my stay would be just a brief footnote before I moved on to something bigger and better.

But now I don't want to be anywhere else. I want to stay at The Vineyard with my pack. I want to be near my grandma. I want to go to college here and finally start building up my life the way I deserve. I convinced myself that I couldn't belong in a small town, that people would never accept me. But those very same people just stuck their necks out and saved me.

Why would I want to go anywhere else?

"Daddy says the others are taking your grandma home," Brady whispers in my ear as he rubs my back. "Trey is escorting us home. It's just us now. We're almost there. Good boy. Good boy."

I cling to him, letting his words wash over me. I'm still trembling but...yeah. I'm really fucking proud of myself. I didn't just lie down and take it from Lowell. I fought back. And my reward was my wolves all coming to rescue me.

They love me.

I think I love them. I'm sure I do. Once my thoughts stop rattling like a pinball shooting around a machine, I'm certain I'll know that for sure.

All I can really trust is that I need to be with all my men tonight. I want them to hold me and not let go until dawn.

I blink as we pull into the driveway. I watch the trees go past the window then the house before we pull into the garage, parking next to Brady's Chevy Bolt. I realize I'm no longer cold and trembling, but I sure am stiff as I slowly let go of Brady and try to get out of the car.

"It's okay, little lamb," Rick says as he opens my door. He reaches over and undoes my seat belt before scooping me up in his arms. "I've got you." I'm not light, but he manages to shrug me into a bridal carry.

Just like he did when he rescued me from my breakdown in the barn.

I don't fight him this time. I wrap my arms around his neck and cling to him tightly as he takes me through into the house. "Brady?" I whimper.

"I'm right here, sweetheart," he says from close by. He rubs my back but then takes his hand away. "I'm just going to wait for Papa, okay? He's parking his bike now."

"Okay," I mumble, trusting that they'll be right behind us.

"I've got you, little lamb," Rick says again, kissing the side of my head. "Everything's all right now. You're home."

"Home," I repeat.

We make our way up the stairs. I'm used to the master bedroom now. My stuff is still all in 'my' room, but I've slept in this massive bed several times since the party night.

There's nowhere else in the entire world I'd rather be right now than here.

Carefully Rick takes off my shoes and socks. Then he eases my jeans down, leaving me in my work T-shirt and briefs. He settles me on the bed, and I watch through half-closed lids as he removes his suit in record time, getting down to just his underwear. He slides onto the bed and wraps me in his arms.

"I've got you," he repeats softly.

Brady and Trey join us not long after. They also hastily get out of their clothes until it's just their briefs left. Brady offers Trey his support as he removes his prosthetic and massages the stump for a minute, groaning in relief. Then they join us in the cuddle pile on the bed. They smell of perspiration and leather and fresh air. I love it.

"I'm so glad you're here," Brady says in a tight voice, clinging to me like a life raft. "I thought we'd lost you. Please stay, Harper. Please. We love you."

Rick laughs. It's a rumble against my body that feels so

reassuring and right. "Our pup has sort of spilled the beans there, little lamb, but he's not wrong. Trey and I were planning on asking you to officially be our boyfriend at dinner, but then you just *had* to outdo us with all that drama."

I chuckle weakly. I don't have much energy to be surprised or overthink anything. "Yes," I say firmly.

"Yes?" Rick repeats.

"Yes, I want to be your boyfriend. I want to date all of you. I want to stay. I want to be a part of your lives."

Trey sighs with such contentment it makes me giggle weakly again. "We literally couldn't ask you for anything more than that, sweet boy," he says.

"Oh, Harper," Brady sniffles. I angle myself so I can kiss his lips. He's the catalyst for all of this. I might be the proud new member of the most amazing polycule, but none of it would have happened if we hadn't run into each other that fateful night at the bar.

I'm going to keep that plastic piece of gold trash until the day I die, I swear. Who needs diamonds or pearls when you have fake doubloons to prove your love?

I'm trembling again, but it's not from shock or fear this time. I'm so dizzy with lust. I feel like I need to be touched all over to remind myself that I am very much alive and well and *home.*

"Daddy," I whine, grinding against him and whatever other body parts I'm in contact with. I'm part of a pile of writhing limbs, already sweating, with a hard cock and a desire to be totally and utterly claimed. I want them to wipe the memory of Lowell ever putting his filthy hands on me from the face of the earth.

"Shh, little lamb," Daddy says firmly, digging his fingers into my skin. "We need to make sure we care for you properly. Daddy is going to ask you a couple of questions, and he needs you to answer them honestly for me. Can you do that for him?"

"Yes, Daddy," I say, feeling so relieved at being given an instruction that I can comply with.

"Good boy," he says, giving me all the warm, syrupy feelings. "Daddy wants to hold you so tightly all night and make sure you're safe. He wants you to feel good. Is that what you want?"

"Yes," I utter. "Daddy and Papa and Baby, please. Don't let me go."

"We won't," he promises with another kiss to the side of my head. "We're here. We've got you. Do you just want snuggles or sexy snuggles? You're in charge. Whatever you want, we'll give you. Isn't that right?"

Brady and Trey murmur affirmations into my ears as they stroke and kiss my skin. "We're here however you want us, Harper," Brady promises me. "You're ours now."

"Ours," Trey echoes.

"I…oh, god," I sob. "I want you inside me. I want you to take me, all of you. I don't want you to chase me. You already have me. Just mark me! Claim me!"

Daddy kisses me hard on the lips as Papa and Baby attack either side of my neck. "Good boy," Daddy mumbles into my mouth. "Such a good boy for telling Daddy what you want. We'll claim you now. You belong to us. You're safe. We've got you."

I gasp and nod, lost in a blur of being touched all over my body. I think I hear Daddy quietly talking with Papa and Baby. The next thing I know is that we're all gently shifting around the bed. Baby seizes my hand and doesn't let go as we rest our heads on the pillows, lying on our bellies. I feel my briefs being peeled down my legs and look over to see Papa is also doing the same to Baby.

"Do you want to take your T-shirt off?" Baby asks me. I

nod and push up on my knees so I can quickly get rid of it. Then I flop back down completely naked and feeling so free. Baby and I have our heads on the pillows facing each other. He grabs my hand again, and I feel more than see our Daddies pulling our legs apart.

I cling to Baby as Daddy starts to eat out my hole, aware that Papa is doing the same to Baby. I try and keep my eyes open so we can look at each other and share this intimate moment. I rut against the mattress, trying to get some friction for my hard, throbbing cock. I don't want to come yet—certainly until Daddy says I can—but I can't help but indulge just a little. I want to be touched all over.

Daddy switches from his tongue to fingers, pushing inside me, stretching me out. I lose track of time as he goes from one to two to three. All I know is that Baby and I never let go. Sometimes he leans over and kisses me so sweetly. I accept everything he gives me, greedy for more.

I'm so hard and horny and exhausted. I don't know how long this all goes on for, but eventually, Daddy comes up and kisses my cheek. "Little lamb?" he asks. I hum. "Brady said you got all negative results from the clinic. Is that right?" I hum again. "Good. That's good, sweet boy. We want to fuck you bareback. Do you understand what that means? None of us would use condoms. We're all clear as well. Is that okay?"

I almost laugh. I trust these men with my life. Of course that's okay.

"Yes, Daddy," I moan. "Please, Daddy."

He smiles and brushes my sweaty hair back from my forehead. "Good, sweet boy. So good for Daddy. I want you to cuddle up with me, okay? I want to fuck your tight, gorgeous hole. Our baby wolf is going to be on top of you, and he's going to fuck inside you as well while Papa fucks him hard. Do you understand? Does that sound good?"

My head is spinning, and for a moment I just blink at

him, my breathing ragged. "Baby and Daddy...will you fit?" I ask weakly.

He laughs kindly and gives my mouth a gentle kiss. I taste myself on his lips and love how primal it is. "I hope we'll fit," Daddy says. "But remember—what do you say if something hurts or feels bad?"

I lick my lips and think properly. "Red," I tell him.

"Good boy. So, so good. And what if you just need to take a breather and see how you feel?"

"Yellow," I say, more sure of myself this time.

Daddy nods, giving me another kiss as a reward. "Exactly. Perfect. So what's your color now? How do you feel about getting fucked so sweetly by your whole wolf pack?"

I groan and drop my head so my flaming face is buried against his neck. "Green!" I squeak. "Green, so green. Please, I want that. Please, please, *please.*"

He laughs kindly again. "It's okay, gorgeous boy. We've got you. You're safe. We're going to take care of you now. Our baby wolf will be there with you the whole time. You're safe, okay? We love you."

I nod, words escaping me for the moment. Then we all start to shift on the bed again. It's almost like I surrender my body, and I'm not quite sure of what I'm doing or who's going where until I feel Daddy's chest against my back, and he's guiding his cock inside me as I sit back against him.

Baby gasps and hovers over me on his knees. He leans down and captures my mouth as I draw my knees up so my feet are by my ass. I think Papa is pushing inside Baby as Daddy pushes inside me. It doesn't take long...maybe. Who knows? Time has lost all meaning for me. All I care about is the fact that we're all here and touching and gasping and sweating and we're together and it's *awesome.*

"Fuck, ah, I, fuck," I say, rambling nonsense. But nobody

minds. Everyone is uttering whatever comes into their heads. This space is safe and free and full of love.

It seems like both Daddy and Papa are settled inside me and Baby. Daddy kisses my neck and strokes Baby's cock. "Are you both ready?" he asks.

Am I? Can I fit *two* dicks inside me?

Daddy knows best. If he thinks I'm ready, I can do this.

"Yes, Daddy," I cry.

Baby seemed to have been waiting for me, because he nods vigorously. "Yes, Daddy. So ready."

"Just relax, little lamb," Daddy says, linking his fingers with mine and sucking on my earlobe as my Baby Wolf starts pushing his way inside me. I whimper. It doesn't seem feasible. But Daddy tightens his grip on my hand. "You can do it, sweetheart. Just stick with me. It's going to feel so good, I promise. We're all here for you. We're all connected now. My beautiful men. My perfect pack."

I pant and writhe and scream, but slowly, Baby forces his big cock alongside Daddy's, claiming and marking me just how I wanted. I'm going to feel this for days.

Good.

Daddy has his arms wrapped around my chest and stomach as Baby manages to push as far as he can inside my hole. I feel like my guts are being rearranged but in a sort of euphoric way. I have no thought capacity to explain it. It's wild and uncomfortable but also incredible.

And then they start to move.

Papa takes the first thrust into Baby, forcing him to hit my prostate, and I simply drop my head back and wail. Daddy starts gyrating, and I'm lost in a mess of touch and feeling and sensation and love.

Two hard dicks work inside me. I see Papa gasp and bite his lip as he fucks my baby himbo's sweet ass. Daddy massages my chest and rubs my nipples with his thumbs, telling me I'm good and perfect and sweet. My solid, tender cock bounces against my stomach, otherwise untouched. I feel like I'm going to explode.

But not until Daddy tells me I can.

I don't know how long we writhe together in a tangle of ecstasy, but then Daddy takes mercy on me and reaches around my stomach, wrapping his hand around my length. "Good boy," he utters, sounding desperate. "Good, sweet boy. So perfect. You did everything right. Come for Daddy now. We love you. We're here for you. Come, little lamb. Come. *Come.*"

I scream. So, so loudly because I can. Because I'm safe and my Daddy gave me permission. I come all over his hand and my stomach, riding out wave after wave of pure unadulterated pleasure. I gasp for air, trying to relax as my wolf pack continues to use my body until their completion. I want them to so badly. I want to give them everything.

Baby starts baying first, like a real wolf. But then Daddy and Papa start shouting at similar times, and in my hazy state, I figure everybody is reaching that beautiful high.

It's pure bliss, and I never want it to end.

Of course it does, but I'm not mad when everyone starts collapsing. I'm hugged from every possible angle, and there are kisses being planted everywhere. I half laugh, half groan as the two softening cocks slowly slide out of my hole. That's definitely going to smart for a few days to come, but I can't say I regret it.

The only thing I regret is that Lowell tried to slither back into my life. But if he hadn't, he wouldn't have been scared off so thoroughly. I hope that eventually I'll see it as a blessing in disguise.

Once I'm able to hold a coherent train of thought again.

"Shh, it's okay," Daddy is saying into my ear. I think he's

been saying it for a while. Oh, *fuck*, I'm crying. It's not a bad thing! It's a good thing!

"I'm okay," I manage to utter, vaguely aware of being carried. "It was amazing. I love you all. I'm green."

Daddy chuckles. He's got me in that bridal carry again. I think I can hear water running. "You're absolutely perfect, little lamb. Crying is good. Let it all out."

I do.

The next however long is a blur of being cleaned and dried and soothed with nice-smelling lotions. Three voices hover around me, telling me how good and special and perfect I am. I know it's all the same stuff repeated over and over again, but that's okay. I need to hear it.

I need it drilled into my brain. I need it to undo all the toxic shit my terrible ex told me. Because that's all in the past now.

These men—this wolf pack—are my future.

And nothing's going to change that.

CHAPTER 25
Brady

I CAN FEEL THAT SUMMER IS ENDING. THERE'S A TASTE IN THE air. The weather is still warm, but the days are getting shorter. It's okay. Usually, the approaching of fall makes me a little sad, even though I love Halloween and Christmas and all that. I just normally feel my best with the sunshine warming my bones.

But this year is different. I don't feel as if something is slipping away from me. It's more like there's something incredibly exciting on the horizon.

I whistle as I lock my car and sling my gym bag over my shoulder. The new semester will be starting soon, and I've been putting in overtime at the gym to make sure that I can keep up with the guys on the team. Coach Drevin says I don't have to. He certainly doesn't. I think he revels in the fact that his pro-athlete days are long behind him. But I want to know what it is I'm pushing the team through and like to lead by example.

Plus, I like being built for my own men.

The house seems unusually quiet for a Saturday as I come into the hallway. Normally, between the four of us, someone has a TV on or is playing music or video games. One of our cats—Chardonnay—comes to greet me by winding around my legs and giving a soft meow. I reach down to scratch her head.

"Hey, sweetie. Where is everyone? Are they off having fun without Baby Wolf?"

She doesn't offer me any insight, but she does wander off toward the kitchen, her fluffy tail swishing in the air. I shrug and follow her. If I've got the house to myself, I might order a pizza or something. I know I just worked my ass off kind of literally, but that just means I earned my carbs. If I'm on my own, I figure I can treat myself.

Except I'm not alone.

I stop as I round the corner into the kitchen, tilting my head in amusement. Everyone's there. Daddy, Papa, and little lamb. Our Daddies have their arms around each other's backs and are beaming at Harper as he practically vibrates with excitement in front of me. Even Merlot is by their feet, and Chardonnay goes to join her. It's a proper family affair. I let my bag drop to the floor and quirk an eyebrow. I notice that Harper is clutching a letter in his hands.

"What's going on?" I ask in amusement.

Harper shakes the letter, tears brimming in his eyes as he dances over to me on his tiptoes. "I got in," he whispers.

My jaw drops. "Got into where?" I say, already feeling excited despite not really understanding what's going on. I know he's been talking about college, but he was too late to apply for this year. Or so I thought.

He grabs my hands in his, crumpling the letter even farther. "Paddle Creek!" he squeaks. "Daddy helped me with my personal essay, and they had a last-minute spot. Daddy said I had to take it. He's covering my tuition. Brady—I'm going to college! Your college! I'm going to study art!"

Emotions overwhelm me as I pull my hands free and

throw my arms around him instead, lifting him off the ground as I squeeze the shit out of him. "Harper!" I yell as tears tumble down my face. I'm bursting with pride and feel almost choked with happiness. "You fucking boss! Oh my god, this is the best news ever!"

He's laughing through his own tears as I put him back down again and give him a messy kiss. "I never thought I could do it," he says. "But I did. Because of you all. I really did it!"

He starts sobbing as Daddy and Papa also come to hug us, kissing the top of Harper's head on his white-blond hair. My little lamb. Who'd have thought when we met at the start of the summer that this is where we'd end up?

"It's an arts major," he explains as he calms down a bit. "So I can study all kinds of new mediums like sculpting and charcoal and all that. But I can also include psychology, English lit, and classics with Benedict and Jackson, and I don't even know what else. Whatever I need to become an art therapist. I'm going to do it, Brady. I'm going to work *so* hard."

I kiss his mouth again and grin at him. "Damn right, you are," I say. "You're going to blow them away. Holy fuck, this is awesome."

"We should celebrate," Daddy announces.

"I was thinking about ordering pizza," I admit.

Daddy's expression is sly. "Yeah, we could do that later," he concedes. However, he then bites his lower lip and gives Harper a filthy look. "But first...would you like your pack to hunt you down and show you *exactly* how special and amazing you are, little lamb?"

Harper's tears dry up immediately, and he takes a shuddery breath as he looks at Daddy with wide eyes. "You want to try a hunt again?" he asks, his voice light and fluttery.

We haven't attempted anything like that since the last

disastrous time. But Harper was putting up a brave front then. I knew he wasn't ready and shouldn't have let him try being chased down and captured like that.

But now a blush is creeping onto his cheeks as he stares up at Daddy with such love and adoration and not a small amount of raging lust.

I think this time he's ready.

Daddy shares a heated look with Papa before addressing Harper again. "We thought you might enjoy that kind of reward. If not, there's always pizza—"

"Pizza can *wait,*" Harper cries, yanking his T-shirt off and throwing it to the floor. Along with it falls the practically destroyed acceptance letter that I make a note to try and save later. Harper grins, bouncing on the balls of his feet. "Just you try and catch me, motherfuckers!"

He shoves his way out of the group hug and bolts for the kitchen door, throwing it open and sprinting into the warm and sunny afternoon. I drop my head back and laugh, loving his enthusiasm. But then Daddy rests his hand on my shoulder, giving me a serious look.

"What do you want, baby boy?" he asks me. "To hunt or to be hunted?"

I shake my head. I still love being prey for my Daddies so much. But this all started because I wanted to try my hand at being the predator. If Harper really is ready, then I want to be that for him, just like how we started back in Creams.

"I'm a wolf, Daddy," I say firmly. "And there's a succulent little lamb out there just begging for us to ravage him."

My Daddies' grins are both feral. Papa leans down and gives me an openmouthed kiss. "Then you'd better get moving, hadn't you?" He winks. "We'll be right behind you."

I give both his and Daddy's hands a squeeze. Then I take off out the back door, following Harper where I assume he's run across the lawn. The barn door is open. We gave him the code a while ago because we didn't want him to feel like there wasn't anywhere he wasn't allowed. This is his home now as much as ours. The lights are on, and when I crash through the door, I hear the sound system is on as well, playing all the ambient forest noises that make a hunt seem so much more real.

I slow down, chuckling darkly as I see the trail of Harper's clothes left like breadcrumbs. "Little lamb," I call out in a sing-song voice, delighted when I hear a frightened squeal in response. Harper isn't trying very hard to hide, but I don't think that's the point of this chase tonight.

Still, I'm as quiet as I can be as I skulk around the corners, searching for my prey. My breaths are fast, and my dick is hard in my jeans from the blood pumping through my body. I hear a rustle around the next bend, so I inhale silently, then *pounce.*

Harper screams as I grab him, and he tries to twist away. He's gorgeously naked, and it makes me feel powerful as I wrestle him to the nearest mattress, throw him down, and loom over him like the predator I am.

"Got you," I say proudly.

He drops his hands over his head and gives me a demure look through his golden eyelashes. His chest rises and falls as he submits beautifully to me. "Got me," he agrees, his voice soft and raspy. "Now whatever do you plan to do with me?"

I capture his lip and drag it through my teeth, loving how he whimpers when I release it. "Whatever I want to, little lamb. You're mine now."

"Yours," he agrees. There's a lot of sincerity in that one word. It makes me lower my head and kiss him slowly, sensually.

"I love you, little lamb," I tell him. I've told him that every day since we rescued him from Indianapolis.

"I love you, Baby Wolf," he tells me back.

I hear a commotion from toward the barn door, but I don't call out. Our Daddies need to find us on their own. And when they do, we can truly celebrate together.

My heart is overflowing. Some days I still can't believe that I'm so fortunate as to deserve the love of all three of these remarkable men. But I am.

And I'll be grateful for that for the rest of my life.

Epilogue

FOUR YEARS LATER – RICK

"That's looking beautiful."

Harper glances over his shoulder at me and blinks like he's coming out of a trance. "Thanks, Daddy," he says.

He rubs his forehead with the back of his hand and turns back toward the enormous painting that he's been working on for weeks. It's part of his final college project, and I appreciate how much he's poured himself into it. I know he wants a good grade to help with his future career, but to me, I couldn't give a shit. I don't really see how you can give that an A or a D or whatever. Art is subjective.

As far as I'm concerned, everything he creates is astonishing.

"Do you think you could take a break?" I ask, keeping my poker face on straight. Harper has no idea what's coming, and that's the way I want to keep it.

He looks between me and the canvas again. He's in the home studio I had converted for him not long after he started his degree, and there are dozens of his creations hung on the walls as well as stacked around the room. Trey encouraged him to set up an online store, so he also does commissions for people and ships them across the country. I think it still baffles him that people like his stuff so much.

It's no surprise to me. There's no accounting for taste, but anyone who tried to argue he wasn't technically spectacular would be an imbecile. His humility after all this time is still sweet. However, I'm hoping once he gets through the thick of this qualification, he'll be able to take a breath and see just how far he's come and what heights he's truly accomplished.

"Oh, damn. Is that the time?" he asks sheepishly as he looks at his phone. "I haven't eaten all day. Yeah, I should probably take a break." He laughs nervously and quickly rinses the brush he's been using. This final piece looks like a surrealist dream to me, full of bold colors and wildly random images bleeding together. I haven't asked him what it represents yet. When he's ready, he'll tell me.

"I think you're done for the night," I tell him kindly but firmly. "Come on. Clean yourself, and let's get some dinner."

He lets out a happy sigh and nods. "Yes, Daddy. Thank you."

There's a sink in the corner where he washes anything that's still tacky from his hands. He dries them, then pulls off his paint-splattered sweats and tee, switching into regular jeans and a Henley. He's still got colorful flecks on his pale skin like freckles, not to mention in his light blond hair, but he wouldn't be Harper if there wasn't a bit of paint somewhere.

"Ready?" I ask, sticking out my hand.

He skips over to me and takes it, beaming at me as he plants a kiss on my cheek. "Ready, Daddy. Are the others in? What did you want for dinner?"

"Oh, I think they're in," I say, holding back a grin as I usher him through the door and out onto the second-floor hallway.

He stops immediately, looking down at the floor. It's strewn with a trail of red rose petals.

"What the...?" He looks back up at me with confusion. "Did you do this?" I shrug, not willing to give the game away. "What is it? Does it go somewhere?"

"You better follow it and find out, hadn't you?" I say, fully aware that I'm teasing.

Harper licks his lips and frowns, but he cautiously walks forward, leading me first down the hall and then the staircase.

It's funny. I might be playing it cool on the outside, but I'm actually kind of nervous. When I did this for Trey, I'd already asked him once before, so I was very certain I knew the answer, even if he'd been high on painkillers the first time. Then with Brady...we never asked. I think him moving in was a bigger deal and showed our commitment to one another right from the start. By the time Trey and I were thinking of doing something fancy for him, Harper came along, and it didn't feel right.

That being said, before Harper arrived, the three of us had already gotten our set of wolf tattoos, each in the same style but drawn in different poses. And then Harper got the most adorable fluffy lamb on the inside of his right wrist last year, designed by the same artist who did the rest of ours. So again, I *think* I know the answer he's going to give.

But this is the first proper proposal I've been a part of, despite having three men in my life.

I can feel Harper's hand trembling in mine as we arrive on the landing. The trail of petals is guiding us through the kitchen. We both laugh as a streak of fur goes rushing past us. Us three decided not to try and stop the cats from interfering with the decorations. They're a part of the family as well, after all, and to them all these petals just look like fun. Especially to our new rescue kitten, Pinot, another British shorthair from Toe Beans in town. It's him who tears past us and dives into the pile of red petals, rolling around in them and meowing in delight.

"Good boy," Harper murmurs as we move around the little ball of feline fury. I like hearing him say that. I say it to him often enough, but it's so sweet the way he dotes on our fur babies. All four of us feel the need to take care of everyone under this roof, even if ultimately, I'm the one in charge.

Harper chews his lip as we follow the roses through the kitchen. Normally, that's against the rules. His body belongs to his wolf park and we're the only ones allowed to mark it. But today is a special day, so I fondly let it slide.

We go out onto the patio, and all the way over the lawn. I'm relieved there isn't too strong a breeze today whisking the petals away, as Brady was adamant this is where he wanted to do this.

Harper looks nervous as we reach the barn. The door is open, and the lights are on inside. "Daddy?" he says in a small voice. Sometimes he's still that frightened little lamb we first met, but that's okay.

He'll always have me to take care of him.

"It's okay, sweetheart." I lift his hand and kiss the back of it before letting him go. "You've got this."

He swallows visibly, but then he nods once and heads inside. I take a little fortifying breath, straighten my suit jacket, then follow him.

I spent all afternoon rearranging the place with Trey and Brady, so I'm not surprised. But I am still extremely proud of how beautiful it all turned out. We pushed the bales around in a semicircle to make a bigger space than we usually have in here for hunting. There's still straw all over the floor as well as a fuck ton of petals.

Brady got the ladder out to hang lengths of gauze and silk

257

in a mixture of pinks, reds, and creams to create a canopy along with white fairy lights. Trey picked out a beautiful playlist of songs that's currently playing instead of our usual forest sounds for hunting. Flameless candles in hurricane jars are placed everywhere and there are a couple of bunches of roses in vases that still have their petals intact.

I set up a couple of basic boxes as a table, but with the red silk tablecloth it looks exquisite. It has a couple of silver buckets filled with ice and ridiculously expensive Champagne, of which I have several more bottles tucked away for further celebration later. That's for when the other guests arrive. For now, it's just a party of four men who love each other very much.

And in the middle of all this is Brady, dressed in nice pants and a shirt, down on one knee with a ring box open in his upraised hands. Trey is standing behind him in jeans and a button-down, his hand resting on Brady's shoulder as he grins unabashedly. I skirt around Harper to go join them, resting my hand on Brady's other shoulder.

Harper is frozen stiff with his hands in front of his mouth. There are tears in his eyes as he looks around the scene in awe. "Brady?" he squeaks.

I feel Brady take a deep breath, so I give him a reassuring squeeze of his shoulder. "Harper Kendall," he says in a clear voice. "We love you so very much. We've told you so many times that we want to build a life together—all four of us—but I want to make it official. We can't all get married, but I'm going to ask if you want to just marry me, so then we can all spend the rest of our lives together. As a pack."

Harper breaks down into pitiful tears that almost crack my heart. He inches forward like a terrified bunny rabbit, staring at the two platinum rings in the box that match mine and Trey's, like he can't believe that they're real. Then he drops to his knees and flings his arms around Brady, almost knocking the little box from his hands.

"Holy *fuck!*" he gasps, and I can't help but chuckle. "Are you serious? I...really? Is this happening?"

I get on my knees as well and offer Trey my hand so he can do likewise. It's harder for him in this position, but he wraps his arm around my back, and I give him my strength.

I will always give all of them my strength for as long as I walk this earth.

"This is happening, little lamb," I assure Harper warmly. "This proposal is from all of us, but Brady wanted to be the one to ask. It'll be you two who are legally married, but we'll all pledge our love in a big ceremony together. If that's what you want?"

He lets out a sob and fumbles until he's hugging all three of us. "It's so much more than I could ever have hoped to want. Oh my god. I can't believe it."

"So is that a 'yes'?" Trey gently prompts.

"YES!" Harper yells, leaning back so he can look at us all. "Are you insane? It was 'yes' before Brady even said anything! Yes, yes, YES!"

I laugh hard, my sides and cheeks aching, my soul brimming with such bliss. That means we won't have to cancel the engagement party later, which is a nice relief. My parents and Trey's family have all flown in. They've met Brady's parents before, and all of them have met Harper over various holidays now. But everyone is dying to be introduced to his larger-than-life grandmother and she's talked of nothing else to me for weeks. All our friends will be there as well, ready to celebrate our first official step together as a foursome.

I'm a man who sees what he wants and goes for it. I've always been that way. And even when I'm so audacious as to ask for the love of three incredible men, the universe still doesn't dare to defy me.

Life isn't perfect. No one's is. At times, it's both miraculous and messy. But my life is undoubtedly mine, just like all these men are. They belong to me, and I will love them until I draw my last breath. They will want for nothing. I'm sure we'll all work on much fancier vows when the time comes, but that is my promise in this moment to the universe, and I swear to whoever might be listening that I will never break it.

This is my pack. I am their alpha. And we will hunt together, now and forever.

———

Thank you so much for reading Harper, Brady, Trey, and Rick's story! If you would like a **special bonus story** of how Rick and Trey met Brady, you can sign up to my newsletter and read **Be Four** now!

Please note, I only send newsletters when I have a new release, a sale, or information about upcoming conventions, so I won't pester you lol. You can unsubscribe anytime, but it's honestly the best way to keep up with my books. Plus, this short story is HOT! You don't want to miss out, so click **here** now.

———

Also make sure you don't miss the next Paddle Creek College book, Hell's Kitten! Nim, the stoic owner of the cat café meets bubbly cheerleader, Jessie. Coming early 2024. **Pre-order your copy now!**

One grumpy biker. One sunshine kitten. Could it be a purr-fect love?

If you want more small towns or Daddies, make sure you keep reading for other books by HJ Welch/Helen Juliet.

———

Thank you to my team!

Cover Design: Cate Ashwood
Editing: Meg Cooper
Proof Reading: Tanja Ongkiehong
Formatting (and general awesomeness): Ed Davies
Love and support: Hubby and our cats

PADDLE CREEK #1: HEAVEN SENT BY HJ WELCH

Two rival jocks. One adorable nerd. A bet that changes everything.

SETH

Being captain of the Paddle Creek Panthers is my life. I wouldn't care that my grades have slipped, except it could not only cost me my shot at the pros, but now the rich kid in town has wagered that if I don't graduate, I'll owe him *big* time. Can this gorgeous little freshman geek Gabe really save my degree and my reputation? All I know is that as soon as I laid eyes on him, I needed him. And I *don't* want to share.

MARTY

I've spent almost four years trying to get my captain Seth to notice me. He's hot as hell and knows how to boss a guy around, even one as big as me. To him, though, I'm just the team clown. But when he drags me into this graduation bet, it's no laughing matter. So why shouldn't this little cherub Gabe tutor me as well? In fact, I don't see why we can't share him in all *kinds* of ways. Seth is clearly a natural Daddy, Gabe thrives being doted on, and I'm happy to Daddy *and* be Daddied. Win-win, right?

GABE

Somehow, I've found myself standing up to the guy whose family pretty much owns Paddle Creek and put my neck on the line for two of the college's star players. Now we're spending every day together as I try and save their grades, and I don't know if I'm crazy but it's like they both *want* me. I've never had a boyfriend. I'm not even out to my overbearing parents. How could I choose between them…or do I actually have to when they *both* want to be my Daddies? After my life comes crashing down, it's their turn to come to my rescue. Maybe what me and these god-like men have isn't just a fling after all?

*Heaven Sent is a steamy, standalone MMM romance. It's the first book in the **Paddle Creek College** series, where it's always the quiet ones who get up to the best kind of trouble. This book features a geek tutoring two hot jocks, two hot jocks tutoring a geek in a completely different way, a trash panda with a heart of gold, a human ice cream sundae, a revenge curse, and a guaranteed HEA with absolutely no cliffhanger.*

Click here to get the Heaven Sent eBook

PADDLE CREEK #2: YES, SIR BY HJ WELCH

Two men. Two secrets. Can true love set them free?

BENEDICT

Just one more year, then I can go back to my beloved Oxford University and leave this tiny town behind me. Teaching is my passion, but I have other desires that I know would get me fired if anyone found out. The only trouble is, my new TA is pushing all my buttons and I'm not sure he even realizes what calling me Sir does to me. That's nothing, however, compared to when he starts calling me Daddy.

JACKSON

Have I got hots for teacher? Oh, yes. Messing around is off the table, though, so in a way it's safe to flirt with him and see him lose that stiff upper lip. It's not like he'd be interested in me anyway if he ever discovered what I love wearing under my clothes. Tough guys like me shouldn't like satin and lace. They shouldn't want to feel pretty. But Sir makes me feel gorgeous, and I want to be *such* a good boy for him.

Yes, Sir is a steamy, standalone MM romance. It's the second book in the **Paddle Creek College** *series, where it's always the quiet ones who get up to the best kind of trouble. This book features two people learning they don't have to be ashamed of who they are, a sassy brat who really wants to behave, a master in the bedroom who's a caring Daddy at heart, role playing so good it could win an Oscar, and a guaranteed HEA with absolutely no cliffhanger.*

Click here to get the Yes, Sir eBook

PADDLE CREEK #3: LITTLE PLEASURES BY HJ WELCH

One jaded Daddy. One brand new boy. A fake relationship that becomes all too real.

XANDER

It's bad enough I have to move back to Paddle Creek with my awful stepmom, but now my half-brother's best friend has decided he has to look after me—even pretending to be my new boyfriend for a family wedding to keep my stepmother off my back. What Ruben doesn't know is that I've been in love with him for as long as I can remember and spending so much time with him is torture. Until it isn't. I can't believe that he's interested in me and even wants to be my Daddy, unlocking something in me I never knew was there. But when my stepmom goes too far, can I rely on Ruben to be there for me seeing as no one else in my life ever has?

RUBEN

When my life-long best friend asks me to keep an eye on his half-brother, of course I agree. Except he's a young man now, not a kid, and he's tugging at every single one of my Daddy heartstrings. Xander has just moved back into town and between finishing his degree, part-time work, and hellish stepmother, he's stressing himself into knots. It's a long time since a boy interested me, but I just want to protect Xander from the whole world. No matter the cost.

Little Pleasures is a steamy, standalone MM romance. It's the third book in the Paddle Creek College series, where it's always the quiet ones who get up to the best kind of trouble. This book features a Daddy introducing a boy to his inner little, the most loyal doggy best friend, a lot of dinosaurs, a heart-stopping rescue, and a guaranteed HEA with absolutely no cliffhanger. CW: Age play but no ABDL.

Click here to get the Little Pleasures eBook

BEARS-4-U (MULTI-AUTHOR SHARED UNIVERSE): KEEP ME BY HJ WELCH

Snowed in for a second chance at love...

BECKETT

It's been over two years since I lost my darling husband, and my best friend is taking matters into her own hands. She's signed me up to a dating app for bears and those that love them, even encouraging me to attend a weekend mixer. I go to humor her, not expecting to rescue the most adorable boy...twice. But I'm not ready to open up my heart again, am I?

LAURIE

My last Daddy was bad news. It's taken a lot of courage for me to reach out on Bears-4-U and go to this mixer, only to find that the new Daddy I've been talking to is just as awful. That's when Beckett swoops into my life like a hero in a story book. I know he's not looking for love, but I want to mend his broken heart so badly. When a scary snowstorm blows in and strands us, I trust he'll keep me safe and warm. I want to be in his life, in his bed, in his heart...forever.

Bears-4-U is a MM Daddy romance multi-author series, featuring a host of delicious Daddy pairings. The Bears-4-U dating app is all about putting Bears and Teddy Bears together for their honey-sweet HEAs. Psst, no real bears involved. Each book can be read as a standalone, but why not snuggle up with all the bears?

Click here to get the Keep Me eBook

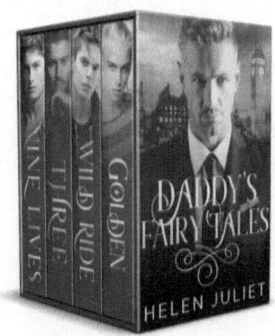
———

Golden

When Goldie's ex-boyfriend leaves him in serious debt with the adult entertainment company he works for, Goldie gets the chance to work off the money…in front of the camera. The idea excites him, but then his favourite throuple—Daddy, Papa, and Baby —*demand* he comes to play with them. No matter how scared he is, he can't miss this opportunity, not even when his past comes back to haunt him.

―――――

Wild Ride

When Red is chased into the woods, he seeks sanctuary at his estranged grandma's house. He doesn't expect to be rescued by his older brother's best friend, the man he was always madly in love with. Could Hunter be the Daddy of Red's wildest dreams? Especially when he unlocks a secret passion of Red's for beautiful lingerie. There's still a threat lurking in the woods, though, and Hunter realises he'll do anything to protect his beautiful boy.

―――――

Three

When three shy best friends sign up to a dating app to finally get some by the end of the year, they don't expect to all fall for the same gorgeous, slightly scary-looking Daddy. The only solution? Let him choose who he wants to bed. Except he doesn't. Daddy Wolf wants to spoil each little piggy, one after another. But when danger comes calling, will their love for each other be enough to save them all?

Includes Halloween bonus scene!

―――――

Nine Lives

When Charlie suddenly finds himself homeless and penniless, he decides to sell the only thing left he owns. Himself. For the very first time. Lucky for him he stumbles across Miller, the own of a London kink club, who saves him from those who would take advantage of him. As Miller discovers his inner Daddy, he also unlocks Charlie's kitten alter-ego. But with both their families meddling, will new love be enough to keep them together?

Click here to get the Daddy's Fairy Tales eBook bundle

It's Halloween and Robin has prepared a sexy little surprise for his boyfriend Dair when he gets home from work. Hold on to your horses, Marine!

———

Troubled Waters

Bodyguard Scout Duffy doesn't know what's worse: the fact that his scorching one-night-stand, Emery Klein, is his bratty new client, or the fact that he doesn't even remember Scout. But Emery's life is in danger thanks to his out and proud charity work, and once he finally recognizes Scout, their chemistry in undeniable.

———

Homeward Bound

Swift Coal just found out he's a father, and his daughter (and her cranky cat) are coming to stay. His best friend's younger brother, Micha Perkins, has nowhere to go and a wrongfully tattered reputation. He's relieved when Swift asks him to be a live-in babysitter. He just has to hide his lifelong crush. Easy, because Swift is straight—right?

———

Bright Horizon

With sixteen years between them, baker Ben Turner and lawyer Elias Solomon have no idea their crush is mutual. But when Ben inherits his long-lost family's estate and becomes an overnight millionaire, Elias swears to protect the innocent younger man from the vultures circling him. To unravel the mystery of the inheritance, they must go to England to confront Ben's estranged relatives...and their feelings for each other.

———

Crossed Paths

Raj Bhat is done living in the shadows. It's time for him to take charge of his own destiny and tell the man he's fallen for how he really feels.

———

Midnight Sky

It's the night before New Year's Eve. Taylan Demir is all alone, and he's just lost his dog. Except when his handsome customer, Hudson Perkins, comes to his rescue, Taylan doesn't just get his dog back. He's suddenly got a hot date, and maybe someone to kiss when the clock strikes midnight.

———

Memory Lane

Angel Shields saved Jay Coal's life in high school, and Jay has secretly loved his straight best friend ever since. Now Angel's back in town with amnesia after a suspicious work accident and it's Jay's turn to rescue him. He pretends to be Angel's fiancé to see him in the hospital, but with his scrambled-up memory, Angel's not sure it's fictional after all. He just knows he loves Jay more than ever.

———

Thin Ice

Kamran's ex broke his heart, tricked him into aiding a bank robbery, and now he wants him to do one last job. There's only one way to say no: seek the protective custody of the biggest, grumpiest FBI agent ever, Lee Marshall. And pretend to be his boyfriend for a week-long family reunion in their giant mansion. Wait, what?

———

Calm Shores

Gorgeous, sophisticated Dante walks into Oliver's bar and orders...a boyfriend?! Dante needs a man to keep his mother from setting him back up with his awful, cheating ex, and Oliver is up for the challenge.

―――――

Fresh Snow

Emery Klein is throwing the best Christmas party ever, but his fiancé, Scout Duffy, and all their friends have something more exciting in mind.

―――――

Each Pine Cove book can be read as a stand alone and has its own happy ever after. But if you read the whole series, you'll see a lot of familiar faces!

Click here to get the Pine Cove eBook bundle

Click here to get the Pine Cove audio bundle

About the Author

HJ Welch is an author of contemporary MM romance series, including the international bestselling Pine Cove series. She lives just outside of London with her husband and two balls of fluff that occasionally pretend to be cats. She began writing at an early age, later honing her craft online in the world of fanfiction on sites like Wattpad. Fifteen years and over half a million words later, she sought out original MM novels to read. By the end of 2016 she had written her first book of her own, and in 2017 she achieved her lifelong dream of becoming a full-time author. When she's not writing she's usually dancing, singing, filming music videos, taking long walks, working on jigsaw puzzles, drinking prosecco, or talking about Eurovision.

She also writes contemporary British MM fairy tale adaptations as Helen Juliet.

———

You can contact Helen via the following:
Newsletter: https://www.subscribepage.com/helenjuliet
Website – www.hjwelch.com
Facebook Group – Helen's Jewels
Instagram – @helenjwrites
Twitter – @helenjwrites
Book Bub – @HJWelchAuthor
Facebook Page – @HJWelchAuthor